Ms. Lily White

BETSY TUTCHTON

PAGE PUBLISHING, INC.
New York, NY

First originally published by Page Publishing, Inc. 2018

ISBN 978-1-64214-988-3 (Paperback)
ISBN 978-1-64298-990-8 (Hardcover)
ISBN 978-1-64214-989-0 (Digital)

Printed in the United States of America

This book is dedicated to Joseph Thomas Tutchton
for he is the only one to have ever believed in me.

Chapter 1

It was Friday, and Jennifer Collins had left her last counseling session for the day in Building A at the Colorado State Prison. The long day had reduced her energy level to zero. Tired of fighting review board member Edward Tuttle—known as the Ol' Man—on every issue, she wanted nothing more than to go home and enjoy a quiet evening, soaking in a bathtub filled with the relaxing aroma of vanilla oils.

"How'd it go today, Ms. Collins?" asked Perkins, one of the guards who usually escorted her to and from her sessions with the male inmates.

"Found another missing piece to the puzzle," she said. Then she looked at him with curiosity. "Mr. Perkins, is there something going on I should know about? Oh, that's right. Next Wednesday's the night, isn't it? The fatal injection for Charlie Bremmer."

"Yes, Ms. Collins," he answered as he stopped to add, "Before we get to our turn up here, you need to be prepared."

"For what?" she asked, looking startled.

"The press and the camera crews are swarming the administration building, wanting a statement about the execution. In the absence of Warden Ellsworth, the prison has no comment," he said as they began walking again. "My job is to get you to your car as safely as possible so you can get out of here."

"But Doralee Anders rode with me today. She was granted a special visit with her son. She has no other transportation," Jennifer said.

"That's okay. She's already been escorted to your car and is waiting for you." He escalated their gait. "Doralee has been briefed on the situation."

"Does Warden Ellsworth know about this?" Jennifer asked.

"She's being tracked down as we speak," Mr. Perkins said.

Turning the corner, they spotted the crews, well equipped with cameras and mikes. The journalists from the state's four largest newspapers had colored identification badges dangling from their lapels. Covering the lawn of the administration building, they seemed to be growing out of control like crabgrass, looking for any warm body that might let them cling like leeches.

Perkins caught their eyes, and the reporters stampeded in their direction. He wrapped his right arm around Jennifer's shoulder and extended his left arm out as though he was directing traffic. Speeding their pace another notch, the pair became oblivious to the nonstop, repetitious questions flying in rapid succession. Struggling to push the mikes out of her face, Jennifer kept her head down and ran in rapid baby steps, battling to keep speed and balance with Mr. Perkins. The ladder climbers of the media pushed and shoved and stepped on her feet, much like anxious children on a school playground all fighting over the same swing. Jennifer thought it obscene that grown human beings would relish any position where the exploitation of others was used as a form of self-achievement and public entertainment.

After Perkins had fought a path to her car, Jennifer quickly hit the unlock button so Doralee could get in the passenger side. After they both slid in, Jennifer relocked all the doors; both women tried to ignore the feeding frenzy of the vultures. And for the first time, Jennifer's serendipitous feelings over having her own parking space faded resentfully. "Are you okay, Doralee?" she asked as she started her car.

"I'm fine, Jennifer, but when we get out of here, there is something you should know about the drug flow through here," she said meekly. Jennifer heard the sound of fear in her voice, but she thought, *Let's just get out of here first. Then we'll talk.* They each took one last glance at Mr. Perkins being hounded for any scraps of controversial information, truth or not, that the public would gladly pay for and ravenously devour.

They fastened their seat belts as Jennifer drove off the prison grounds in the 2007 Subaru Forester. She started to ask Doralee what she was talking about when something suddenly slammed against the back of her seat. The man rose quickly, clamping his hand tightly around Jennifer's mouth and pointing a gun at Doralee's head.

"Keep your eyes on the road," he rasped. The women were terrified. Jennifer could smell the odor of alcohol and car oil on his calloused hand. Nothing in her life ever prepared her to handle what she feared could happen next. *This just doesn't happen in real life,* she thought. *Only in the movies.* She knew what she was feeling was real—and life-threatening.

She may not have been prepared for this kind of situation, but she knew instinctively to keep things on an even keel: no screaming, no crying. This wasn't a movie where the clueless victim shouts, "When I get loose, I'm going to call the cops!" For one thing, no one with a full picnic basket would actually yell that out at a time like this. By now, Jennifer's fear was for Doralee more than herself, but she couldn't help wondering why Doralee was calm—even serene.

"What do you want?" Doralee asked as if she were asking him to please pass the salt.

"What I want is for your friend here to be dead. That's what I want! If I were you, you stupid shit, I'd shut my damn mouth and I'd keep it shut so maybe, just maybe, I wouldn't have to kill you too!" He said, pulling the grip tighter around Jennifer's mouth, blocking the air from one nostril. He held the gun as steady as possible at Doralee's head. "Keep driving, bitch, until I tell you to stop," he slurred over Jennifer's shoulder.

Jennifer was shaking as she gasped for air. Suddenly, panic caused her legs to jolt upward, forcing both knees into the steering wheel column with such force they were commanded to plunge back down with one quick thrust, her right foot slamming the accelerator pedal to the floor. As the pain from her knees consumed her, Jennifer grasped the steering wheel, exposing white knuckles as the racing car reached uncontrollable speeds. Her left foot searched frantically for the brake pedal while her right fought a muscle spasm that held the accelerator pedal to the floor. The car was now veering out of control; tires screeched while it swerved from one side of the road to the other.

Suddenly, the gun went off, followed by the explosive sound of the back door of the car blowing open, and the mysterious hand jolted loose from Jennifer's mouth and air slowly filled her lungs.

The nippy breeze of November whirled as Jennifer negotiated a barbed wire fence that flashed in front of her. She drove in between two fence posts, ripping them from the ground as though they had been planted in shallow loose sand. Finally, her left foot found the brake pedal as the right relaxed and slipped off from the accelerator. The back tires hit the ditch forcefully with a sideways motion, causing Jennifer's head to be thrown into the rearview mirror, snapping it off. Then the car came to a rapid stop. In seconds, blood poured from the resulting gash. The hood popped open, and steam spewed out from the radiator into the atmosphere, forming a hazy white cloud.

Jennifer's heart pounded, and her hand shook so badly she couldn't grasp the key to turn off the ignition. Disorientated, she struggled to decipher between what she believed to be her reality and the reality that just happened; the horrifying experience simulated the awakening from a two-hour nightmare, and perspiration beaded her eyebrows, mingling with the blood that was running down her face. Seconds passed as she realized that this was no nightmare. What had happened was *real!*

She looked over at Doralee and asked, "Are you okay?"

There was no answer. Doralee's gray head of hair was resting on the door, her seventy-eight-year-old body was held in place by the seat belt. She looked thin and frail. Now Jennifer could see that Doralee had been shot in the chest, and she cried and repeated loudly, "Doralee, Doralee!" She reached for her wrist to see if she could feel her pulse—nothing. She pressed three fingers on the side of Doralee's neck, trying hard to establish a heartbeat. Jennifer heard soft sobbing and looked at Doralee's face, but there were no tears. She cupped her own wet face with two quivering hands, head resting on the steering wheel. *It was me*, she thought, startled. *It was me who was crying.* Through tear-blurred vision, she saw her cell phone on the floor by Doralee's feet and leaned over to pick it up but stopped immediately to grab a VIP badge from a well-known newspaper. The name Tim Xavier was in large print. She pushed 911 and gave her location but was unable to stay conscious long enough to call Jeff, her best friend.

Paramedics were holding ice packs to Jennifer's forehead and knees while the ambulance sped to the hospital. They were happy when Jennifer started talking. But she was only comforted by the thought that Dr. Beadle was on duty in the emergency room. He was one of Jennifer's favorite people in Clear Water Springs. His snow-white hair was rarely groomed, but that didn't seem to matter to anyone, probably because his simultaneous warm smile and quick wink were present for almost all occasions, endearing him to the community for the past thirty years. People would comment on how much weight the Doc had been putting on and then turn around to give him a home-baked apple pie or his favorite cheesecake.

Dr. Beadle had seen the people in town through critical times in their lives—death, marriage, divorce, and even an epidemic or two. He always used caring, and sometimes philosophical, humor to assure them things would be okay. Even small children didn't mind getting their immunization shots from Dr. Needle, a fond nickname pinned on him from the beginning. Or maybe it was because he always gave the children a coupon for a free ice-cream cone whether they cried or not while getting their shots.

The nurses had Jennifer pretty well cleaned up by the time she saw the Doc. He walked to her side with a broad smile, saying, "What are you doing in such a hazardous occupation, young lady?"

"Oh no. This didn't happen at the prison," Jennifer said wide-eyed.

"I know," he said, helping her lay back on the exam table. "I heard about the accident on my police radio. Okay, I think we better sew this up for you." He examined the cut on her forehead. Doc poked and prodded until he was satisfied that Jennifer didn't have any internal bleeding. "Your X-rays on your knees and legs all look surprisingly good, but you're going to hurt for a while. Why don't you take a week off from work? I'll write a note."

"Who are you, my mother?" Jennifer asked.

"It's a tough job, but someone has to do it," he said with a wink.

"That's just what Tuttle would want," Jennifer said unwaveringly.

"Who cares what *he* wants? Besides, do you really think you need to be so tough all the time?" he asked sincerely with a sweet smile.

"Yeah, I do! That's the point," Jennifer said.

After the stitches were in and Jennifer was ready to leave, she asked, "Could you please call Jeff for me?"

"Don't have to. He arrived here before you," Doc said, helping her down from the table. "Besides, *where else* would he be?" He winked as though he knew something she didn't. "You know, it wouldn't be such a bad idea if you spent the night here. You could have a concussion, you know."

"I love you. I love your hospitality, but I'm outta here," said Jennifer in a determined voice. "And incidentally, how does Jeff know I'm here?"

"News travels fast when there's an accident like the one you were in. Clear Water Springs is not that big of a town yet where you have to wait for the morning paper to know what happened the day before," the Doc said.

Jennifer tried hard to prepare herself for the ride home with Jeff, knowing his concern was justified. He knew more than what just happened today. He knew Jennifer had been being bothered by unwanted phone messages that had now escalated into threats of violence.

There wasn't much that Jeff didn't know about Jennifer's life and vice versa. He had been adamant about Jennifer not publicly supporting her interest in two of Colorado's House bills, HB 134, pushed for inmates, while still serving time, to retain their voting rights. She was steadfast about keeping the inmate in touch with the real world outside of the prison gates. Prison should never have been a place to force one not to care about their country or the government that runs it. Whatever goes on in their country does matter, and they're still an integral part of it. Studying government and politics in prison hones their decision-making and analytical skills while lifting their social awareness. Keeping them out of society's loop contributes to a higher recidivism rate through alienation.

House Bill 135 would allow the nonviolent inmates to shave time off their sentence if they are willing to drop a urine analysis three times a week to prove they have no illegal drugs or alcohol in their system. The days would be randomly selected by an outsider and two witnesses. The measure promotes wellness for the inmate and a sense of security for employees as well as the general public for when they are released. Prisons have fewer incidents when inmates stay clean and sober and they also cooperate in a friendlier manner and are more equipped to control their anger. The everyday citizen isn't so naive as to think that drugs and alcohol aren't available behind prison walls. Society could feel safer knowing that the early-released inmate has been clean and sober for years. Any classes or rehab meetings that are offered or mandated make a far better impact on the inmate when their personalities are not altered. Although some taxpaying voters may feel that this is just another added expense to the prison budget, it's still cheaper than recidivism. Training employees of the Department of Corrections to perform the urine analysis would cut cost by more than half versus sending it to labs.

Because of Jennifer's passion about the criminal justice system, Jeff stayed well-informed on how the public viewed these house bills: some taxpayers felt none of the inmates should have even one privilege regardless of any circumstances. According to these people, mitigating circumstances are just words that the judges use to justify their sentencing. Others believe it all depends on the judge's mood that day. On the opposite slide of the spectrum you have those who overdose on rehabilitation to an unsafe and unrealistic sense, suggesting any childhood trauma should be considered mitigating regardless how many chances the criminal justice system has given them in the past or how much free help they had been given.

"Jen, you must be thinking what I'm thinking," Jeff said gently as he started to drive her home.

"What? That the accident today has something to do with the obscene phones calls I've been getting at home on my phone recorder, right?"

"That was *not* an accident. When someone has been threatening you with bodily harm and you end up with a creep like that in the back seat of your car trying to kill you, that's not an accident," he said quietly, in a tone she'd heard more than once.

"Well, what can I do about it?"

"Jennifer, you have to call the police to your home and let them listen to the threatening messages. That was no accident today, not when you end up with a creep like that in the back seat of your car. You should have called when those calls began," Jeff said in a tone she'd heard more than once. "You need to start taking all this seriously."

"It's just that it has been so crazy at work. But okay, as soon as I get home I'll call them," she said.

"That sounds like a deal," Jeff said. "How do you think this guy could've hidden so well from all of you in the back seat of your car?"

"It's taken me a little longer than you, but I was starting to wonder about a few things myself," Jennifer said. "I mean, I don't keep a lot of stuff in the back seat. When I got the car, I tossed in a sleeping bag, a wool blanket, and a flashlight. I work in the Rockies, anything can happen unexpectedly—especially the weather. I guess I'm just used to ignoring the back seat."

"Yeah, I think most people wouldn't have thought to look," Jeff concluded. "Plus you wouldn't think you'd have to worry about it." The two fell silent.

Dr. Jeffrey Hanes was a tall, slender man in his mid-fifties who carried an unidentifiable charisma in his stature. He looked distinguished long before the pepper gray hair appeared, which seemed to happen almost overnight. It came at a time in his life when his wife was dying, and there were no remedies. The crow's feet surrounding his ocean-blue eyes only served to magnify his caring concern of others. His serene approach to any given situation lent a calming effect, like being gradually submerged into a hot tub, commanding all muscles to relax and the day's disturbances to disappear.

Jeff became an invaluable friend to Jennifer years ago, initially of need more than desire. He was an established, well respected psychiatrist whom both the public defender and the district attorney often used for expert testimony. Although it was unusual for either of them, they formed a fast and binding friendship when volunteering for a mental health fair the city council arranged as an extension of Drug Abuse Resistance Education.

Jennifer held a special regard for this man, one that she never found necessary to analyze or to explain—to anyone. Though it was true that feelings of adolescent emotions resounded while in his presence, she brushed it off as respect. She just wasn't ready to get honest about her feelings for the man, mostly out of fear that if she did, she'd lose what she already had. *That* she could not bear! She had convinced herself that her feelings were in the right place and that she was only mesmerized by his uncanny insight into the human mind. Jeff was destined to do exactly what he was doing, which was helping others.

Jeff had ample time to wonder what kind of a monster would want to hurt Jennifer. If there was ever a person without an enemy, it had to be her. Some who didn't understand her or her occasional playful humor in somber moments may see her wit as sarcasm. But it seemed transparent to him that on those occasions, she'd try to camouflage her anger—or her fear. And, sure, he had heard that she could bear down pretty hard on clients in her private practice, trying to urge them to expose and examine their own truths. She could dig her heels in when battling Tuttle's inhumanities, and she was also more than capable of setting a stranger straight if they tried to propose improprieties. Even in her neighborhood, when Jennifer had had enough, she'd had enough! She'd blasted Angela Colder before, but all that did was give "the crowned princess" ammunition—something to make Jennifer look bad, which was all Angela ever wanted anyway. But neither Jennifer's straight-laced honesty nor her expectations of integrity had ever provoked someone into threats of violence. These qualities commanded only respect.

Jeff opened the front door of Jennifer's home, looked around quickly inside, and said, "Do you remember the day you asked me to look at this house before you bought it?"

"Yeah, you thought it was a wreck," she answered, hanging both their coats on hangers in the front closet.

"But look what you have done with this so-called *wreck*," he said.

Jennifer's medium-sized, three-bedroom brick ranch home in an older subdivision had been remodeled following her specific instructions: remove all nonbearing walls connecting the kitchen, dining room, and living room. Jennifer loved the feel of openness. After some texturing for the walls, she painted the kitchen and dining room sand dollar white, a flesh color without the hint of pink. The kitchen, the most costly to renovate but the easiest on the imagination, was outdated by three decades. It was originally designed for the greatest amount of function. Now natural oak cabinets hung from the walls, white ceramic tile covered the countertops with a small flower border, and a blue-and-white checkered ceramic floor set the kitchen apart from anything she'd ever seen. Her quest was uniqueness.

"So what's your point?" she asked.

"This home belongs to an open-minded person with a flair for precise decor. A home says a lot about you. For instance, even if I had never met you before, I could tell you tend to be trusting," Jeff said as he sat down at the kitchen table.

"How would you know that?" She was genuinely curious.

"Well, for one thing, you have an open floor plan," Jeff asserted.

"That may be true, but what you're really saying is that you think I'm just a little too trusting, don't you?" she asked as she was dialing the police as promised.

After waiting and listening to Jennifer's end of the conversation, he answered, "Yes, I do sometimes think you're too trusting—but just sometimes." He watched her place the phone in its cradle. "What'd they say?"

"That they are sending a detective over who is already in the neighborhood."

Jeff laid his hand on Jennifer's as they sat at the kitchen table in a contemplating but comfortable silence. He knew she needed time to absorb the day's events and to ponder the days to come! She was always a strong person, but he also was privy to the other side of Jennifer Collins: the side that was vulnerable, the side she'd never admit to anyone—except occasionally to herself.

Finally, Jeff asked, "You thinking about Doralee Anders?"

"It was just so awful, Jeff. I mean, it's not like she and I were close friends, but we were still friends, actually the only one I had in *this* neighborhood. She learned through the local newspaper that I had been granted the Homeward Bound Program out at the prison. She asked me for just one favor—one favor!—and look what happened!" Jennifer said, almost in tears. "She had her last visit with her son, knowing that she only had about a month to live and most of it was going to be in bed. Cancer! The damn cancer! I imagine her son knows about what happened by now."

"Hey, wait a minute, you can't blame yourself," Jeff said in a low tone that always got her undivided attention. "First of all, you are not the one who shot her. And although you may not want to hear this, Doralee was lucky in a way. God stepped in so she wouldn't have to be subjected to the kind of pain that no one should ever have to endure in the final days before going home."

She patted his hand, saying, "Thank you, Jeff. Thank you for giving me another way to look at this."

Jeff heard the knock on the door and walked over to open it; Jennifer followed close behind.

"Sorry 'bout the way I'm dressed," Detective Malloy said after stepping into the house. He realized why the couple's inquisitive looks had become fixed upon his attire. "I've been working the vice squad all day and all evening, and I haven't had a chance to change—or eat, for that matter. I don't normally dress like this, believe me." Malloy tried to explain why his thirty-five-year-old body looked more feminine than Marilyn Monroe's did in the early sixties.

"That's okay," Jeff said, trying to hold back his laugher. "Come on in and have a seat."

The pair watched while Malloy took a seat at the kitchen table and pulled the blond wig from his balding head. He used a handkerchief to wipe off as much of the makeup as he could. Then he yanked off the false eyelashes. Jennifer cringed. He pulled out the falsies from the top of his dress and sighed deeply as if the weight of the world had been lifted. Jeff smiled tight-lipped.

"Can I get you something to eat, maybe a sandwich or something?" Jennifer asked.

"No, no, but thank you. I'll be heading home to a warm cooked meal as soon as we're done here, but I appreciate the offer," he smiled.

Jeff knew Detective Malloy was one of the best in his field in Clear Water Springs. Malloy had been presented with a couple of medals for heroism, but what impressed Jeff the most was that Malloy never let a case go as unsolved even when his captain said it was time to let go of it. Malloy had a memory like a computer. He might be on the trail of a recent suspect, but he never forgot the unsolved crimes.

Malloy took from his inside pocket a small pad and pen. "Now, Ms. Collins, because of your line of work, I'm going to have to ask you about any known enemies, past or present."

"If you're referring to the men in the Homeward Bound . . . " she started to say, then remembered Malloy's only knowledge of the program came from the local newspaper.

"Look, we have to start somewhere," interjected the detective.

"First of all, the messages are being left at a time when I'm either with the men or at times when they don't have access to a phone. Second, the messages repeatedly say, 'You've ruined my life, you must pay' and 'You should've minded your own business.' After that, then there's always a various stream of obscenities. Anyway, I haven't been working with the men long enough to ruin their lives or to get into their business," she said with a forced, quick laugh, trying to relate the ridiculousness of what he was thinking.

"Wouldn't phone records indicate the origin of the calls?" Jeff asked.

"We'll be checking that out and also putting a tap on Ms. Collins's phone," the detective said.

"I already know these calls are coming from a pay phone, maybe a variety of pay phones, because I can hear a diversity of background noises," Jennifer said. "Plus, I have caller ID. But more and more he is using prepaid cell phones, so then there's no caller ID."

"That's a start," Malloy said. "Are you seeing anyone presently? I mean, romantically?" He was taking notes.

"Just Peter, Peter Winslow," Jennifer said.

"Yeah, I know Peter. It's not that big of a town yet. He owns his own insurance company, right?"

"Yes. Yes, he does," Jennifer said. "He takes care of all the insurance stuff for me."

"Apparently," said Malloy.

"What do you mean?" asked Jennifer.

"Well, Ms. Collins, after the accident today, he was right out there promptly—with an insurance adjuster, I might add," said Malloy.

"Oh, no! My car is totaled, right?" Jennifer asked cringing.

"No, not at all. From what I heard, you just need a few repairs. A new hood, front bumper, windshield, dents removed, and some paint are about it. The engine wasn't damaged at all. Subarus are very durable—a damn good car. One other thing, Ms. Collins, how many people know about these threatening phone calls?"

"Just Jeff," she answered with a shrug.

"Let's keep it like that. We don't know who's doing this yet, and you might say the wrong things to the wrong people," Malloy said, standing to leave. "Well, that'll be all for now. I'll stay in touch." He picked up the pieces of his costume as he headed for the door. "Oh, Ms. Collins, before I leave, I need to hear the messages."

"Certainly!" she said as she pushed Play on her phone.

"Yep! That's pretty nasty stuff." Malloy nodded. "Jennifer, if the messages change at all, even a little, please call me," Malloy said. "May I ask you something?"

"Sure, if it will help," said Jennifer.

"You must know there's been a hike in drugs being smuggled in the prison lately," Malloy said.

"Not really, just that Doralee said something about it right before our intruder jumped us. I shared that with the police. Why would I know anything else?"

"Aren't you working with the convicts?"

Geez, she thought to herself, *that mind-set! Where does it come from? Where does it end!* "So you think that gives me an inside track? I'm working with people who have made some mistakes in life and have chosen to not make them anymore," she said coolly.

"Okay, whatever, talk with you later." Malloy waved goodbye.

After Detective Malloy left, Jennifer and Jeff settled down on the oversized paisley camelback sofa. With the walls gone, there was spacious walking room and a few select pieces of nearly contemporary furniture. Lighted wall paintings adorned the walls and refused to be washed out by the plush, white pile carpeting. The oak-and-glass, claw-legged coffee and end tables were assembled around the sofa, paying homage. The right wall was exclusively devoted to a mammoth collection of the philodendron family, displayed from floor to ceiling. Directly across the room from the ever-growing botanical garden was the new expanded bay window, whose job it was to provide an abundance of sunlight for the jungle. In a corner, just a few feet from the bay window, was a small but efficient wood-burning stove that produced warmth while the chiseled white-bricked wall behind it emitted soft light.

"You didn't tell Peter about these calls?" Jeff asked, basking in the warmth of a secret he alone shared with Jennifer.

"I've told you how Peter is about my personal safety, and you've seen how he keeps my car in perfect running condition as though it carried the Queen of England," Jennifer said as a reminder.

"I was just thinking maybe he could look around a little when the two of you are out together. You know, to see if anyone's following you," Jeff said.

"Are you crazy?" Jennifer's voice flew up two octaves. "Peter would be so conspicuous if he knew what was going on that they'd have to haul him away in a white jacket labeled paranoid," she said, furrowing her eyebrows, then quickly felt her hand touch the stitches that tugged on her forehead. "You know how he is!"

"In that case, let's just leave things as they are. But let me ask you something. Why didn't you mention Angela Colder to the detective?"

"Oh, Jeff, don't be silly," she said with quick sarcastic grin. "You mean the ol' bitty down the street who is so obviously narcissistic that I can't even take her seriously?"

"She doesn't like you and she has made trouble for you in the past," Jeff reminded her. "It's happened enough times that people in your neighborhood have turned their backs on you. She somehow got the owners of Rock Hard Steak House to make you so uncomfortable that you won't go there anymore. Robert says it's because of the owner's wife, her being so jealous of you and all."

"Well, first of all, Angela never does anything on her own. She has little *guppies* to do all her dirty work. She thinks it keeps her hands clean; God thinks differently. Second of all, his wife is jealous of *every* female that walks into their restaurant. You know, fidelity isn't exactly Max Short's long suit. But that aside, let's get real—*him* and me? For anyone to believe that, they would have to live in an alternative universe." Jennifer furrowed her brows.

"Still, I think she is capable of hurting you," he stated. "I'm going to have a talk with Malloy."

"Go ahead, but she's just the type that must have control over everyone—what they wear, how they cut their hair, how they mow their lawns, remodel their kitchen."

"Aha! You *do* remember the fuss she made over your ideas to redecorate," he interjected. "I thought the woman would have heart failure when you wouldn't do it the way she wanted it done."

"No such luck. Now let's drop it, okay?"

"Okay! I'll change the subject. Did you happen to hear about Charlie Bremmer's execution date at your new place of employment?" Jeff asked, purposely exposing his nonchalant attitude. He knew he had hit an anxiety button that would either cause Jennifer to clam up or send her off into a twenty-four-hour congressional filibuster, protesting all the inequalities of the death penalty.

"Don't even get me started," Jennifer said, keenly aware of his intentions. "Are you just trying to irritate me?" She hit him with a sofa pillow.

*****

A week later, on Monday morning, Jennifer approached the conference room in the Colorado State Prison. Her knees, no longer swollen, were sore and bruised various shades of green and purple. This was the first time she was glad the dress code for her was dress slacks only—no dresses, no skirts. The stitches from her face had been removed, and carefully applied makeup hid the redness. The hard soles of her pumps hit the chipped tile floor as though they were stamping out a small campfire. Seconds later, spasms of anxiety fluttered from her stomach into her throat. Anger had been born from anticipation that her program was about to fall under dire scrutiny. The uncomfortable feeling settled in the pit of her stomach the moment the prison grapevine echoed the criticism, which had come from a disgruntled review board member, Edward Tuttle. He was annoyed by what he thought had become a disregarded stipulation of the Homeward Bound Program (HBP), which Jennifer had initiated and gained approval for just a month ago.

She remembered their first encounter as well as all the ones that followed: "After all, I am the chairman of the review board from the operations division of the Department of Corrections. I also perform audits and conduct regular reviews of budgeted programs," Tuttle would state as though crucial information was being released for the first time. Oh yes, this wasn't their first trip to the mat, but she'd hoped that after negotiations were settled, their verbal volleyball would cease.

Edward Tuttle, a short man who hadn't missed many meals in his fifty-some years, squinted from under bushy eyebrows as Jennifer walked into the room. The Ol' Man sported an ostentatious handlebar mustache in an egotistic manner by rubbing, twisting, and twirling it whenever he spoke. Jennifer speculated the mustache provided an emotional shield that heightened the small-man image he carried of himself.

"Good morning, Ms. Collins. Please take a seat," Warden Elizabeth Ellsworth said.

"Thank you," Jennifer said, sitting at the large, oval conference table. The prison board members shied from making eye contact—all, that is, except for Tuttle, whose pressed lips, furrowed brows, and squinting eyes revealed aversion.

"Jennifer, we asked you to join us today because there seems to be some concerns about your application of the Homeward Bound Program," Warden Ellsworth said.

"And just what might they be?" Jennifer asked, hurling a look of accusation at Tuttle.

The warden leaned back in her chair, parting her lips to speak, but the loud authoritarian growl came from Tuttle. "Why aren't your six cons working anymore at their regular jobs? I thought we all agreed they would still work even after your persistence, and Special Operations approved your program—against my better judgment, I might add."

Jennifer scanned the now-wide-eyed faces of those on the board hoping what she had to say would make her feel a little less alienated from this male-dominated, as well as Tuttle-dominated, group.

"What we agreed upon was the work in the HBP came first and if there was time left over, the inmates could work at their menial jobs, for which they are paid about one dollar a day," Jennifer said.

"How much they're paid is irrelevant. This isn't about money, it's about teaching responsibility and discipline," Tuttle said as the veins on his neck began to protrude over his collar.

"And just what do you think the Homeward Bound Program provides? A retreat from the world's harsh realities?" Jennifer flashed into sarcasm, sensing he'd already proposed to the others the program be terminated. She thought of screaming, *Borrow a clue! What part of high recidivism rate don't you understand! How many times do the same faces have to reappear at your prison gate before some sort of genuine prison reform is implemented?*

But a calmer attitude surfaced for effect before Jennifer continued, "You can't honestly expect me to believe this isn't about money, albeit the free labor. Our society has spent millions of dollars building new prisons, and 50 percent of the offenders recidivate in less than six months. Except for a brief period during the late sixties and early seventies, our prison institutions have opted for punishment to deter crime almost exclusively over rehabilitation. When are we all going to learn that punishment by itself doesn't work? Or is that the whole point? To set the offender up to fail?"

"I resent that!" the Ol' Man shouted, his bushy furrowed eyebrows scrunched together to form one solid line of hair.

"So do I!" Jennifer said with an escalated voice, leaning forward.

"We give the con every possible chance to succeed," Tuttle said at full volume while twisting facial hair.

"How?" Jennifer asked, hearing her voice grow again with intensity. "You lock them up, you lock them down, and in between you give them work. But you offer no tools for living, the very thing that would help keep them out of here. This treatment is perfectly fine for known terrorists, but for the rest—"

"Excuse me, Ms. Collins," interjected Gordon Fairchild, a review board member. His voice was dripping in superiority. Fairchild's thick, fluffed white hair clung motionless to the sides of his head while a large bald spot shined like the silvery moon. "The inmates here attend rehabilitative meetings such as AA, CA, and domestic violence classes."

"Which are all a joke, and everyone in this prison knows it. Okay, some *do* probably benefit from those meetings, but the majority only attends to spruce up their resumé for their parole hearing. The fact remains inmates need more than just society's worn-out traditional rehabilitative methods, which haven't yet produced any positive long-term effects," Jennifer countered.

"Their rehabilitation is their responsibility. Our responsibility is to help them adjust to prison life," Tuttle said as though he was the alpha and the omega of the prison system.

"Well, you're doing a great job!" Jennifer snapped. "They're so well-adjusted that they keep coming back! Too bad your responsibility doesn't extend to teaching them how to adjust to the real world," she added with a slight mocking voice.

"We do not set them up to fail!" Tuttle reiterated, tapping his pencil on the table with rapid wrist motion.

"Or to succeed either, obviously," Jennifer said, restating the number one reason for the high recidivism rate. She viewed the faces around the table, listened attentively to the dead silence before continuing. "Don't be so damn obtuse, Mr. Tuttle. The entire structure of the criminal justice system sets them up to fail. Do you think it would be necessary for this prison's payroll to carry two hundred employees if the recidivism rate was 1 percent?"

"What are you saying? Do you actually believe our state builds more prisons to lessen its unemployment rate?" Tuttle asked with deliberate sarcasm.

Exhibiting a shrug of confidence, palms slightly exposed to the heavens, Jennifer muttered, "Well, if the shoe fits . . . "

"Your flagrant liberalism obstructs public safety. Surely you agree the public deserves to feel safe from threats of criminality," Tuttle asked in a patronizing tone.

"Of course, but you have to understand that it's the fear of crime that shapes our criminal justice policies, not the crime itself. Take a long hard look at what we've done to feel safe in just the last ten years. We've passed several comprehensive crime bills, we've made new sentencing guidelines to ensure that everyone is being treated fairly, we've spent millions of dollars building hundreds of new prisons, we've incarcerated more people per capita and inflicted the death penalty on more prisoners than any other country in the industrialized world! And yet we still don't feel safe from threats of criminality. So it's easy for me to conclude it's not new prison structures we need, but new prison infrastructures," Jennifer said. "*And now*, prisons claim that they are understaffed, overpopulated, so we let the criminals out anywhere from one to four years earlier than their sentences. They justify this by claiming the inmates who are prereleased are nonviolent—as if they'd know!"

Feeling provoked, Tuttle asked, "So your solution is what?"

Calmness returned before Jennifer allowed herself to say, "It's the same as yours. It's the same as everyone's in this room. It's to lower the crime rate. First, of course, we need to lower the recidivism rate since that's our heaviest traffic flow. However, our two very different techniques on how to achieve that goal have reached an impasse due to opposing forces in society: punishment versus rehabilitation."

"To hell with rehabilitation! How do you think it makes the other cons feel, knowing your men don't have to work?" he asked, twirling a side of the wadded mustache.

"First of all, they do work. They work very hard. But to answer your direct question, they probably feel a little resentful. But they have to understand that the men I'm working with are up for parole in less than six months, and more than once, they've returned to this prison. Punishment alone has failed to produce any long-term, positive effects. Repeating the same act, expecting different results is nothing short of insanity. Even an animal won't repeatedly touch a hot surface," she said.

"So you think treating the con as though he's . . . he's . . . "

"A valuable human being?" she said, offering the missing ingredient.

"No!" he said, shaking his head with force, deriving virile stimulation from a tasseled mustache. "As though he somehow deserves the attention you're giving him."

"He does. We owe it to him. We owe it to ourselves."

"We don't owe them a damn thing!" Tuttle said, slamming his closed fist down on the table.

"If nothing else, we owe them the gratitude. Without the offender, none of us would have a job, including you," Jennifer said with premeditated calmness.

With charged ego, the tyrannical voice spoke, "The fact is, Ms. Collins, since your program is not only experimental, but also probationary, I see no reason to continue this—"

"What we might do to settle this difference is schedule all of Ms. Collins's sessions with the soon-to-be-released inmates for afternoons, leaving the men free to work mornings," Thomas Otter interrupted, a salt-and-pepper-haired review board member who usually remained mute. Otter was always attentive to Tuttle's whims. He removed his John Lennon look-alike glasses that never left his face except for cleaning. The eyes in the room watched as he methodically wiped the lenses clean with a handkerchief drawn from his pocket. Then with apprehension, the other review board members nodded in concurrence despite Tuttle's prearranged attempt to dissolve the program.

"Well, you've won this one, Ms. Collins, but I'm warning you," Tuttle said. "I'll be keeping a close eye on any mollycoddling of the prisoners." He tapped a pencil on the table while scanning the faces of the board members whom he thought had betrayed him.

Jennifer left the conference room remembering only the barred windows, which were now etched in her mind indelibly. Not recalling pictures that hung or prevalent smells each prison room seemed to adopt, she wondered if that was all there was to remember. Bleakness.

She relied upon her intuitive skills to receive accurate insight with precision timing, which was an enormous asset in counseling session. Often this quality would be overlooked by others, partially due to her petite frame of 5 feet, 2 inches carrying 120 pounds, but it was also due to her triple-dimpled smile, which gave others a mixed conception about her vulnerability as well as her age of forty-something. But regardless of the big brown eyes or the way she unconsciously tilted her head that shook the loose, brown curls, her ability to exhume information from the unsuspecting grew to a talent beyond her own recognition.

She had been keeping an ear open to all the high-profile scuttlebutt in books and tapes about *How to Develop Your Intuition through Spirituality*, and it reminded her of a Barbara Mandrel song: "I Was Country When Country Wasn't Cool." She felt she knew exactly how Barbara felt. Jennifer didn't think there was anything wrong in teaching people to develop their intuition by becoming more spiritual, but what disturbed her was allowing people to think that this form of self-awareness hadn't been practiced for thousands of years. She had been born with a keen sense of it.

Having left the administration building with Mr. Perkins right on her heels, she heard "Ms. Collins!" She stopped abruptly.

"Ellsworth would like to see you in her office. You can use her private door."

Perkins, a large black man in his late fifties, wore his navy blue prison uniform with dignity. He always had a huge wad of keys dangling from his belt, handcuffs hanging out the back pocket, and a solid, soft-blue tie that hung meticulously straight. His amiable poise intrigued Jennifer, inviting her to perceive him more as a greeter for the welcome wagon than a prison guard—or officer, as they preferred to be called. She had yet to witness the same demure attitude in most of the other guards. To the contrary, they were better known for their harsh and vulgar speech.

The long corridor leading to the warden's office was drab and neglected. Jennifer winced and gaped again at the chipped tile floor, cobwebbed pictures with dusty frames hanging unevenly from the yellowing walls, and the chipped painted baseboards that were once stained natural wood. She still wondered, *Why?*

The warden's office, however, had been refurbished with scenic Rocky Mountain paintings mounted in designer frames on freshly textured, eggshell-colored walls. The beige pile carpet presented a rich contrast between the dark solid oak desk and filing cabinets. But the highly visible clock hanging on the warden's wall gracefully invited Jennifer to feel the irony of its presence. The Roman numerals were ticking off every minute of every hour of every day in absolute synchronized strokes.

Elizabeth Ellsworth was a stout woman in her early fifties who wore dresses and skirts just below the knee. A white high-collared blouse with loose-fitted sleeves was her everyday attire. The wire-rimmed reading glasses were seldom used except for board meetings. Every strand of graying hair was pulled tautly into a round bun that rested undisturbed on the back of her head; no jewelry had ever been witnessed. Jennifer always felt there was something deep and covert residing inside the warden's heart that wanted to be free, but it could never find its way to the surface. What really captivated Jennifer were Ellsworth's quick, penetrating eyes that seemed to set sedately in the background of an unblemished salmon-like complexion. They were her one feature that people listened to much more than her words.

"Ms. Ellsworth, you wish to see me?" Jennifer asked, poking her head into the warden's office.

"Yes, please come in," the warden answered, getting up from a desk heaped with stacks of files and unattached papers. Walking to the door to close it behind Jennifer, the warden offered her a seat in one of the two mint green, overstuffed corduroy chairs that faced the oak desk.

"Ms. Collins . . . Jennifer. May I call you Jennifer?"

"Yes, please do, Ms. Ellsworth," Jennifer said, hoping the warden would extend the same courtesy to her.

"Tell me how things are really going for you with the men in the HBP. Has there been any noticeable progress?" she asked in a tone filled with sincerity. She didn't ask to be called Elizabeth, however, which would've made Jennifer a little less apprehensive.

Jennifer wanted, more than anything, to be friends with this woman, to have her as a confidante. But Ellsworth hadn't exactly been her ally during the negotiations for the HBP, but then, nor had she been her adversary. *What does she really want?* Jennifer thought. Leaning back in her chair, Jennifer answered the question with appropriate caution, "I think things are going as well as can be expected, considering I've only worked with the men for a short time."

"You know, Jennifer, you probably can't expect the same kind of results here as you elicited in your private practice as a psychologist," Ellsworth continued. "You're no longer dealing with kleptomaniacs, housewives struggling to find their true identity, unfaithful husbands, or someone on the brink of confessing their closet alcoholism. Here, it's a different world, and you need to be prepared. It can get rough, rougher than what you've experienced from Mr. Tuttle." The warden maintained strict eye contact throughout their conversation. "But not to worry. There will be a guard no farther away from you than twenty-five feet or less at all times."

Jennifer was witnessing a side of the warden that she hadn't been privy to before, a side that disclosed candor. No longer was she hearing the voice of a bureaucrat lecturing about prison pitfalls to the bleeding-heart liberal. Instead, she was hearing a poignant voice coming from a thirteen-year veteran warden who had experienced indisputable disappointments in the prison system.

Although Ellsworth had captured Jennifer's undivided attention, this new, temporary prison psychologist didn't share the same preconceived hopelessness.

"I was persistent about implementing the HBP for one reason only, and that was to discover firsthand why the recidivism rate is so high. If I can help in any way to lower it, then all the better," Jennifer said.

"Be careful, Jennifer, about minding all the stipulations the review board has passed down, especially the one about you having a guard escort while on the premises," she warned in a manner that wouldn't have fit Tuttle's style. "Don't give them ammunition."

Jennifer recalled the one time she left Building A alone to retrieve a paper from her locker but was sure no one had seen her. "I'll be more careful about that," Jennifer said, wondering if the warning meant the warden was on her side after all.

"You have great ideals, Jennifer, but remember, there are no secrets in prison. Keep me posted on your progress, and if you ever have any questions, please feel free to call upon me," Ellsworth said, dismissing her.

Jennifer could only hope Ellsworth's sincerity was genuine. But the recognizable comfort zone was to proceed with prudence in any relationship connected with the review or parole boards, especially with the warden, where Jennifer felt the most vulnerable.

Even though Jennifer had told the warden that her main goal was to lower the recidivism rate, it wasn't her only goal for her six charges. She wanted so much more for them than just their freedom from bars and concertina wire. They needed to believe that their past couldn't define them any more than their home life or substance abuse could. She was well aware that she couldn't give them self-confidence; that was something they would need to earn by accomplishing small positive changes in their everyday lives. It certainly was clear that if she was ever going to be able to assist them toward their dreams and purpose in life, she has to get to know them first—at least at some minimum level. Seeing them only in the afternoon could be a deal breaker.

Jennifer longed to reach out to each of her men and tell them that life doesn't have to be the way they have been living it. She wanted to say, "I know because I've been where you are now. No, not in prison, not like the one you are in, but one I built around myself." She was well acquainted with loneliness, despair, and feelings of inadequacies. They once were her constant companions, her only companions. But one day, those feelings had been replaced with honest, loving friends, hope, and the thrill of God's love.

Although it was assumed that Jennifer received most of her information through college academics and keeping up on responsible research, the truth was much more sinister. She came from a long line of drinkers, druggies, and abusers. She never invited friends over or had dates pick her up at home. How she managed to be such a high achiever throughout her public schooling was nothing less than phenomenal. Later, she came to believe that studying hard, getting good grades, and earning respect from all the teachers were what caused her to not just survive but actually thrive.

Not surprising, after graduation, Jennifer moved far away and attended UCLA, earning a BA in sociology and later an MA in criminology at the University of Colorado-Boulder. She'd realized since grade school that education was the way out and dreamed of the day when she'd own her own car, had her own place to live, where nothing smelled bad, and no one could ever hurt her again.

Unfortunately, along the way, she acquired a taste for the grape. Wine would relax her on those uptight nights, or days. Moving to LA not knowing a soul and carrying all the expectations from previous teachers overwhelmed her. They were the only ones who ever cared about her; she couldn't let them down. A glass of wine—or six—also enhanced her studying time, helped her make better first impressions at parties, and become instrumental in creating new relationships with both sexes. Then it became her number one reason for leaving California. The respect and admiration she once enjoyed with students and faculty at UCLA had not only faded but also vanished due to her love affair with vino blanco. When someone talked about her drinking, she'd say, "Oh well, I'm not that bad yet. After gradua-tion, I won't drink anymore." She managed a 3.9 grade point average, which got her into grad school in Colorado.

Jennifer survived a horrendous life-altering car accident and spent two months in the hospital. She got acquainted with time and lots of it. The roller-coaster ride had finally come to an end, and help had arrived. Her mission was clear from then on: she would be com-pelled to pass on everything she learned.

As the late November snow flurries were drifting in and out, Jennifer began to relax. She turned all thoughts to Thursday's ski trip to Aspen over the upcoming Thanksgiving weekend with her latest beau, Peter Winslow. She felt the break would rejuvenate her; he'd fill the air with laughter.

The snow had turned to a steady rain as Jennifer pulled into her driveway. Discovering that the front door was unlocked shook her sense of security, but scrambling to answer the phone postponed any anxiety—at least for the moment.

"Hel-hello," she said, breathing hard.

"I-I didn't think you'd be home this early. I was just going to leave you a message," said Jeff Hanes. "How'd things go today?"

"As I expected with the Ol' Man, but I'll tell you about that later. What's up?" she asked.

"I've been more than a little worried about you," Jeff said.

She knew there was no sense in pretending the threatening calls left on her answering machine hadn't been frightening. He knew her too well. "I know, but I'm taking them more seriously now."

"Good. I'd like to stop over and talk with you, if you're not too busy," Jeff said. "I bet you haven't even eaten yet, have you?"

"No, I'm not too busy. Come on over," she said.

Jeff's analytical mind was set into motion as he drove. He strug-gled to pinpoint the personality of the guy who'd left the phone mes-sages. The man's threats and vulgarities weren't much to go on. The only other information he had was the perp smelled of car oil and alcohol and his hands were calloused. That could indicate that he worked in a garage. Whoever was able to get into Jennifer's locked car had to know some trade tricks, probably some that he learned in prison. He's a pretty good actor to have gotten through the guards' gate; he'd have to be in order to insinuate himself in a group of reporters. So are there two men with separate motives? Or is it just one man with his own agenda? Or is it even a man?

Could Angela Colder possibly be a part of this elaborate scheme? Would she really go as far as to *kill* Jen? He was well aware of the choke hold she held on the residence in Jennifer's neighborhood—in fact, more so than Jennifer was able to admit. But murder seemed a little much, even for someone as vengeful as the aging "princess." It wouldn't be the first time that narcissism had led to murder. Torturing the victim first would simply be a perk. And there was always Helen to consider, Angela's very own young puppet who obeyed Angela's every command—sometimes before it was given. He couldn't recall Helen's last name and decided that he didn't commit it to memory because it would only clutter his attic.

After all, what had Jen ever done to this woman? From the time she moved into her home, and even during remodeling, she was always having the neighbors over for one reason or another, always serving drinks and homemade tasty morsels, retrieving recipes found in a magazine. She held the Homeowners Association (HOA) meeting. She put forth this effort because of her strong belief in community ties, not to show anyone up. Now Jennifer was no longer even invited to those meetings, but Helen, Angela's puppet, graciously allowed her to give a proxy vote to any other neighbor. No, Angela can't be ruled out—not yet. She could have easily found a man to do the obscene calls and the car attack; it's not like she ever did her own dirty work anyway. *It never ceases to amaze me how narcissistic people always come across looking so righteous!* He'd learned a long time ago from a famous poet, "When people show you who they are, it's best if you just believe them."

*****

Jennifer was startled for a second when she heard the knock at the door.

"Hey, anyone ready for a double-cheese pizza?" Jeff called as he entered Jennifer's house.

"Yes! Come on in and we'll feast out in the kitchen," Jennifer said, grabbing a couple of plates, forks, and napkins and setting them on the kitchen table, listening to her heartbeat return to normal—almost normal.

"I even remembered to bring that orange drink you like so much," he said.

"You *are* an angel," she smiled.

"I was hoping you'd notice." He smiled back at her in a way that could've been interpreted as flirting, if Jennifer wanted to see it that way.

"I would *always* notice double-cheese pizza with my orange drink!" she said, knowing that wasn't what he was referring to. "So what's up?"

"I thought you'd probably like to know something I found out from Malloy," he said, diving into the still-hot pizza.

"Shoot," she commanded, pouring the drinks into large glasses.

"The perp in your car left a .38 under the back seat, but unfortunately there were no prints," Jeff said as he swallowed a gulp of the ice-cold drink. Then he saw the look on Jennifer's face. "What? What's wrong?"

"I'm kind of flashing back. Now I remember that he did have a glove on his right hand, the one that held the gun to Doralee's head," she said, swallowing hard to get the pizza down. "What else?"

Jeff reluctantly proceeded, "The badge was falsified. There is no such person as Tim Xavier who works for any newspaper in Colorado," Jeff informed her. "And one other thing. Doralee wasn't shot in the chest. She was shot in the back, and the bullet came out the front, passing through her heart and into the dashboard." He could see Jennifer was still struggling with Doralee's death, and what she really needed was a big hug—but not enough to let it happen.

C h a p t e r   I I

Tuesday evening, Warden Ellsworth closed Charlie Bremmer's
file and slid it into the top drawer of her desk. The clock hands
ticked past the Roman numerals and soon declared it was 11:00 p.m.
Leaning back in the cushioned chair, an unyielding thought persisted
about the last time she stayed this late at the prison.

It was ten years ago. Charlie Bremmer, convicted of first-degree
murder, had been sent to her prison to die by lethal injection. Each
minute of that day was as firmly planted in her mind as a hundred-
year-old oak tree flourishing in a forest.

That day, she'd told the guards to call her the minute the new
inmates arrived. When they did, she walked to the admitting building where new prisoners were given physical and psychological exam-
inations. They were briefed on rules and regulations, body searches
were conducted, showers and haircuts took place, and urine samples
were collected before prison uniforms were issued.

Upon entering the area, Warden Ellsworth found the induction
guards waiting before they proceeded with their initiation tasks. She
always gave the same speech to all the new prisoners, but this time,
she avoided looking into one prisoner's eyes, the only one headed for
death row. Finishing a well-rehearsed, coordinated speech but fore-
going the question-answer period, she walked back to her office. She
felt the beads of perspiration collect across her forehead as the relentless pounding of her heart vibrated in her ears.

Elizabeth struggled to clear the confusion she felt, which made
her feel as though she was spinning out of control. When she failed,
one thought persisted: *My God! Was that really Charlie?*

That night, Elizabeth stayed until 11:00 p.m., finding mean-ingless paperwork to occupy time and divert thoughts. When all the inmates were locked down for the night and without a word to any-one, she walked to Building D, which was death row. She hated this building. It always smelled unfit for human habitation. The odor of death, whether actual or preconceived, permeated the entire struc-ture and its contents, oppressing all other senses.

"Good evening, Warden Ellsworth. Are you here to see Bremmer?" asked one of the two guards she knew well.

"Yes, it's my administrative visit," she answered in an official tone, watching the guard fill in the time on a preprinted form. "This visit will take place in the room at the very end of the hall, the room that's usually used for the guards' breaks. When you bring Bremmer, I want you to take his handcuffs off and leave your cigarettes and lighter on the table. I'll return them to you later."

"But, Ms. Ellsworth," the guard said, protesting as though the warden had forgotten prison protocol.

"I don't need to be told that this is seriously irregular, just as I'm sure you don't need to be told some of your activities here on Friday nights are seriously irregular," she said in a dry, authoritarian voice.

The two guards looked at each other. *How could she have known about our Friday-night poker games and delivered pizza?* Then they heard her unspoken words as she breezed by, glaring at them. *There are no secrets in prison.*

That Charlie would still be in leg irons and a two-guard post would remain just outside the door was enough. Elizabeth couldn't cope with seeing him in handcuffs for their first visit in almost eigh-teen years.

"Why would the warden want to see *me?*" Charlie asked when the guards appeared in his cell.

"It doesn't matter why. You don't call the shots in here," the charge guard said, jerking him from the cot.

Charlie felt his body tremble as though an earthquake had just begun. *Oh, Elizabeth, you don't need to jeopardize anything for me.*

The guards shoved Charlie toward the break room as though he was a piece of furniture too heavy to carry. After thrusting him into a chair—a reminder of his new subservient position—they threw the cigarettes and lighter down on the table. Suddenly, they felt the burning, piercing eyes of Warden Ellsworth standing in the doorway.

"Will there be anything else?" the charge guard asked, rapidly acquiring a more pleasant disposition.

"No, I think that's quite enough," she said in a warning tone. She took a seat across from Charlie as the guards closed the door.

Although the small room had been recently updated and repainted to please the guards, the odors clung like forgotten tennis shoes dumped in a gym locker. Several vending machines had been replaced, along with new refrigerators and microwaves. Formica-covered tables with chrome and cushioned chairs replaced the old beaten-up wooden tables and chairs. Although the burned and scratched wooden floor and chipped countertops had been replaced, they were already showing signs of defacement. Political cartoons degrading the inmates, making a mockery out of the prison system, and portraying the guards as the real prisoners already plastered the tan-colored room.

Elizabeth noticed Charlie's confused look when the handcuffs were removed. Although he had never been on death row, he was familiar enough with prison procedure to know an exception had been made—and who made it.

Charlie groped to find the right words, hoping the trembling in his body and mind would cease. *God! She's still as beautiful as I remembered.*

"Ms. Ellsworth? Or Mrs. Ellsworth?" he asked.

"I married Steven Ellsworth about two years after our divorce, Charlie. He died a few years ago. I use Ms. as a politically correct subtitle for professional reasons," she said, scrutinizing every inch of his face.

The deep, embedded lines that crossed Charlie's forehead, the red scar just below his right nostril, the dentures, and the completely gray head of hair were not present in the days when Elizabeth knew him. The only familiar characteristic was his height of 5 feet, 8 inches. Even his weight had changed dramatically, from 170 to 140. His forty-eight-year lifestyle had produced a sixty-year-old man.

"Well, Mzz. Ellsworth," he accented with humorous banter, attempting to shake the perpetual chill that filled his frail body.

"Don't, Charlie. Don't do that," she said.

"I-I'm *sorry*, Elizabeth. I-I'm not trying to be a smart-ass," he said, leaning forward in the chair, centering both hands in the middle of the small table. "It's just that I'm so overwhelmed by the sight of you. I mean, look at what you've done with your life, and then look at what I've failed to do with mine." His voice was cracking. Tears would've followed if it had been anyone but Charlie.

He composed himself before continuing. "About three years ago, after I was released from a prison upstate, I heard you were appointed Warden here. I actually thought about looking you up, but by that time I'd had enough of the judicial system," he said with a chuckle, thinking of the irony of his present situation.

Elizabeth remembered this side of Charlie well, the side that was much more willing to let emotion out through laughter than through tears. Seeing him, maybe for the first time, she thought, *Oh, Charlie! Our lives could've been so very different!*

"Life never does seem to go much like we plan, does it, Charlie?" she said before reminiscing. "I remember when we were first married. You were working at the bank in the accounting department, and I had returned to the University of Colorado for my master's degree in criminal justice and criminology. Everything seemed so perfect then. You were young, but bright. All I ever knew was about three years into our six-year marriage, you began to slip away into something I had no way of relating to, let alone curing."

"Cocaine. I was slipping into the wrong crowds doing the wrong things. One of those wrong things was losing you, Elizabeth. I have no idea why you stayed the last few years of our marriage," he said. But he *did* know. He knew how much she had loved him and would've done anything to put him back together again. But only he could've done that, and he wasn't ready. And she didn't know if he ever would be.

"Are you clean now, Charlie?" she asked, lacking the need to dwell further on what couldn't be changed.

"Yeah, I am. I attended Cocaine Anonymous while serving six years on a twelve-year sentence for attempted murder. I'd been under the influence of the deadly white powder. I decided right then I'd never touch the stuff again. And I never have. I had my chances while still in prison. Cocaine flowed like water through there. But CA saved my life," he said, chuckling once again over the irony that hung between the life he saved and the life he was to lose.

"Then what happened, Charlie?" she asked, feeling the regretful words squeak through a tightening throat.

"I dunno. I-I got out of prison, found a pretty decent job, and attended CA meetings for about a year, maybe longer. You know the absurdities of my ego. It kept telling me that I was in the driver's seat again as long as I didn't blow snow. I got pretty lonely on the outside, so I started to stop by a local neighborhood bar on my way home from work," he said.

"I don't recall you being much of a drinker, Charlie," she said.

"I wasn't when you knew me. But later, I needed it to bring me down from the coke. I learned from CA if any of us druggies were using alcohol, we were only one step away from blowin' powder again, regardless of our drug of choice. But that was just intellectual knowledge, not to be confused with experimental knowledge."

"Since I didn't stay in touch with your trial, how did Eddie Wallace fit into the picture? Isn't he the one you suspected did the killing?" she asked.

"Yeah, he couldn't be found before, during, or after my trial. He didn't have any priors, so there was only a pseudo-search for him," Charlie said, reaching for the cigarettes. "I used to smoke these."

"I remember. Did you quit?" she asked.

"Yeah, about four years ago. You'd think I'd be smart enough not to light up, wouldn't you?" he asked, lighting the cigarette and taking a short drag that prompted a small choke. "Addictions are strange creatures, like parasites. Once they attach themselves to you, they don't ever want to let go. And they're so patient. Even if you find the strength to leave them, they'll wait for your return."

"So you and Eddie were . . . what? Friends?" she asked, using a humorous and exaggerated hand wave to disperse the cloud of smoke that hung between them.

Charlie smiled, remembering the era when she smoked a pack a day.

"Eddie and I were more like boozin' buddies," he said. "We played pool and drank some beers, and he enjoyed looking out for me, his size being so intimidating and all. He didn't just *look* tough. He *was* tough. Pretty soon I found myself matching him beer for beer about three or four nights a week. I still went to work, paid my bills, and refused offers of coke from bar customers. I thought I was doing okay."

Elizabeth got up and walked to the counter where fresh coffee had been brewed. "You didn't start using cream or sugar in your coffee, did you?" she asked with a coy grin.

"No," he said, smiling, remembering the times she used to get up early on the weekends just to fix him breakfast with piping hot coffee, the only way he liked it.

"It's not exactly piping hot," she said.

"I'm sure it's fine," he smiled with a broad, toothy grin, feeling blissful she remembered.

"What made you think Eddie had killed that man?" she asked, bringing the two cups of coffee to the table.

"You probably haven't been to a lot of *these kinds* of bars, so let me tell you about the atmosphere at the Brandy Snifter," he said, sipping his coffee, mindful of her every movement and facial expression. "It's a good-ol'-boys bar, neighborhood owned and operated, mostly reserved for the blue-collar worker. It saves a lot of the locals from getting DUIs because they can walk home. The few true family men leave by six or six-thirty, but the rowdy regulars, as they like to call themselves, stay the night. It's got two or three pool tables that are hot all the time after five. There's usually a dart game or two going on, and someone is always flipping a coin with the bartender to see who'll pay for the jukebox, which gets louder as the night grows longer. On weekends is when you're apt to see a fight or two break out over a pool game or some chick. Charlie threw her a boyish smile.

"It's okay, Charlie. I've heard most all the words you've heard by now, including feminine pronoun slang that hasn't been nearly as cleaned up as *chick*," she said with a short chuckle.

"Well, anyways, those fights are usually short-lived because the customers break them up to avoid police contact," he said, watching her face closely.

"Is this the bar where you met Eddie for the first time?" she asked, now noticing the look in his eyes.

"Yeah, Eddie and I only saw each other in the bar. We had no other outside socialization, except for the night of the murder," he said.

"Where were you at midnight on that night?" Elizabeth asked.

"In a diner down the street from the Brandy Snifter—with Eddie first, then the waitress whom I stayed behind to talk to."

Elizabeth was wondering where her strength and courage came from to request trial information that she had purposely and adamantly ignored up until now. "Charlie, tell me what happened that night, starting with the moment you walked into the bar."

"I've lived that night a thousand times," he said, lowering his head for a moment, imagining the reflection of a distraught face in the dark-brewed coffee. "That night started out like all the rest. It was about nine on a Friday when I walked in and sat at the bar next to Eddie. We talked about what men talk about: work, sports, and weather. Not always in that order. We drank some beers and put our quarters on the edge of the pool table. After we played for a while, in walks this guy that stood about six-foot something, had a big mouth, and wore a tanned cowboy vest with long fringes. There was no doubt this guy was either coming from or going to a rodeo. Or maybe he was just a wannabe cowboy. I've met plenty of them. But he sure was rodeoed! Practically falling down drunk. Called him Stix. Why? I have no idea since he wasn't slim, and his pool game was no indication he could play worth a sh——. I suppose it was to impress the other pool players. I kept having the feeling that Eddie and Stix weren't strangers."

"How do you think they knew each other?" Ellsworth asked.

"I've had time to think that over clearly. I think Stix was in over his head financially to Eddie, probably for coke. It's just one of those things you can feel, especially if you've ever had a personal involvement with the stuff, and the business that it's attached to it," Charlie said reassuringly. "Stix was carrying. I saw some in his shirt pocket, and believe me, so did Eddie.

"After he and Eddie played a few games of pool for beers, Stix says, 'Hey, how 'bout making this game interestin' with a little side bet?' Eddie knew Stix could play pool about as well as I could stay out of trouble, so he told him, 'No can do. It's against the law.' But Stix wouldn't let up. He'd say things like, 'Are you chicken? Here's my twenty bucks. Are you with me or against me?'

"Eddie played him for the twenty and won, played him again and won another twenty bucks. I moved to the bar, knowing how this would most likely end—in a fight. And sure 'nuf, in less than an hour, they were going fists to cuffs. Several of the regulars had it almost broken up before I got over there. When the bartender told Stix he had to leave or he'd call the police, Stix started to scream he was going to kill Eddie. But no one took the threat seriously. Everyone knew that it was just the alcohol talking.

"For some insane reason, I think Stix thought if he found Eddie before Eddie found him, he'd be able to give some sort of reason why he hadn't come up with the money yet. That would end up being the next to the last stupidest thing he ever did," Charlie deduced. "Eddie was probably using this time with Stix at the pool table to get the money that was owed him. These kinds of people don't fool around with you when you owe money. At that moment, unless you can pay the debt or give the drugs back, you might just as well bend over and kiss your ass goodbye. I imagine Stix was making excuses left and right. Drug dealers don't want to hear, and clearly don't care, if your home burned to the ground, killing your four children and wife, and if your parents are in an abusive nursing home on the wrong side of town. They just simply don't care!

"My infamous threat, which later was taken out of context in court and not challenged—'I would have killed him'—was said to Eddie as I pulled him out of the bar. Of course, I was referring to the pool game, but the jury didn't know that. I finally convinced Eddie we should go and grab a bite down the street. It was well past midnight by the time we finished eating and sat to talk a while. Then Eddie reached in his pocket and said, 'That son of a bitch stole my wallet!' I told him that was okay. I'd be glad to pick up the check. Eddie seemed fine and said he'd had enough for one night and was going to walk home. After he left, I stayed to talk with the waitress, which, as it turned out, was used against me in court."

As Elizabeth studied Charlie, her mind began to put the pieces together. "And this is when you think Eddie stabbed Stix?"

"Yeah, I do. Stix coming back to meet up with Eddie was his last act of stupidity. A fine example of a reckless drunk," Charlie said. "Eddie was there waiting for him as if he knew Stix would be insane enough to come back. Dealers read people well. It goes with the territory.

"Eddie wanted the murder to happen in front of the bar, not some place where there was a chance that the crime scene would be preserved with any amount of integrity. He knew I was coming shortly behind him and suspicion would be thrown my way and the crime scene would be contaminated by at least fifty people from the bar all wanting to see the body before the police arrived. By then, word had spread up and down Capitol Hill about the stabbing. Eddie used Stix as an example of what could happen to others who owed him money."

"What did you do next after talking with the waitress?" she asked.

"I was heading back to the bar just in time for one last drink before going home. Then I saw a body lying flat, facedown in a pool of blood, in front of the Brandy Snifter. At first I thought it was just some drunk who had the misfortune of passing out there. But when I recognized the tanned cowboy vest with long fringes, I knew it had to be Stix. I crouched down beside him and saw the knife in his back and blood streaming down the sidewalk, and I simply panicked. I pulled the knife out of his back and started screaming, running into the bar. Unfortunately, the bloody knife was still in my hand. That's everything that happened," he said, gesturing simplicity and honesty, with both palms open to heaven.

She looked astonished, then asked, "My God, Charlie, where was your lawyer? Out to lunch?"

He snickered a little before saying, "Only when he wasn't snoozing. The truth is, I couldn't really afford a lawyer, so the court appointed me a public pretender."

Elizabeth grinned. The overused term had become a way to connect in prison lingo. "But, Charlie, you said you had a decent job and your bills were all paid."

"That's true, but a good criminal lawyer wants twenty to thirty thousand dollars as a retainer in cases involving first-degree murder, especially when the accused has a prior conviction for attempted murder. And the fee could've doubled, even tripled, depending on the hours put into the case. I didn't have that kind of money." Charlie paused a moment to reflect. "I had the money to fork out on the last mess I was in, and I saw little difference in the outcome."

"What was your defense based on?" she asked.

Squinting while wearing a quizzical look, Charlie spoke, "Where do you live, girl? That's not what public pretenders do. Mine spent his time trying to convince me to plead guilty to a lesser charge. I told him again and again I wouldn't plead guilty to something I didn't do."

Elizabeth felt compelled to ask, "Any regrets?"

His eyes focused on the table for a moment before speaking in a melancholy voice, "See, even though I didn't kill Stix, that only really means I'm not guilty of murder. It doesn't mean, in my opinion, I'm innocent of my situation. I had no business hanging out in a bar."

"You mean legally?"

"I mean legally, morally, emotionally, or psychologically. The laws of the universe will eventually catch up to you. You've heard of the ol' cliché, 'If you keep playing with fire, you'll get burned.' Well, that's why it's a cliché. It'll always apply," he said.

"So are you telling me that because of your emotional immaturity and bad judgment, you deserve to die?" she asked.

"I could answer that two different ways, couldn't I?" he asked. "I could answer it 'Yes, I deserve to be punished in the form of death' or 'Yes, I deserve to be rewarded in the form of death.'"

"Which is it?" she asked, knowing she might regret the answer.

"Because of my Higher Power, I'm prepared to accept what may come," he said. "If the State of Colorado puts me to death for a crime I didn't commit, then my Higher Power wants me somewhere else. My faith tells me it wouldn't be a punishment."

No matter how admirable Charlie's strong spirituality was, Elizabeth wanted out of any more discussion involving his demise. "Let's talk about some specifics involving your trial. What was the evidence that you think actually got you convicted?" she asked.

"There were several pieces of evidence that convicted me, which could've been easily overturned by most any competent lawyer. The prosecuting attorney, Robert Henderson, led the jury to believe that I had lied about a certain statement. Of course, that left the jury speculating about what else I'd lied about, and—"

"Wait a minute, Charlie," she interrupted. "What was it they thought you lied about?"

"I had already opted to take the stand in my own defense, hoping I could undo some of the erroneous innuendo that my public pretender didn't want to confront. I told the jury and the judge that I didn't know Eddie 'cept from the bar. But then Henderson pulls a surprise witness, the waitress I told you about. She testifies that she saw Eddie and me in the restaurant the night of the murder. It looked like I lied. I lost any credibility then," Charlie said.

"They wouldn't have been able to bring up your past convictions if you hadn't testified," she said.

"How far do you live from the realities of the criminal courtroom in our judicial system?" Charlie asked as the quizzical look swept over his face again. "That's not how it works. That's how it's *supposed* to work. My past convictions were already mentioned before I even agreed to testify. Even though the judge instructed the jury to disregard the damaging statement about my past convictions, it doesn't necessarily erase it from their minds."

"Right then were grounds for a mistrial," she said.

"Well, yeah, if I would've had a defense attorney instead of Rip Van Winkle defending me," Charlie said, shaking his head.

"What about circumstantial evidence?" she asked.

"Oh yeah. Henderson calls several other patrons from the Brandy Snifter to testify, asking each one of them to analyze the relationship between Eddie and me. They all talked as though we were best friends instead of boozin' buddies. This was when I was erroneously quoted as saying that I would've killed Stix. The jury was convinced I would have killed for Eddie. And of course, my public pretender had nothing of any substance to say in my defense. He didn't believe I was innocent of murder. Therefore he couldn't transmit that to the jury. You can't give someone something that you don't have."

"Was there any concrete evidence?" she asked.

"Well, it depends on who you're asking," Charlie said, leaning back in the chair, taking a long drag from another cigarette. "Henderson said the murder weapon only had my fingerprints on it. But since the knife that killed Stix belonged to Stix, why wasn't there at least two sets of fingerprints? Because Eddie was smart enough to wipe the knife off, that's why."

"A conviction of first-degree murder, resulting in the death penalty, almost always requires DNA and an eyewitness," she said.

"There *was* an eyewitness who claimed that from a smoke-filled barroom, after drinking for several hours, he looked out the window at the very moment I was supposed to have stabbed Stix. I kept waiting for my public pretender to ask the eyewitness questions like 'How much had you been drinking? What was the lighting comparison inside to outside the bar? How can you be sure that what you saw wasn't Charlie Bremmer pulling the knife *out* of Stix, not pushing it in?' But my public pretender seemed to be asleep."

"So that's how they obtained the DNA. What about any other patrons?" she asked.

"None of them claimed to be eyewitnesses, but all of 'em were consistent in their testimonies. They said after I came running into the bar with the bloody knife still in my hand, I said, 'Call an ambulance! Stix is dead!' Of course, Henderson said to the jury, 'How did Charlie Bremmer know that Stix was dead and not just injured?'"

"What did counsel for defense have to say?"

"Nothing. I couldn't wake him. Damn, I'm not even a lawyer, but the logical thing would've been to ask the jury in closing statements, 'Wouldn't most of you infer that a person who was lying on a sidewalk at night in front of a downtown bar, facedown in blood, with a knife in their back, was dead?'"

"When will you appeal? As you already know, when you're sent to death row in this state, your first appeal is automatic. We have a law library, and I'll have some books sent to your cell," she said. "Later, you'll be able to go to the library with guard assistance."

"Why would you want to do that for me?" he asked, hoping she still cared.

"I'm not doing anything for you I haven't done for others in your situation," she said. "Charlie, before I go, I want you to know I respected the way you handled yourself today in the admitting building. The fact that we were once married and now we have opposing positions, well, to be honest, I didn't know what to expect. There was a time I would've seen bitter anger on your face."

"No, Elizabeth. The anger that once owned me, that once gave me a euphoric high was removed by a power greater than either one of us. When I saw you today, all I could think about was how badly I'd blown life. Twice! Our marriage failing had nothing to do with you," he said, hoping his tear-filled eyes wouldn't spill. "I still love you. I never remarried or had children. I never allowed myself to be close to anyone like I was with you."

She listened to the stillness of the room, watching Charlie's tears trickle down and drop onto the table. *Did it take death row for him to release what had been locked inside for so long?* she wondered. With heartfelt deliberation, Charlie stretched his hands across the table, hoping she would reach out too. And she did.

Elizabeth knew that this would be one of those days in her life that would always surface from time to time. But instead, her conversation with Charlie remained persistently in a small cranny of her mind for the next ten years. Maybe with new evidence Charlie could be set free someday, hence, setting her free once and for all.

*****

As Jennifer pulled into her parking spot on Wednesday afternoon, her curiosity peaked after noticing Robert Henderson's car also parked in front of the prison administration building. Not only was he the public defender now for the district attorney's office, but he was also Jeff Hanes's closest friend. His stature and mannerisms were very close to Jeff's, except he outweighed his friend by about twenty pounds.

Perkins greeted her at her car door in his usual affable way. "Well, hello, Ms. Collins. I see everything must be turning out okay. They haven't scared you off yet."

"I don't scare *that* easily," she smiled as they headed toward Building A. "But you probably already knew that. You know about a lot of things that go on around here, don't you, Mr. Perkins?"

"Well, there aren't any secrets in prison."

"So I've heard," she said, producing a quick smile. "What's Mr. Henderson doing here?"

"He's probably hoping to see Ms. Ellsworth," he said, quickening his gait.

"Why?" she asked, sensing his discomfort.

"You know, Ms. Collins, I've been here a long time. I'm only four years away from retirement. I mind my own business," he said.

"I understand. I'll ask Ms. Ellsworth today when I see her," she said.

"You won't be seeing her for a few days. She left this morning for a long overdue vacation," he said.

"Oh? She didn't tell me," Jennifer said.

"Ms. Ellsworth's a very private person, Ms. Collins. She doesn't tell anyone much of anything, unless under obligation."

"She confides in you though, doesn't she?" Jennifer asked.

"Yeah, sometimes. Sure looks like the weatherman was wrong about it snowing," he said, gazing at the cloudless sky.

"Indeed, it does," Jennifer said, recognizing Perkins's regard for the warden would remain intact.

He guided her to Building A, which was the equivalent of about one-and-a-half city blocks. Making a right turn at the first intersection past the administration building, Jennifer saw the outdated red-brick buildings all in grid rows with steel-barred windows. The well-kept grounds distracted from the narrow, cracked sidewalks leading to the buildings. Double concertina wire wrapped the top of the chain-link fencing that encircled the prison buildings. The wire gleamed in the sunshine, producing hundreds of starlike images. Its symbolic irony, mixed with a dash of idealism, struck Jennifer.

After Perkins left her at the door of Building A, Jennifer felt a soft buzzing vibrating in her head—a signal that something quite significant was happening or was about to happen. She struggled to shake the feeling before Hank escorted her to a counseling session.

Hank Poovey's six-foot frame was moving 230 pounds with each step he took. He wore a wrinkled guard uniform that either had been left in a hot dryer too long, or he had grown two sizes and didn't care enough about his appearance to ask for a larger uniform. A three-day beard added to his unkempt look and caused Jennifer to speculate that he didn't take much pride in himself or the position he held. The cocky attitude didn't inspire much confidence either. It was worse than just neglecting personal hygiene. The palpable problem was the role model the inmates weren't getting. Not even they could respect someone like Poovey. He thought it was reverence that he had earned from the inmates, but it wasn't, nor was it fear, which he would've relished even more. They had all come to the same conclusion: Hank Poovey meant nothing to them, which is easy to understand, since he never showed them the least bit of common courtesy. It wasn't necessary for him to treat the men as if he were Dr. Phil, but on the other hand, they all deserved his respect—at least until one showed him differently. *Why is it such a quantum leap to understand that respect works best when it's a two-way street?* And it shouldn't depend upon one's status in life, only on one's willingness. The men knew that they had to obey him, but they sure didn't have to be like him. *I guess the inmates have already been subjected to too many Pooveys in their lifetime. It made respecting guards even harder.*

"Tell me something," Hank said as they walked down the hall to the counseling room. "What do you expect to gain from this counseling nonsense? These kinds of people don't never change. I'd think you'd know that because everyone else does. Well, 'cept for maybe a few new recruits, but they soon find out."

"And I bet you and the other guards help them see things through your eyes," she said.

"We have to. The new guards come here full of hope and notions of treating these cons like they're people. They're not, you know, or they wouldn't be here. In fact, most of them are animals, so that's how we treat 'em," he said with an air of supremacy.

"Oh! So you're saying that if you treated the inmates as though they were *real* people, then they would act like they were *real* people, right?" she asked.

"That ain't never gonna happen," Hank said with the utmost assurance.

"Which? The guards treating the prisoners like they're real people or the inmates acting like real people?" she asked.

His voice became consumed with self-satisfaction when he answered, "Neither one."

"Well, Hank, I can only venture a guess that if these cons acted like people, then it would diminish your false sense of superiority that you believe you have over them," Jennifer said, then quickly breezed past him into the counseling room, leaving him outside, then realized her error in assuming Hank didn't have pride. He did have pride. *Demonic* pride.

*****

Chapter III

Building A housed about a hundred male prisoners. The main floor, which was all Jennifer would ever see, was used for recreation, preparation of meals, offices, and other operational functions. The female prison population had separate quarters on the following block.

Entering the large counseling room Wednesday afternoon for a one-on-one session with Ronald Bookman, Jennifer felt embraced by the three floor-to-ceiling windows that were recently installed for security purposes. Known as Rec Room One, the sparsely furnished room had but one almost-empty bookcase sitting by a television in a corner. A big worn sofa occupied a small space against the windowless wall. The rest of the room had only two round orange Formica-covered tables surrounded by eight chairs of different styles and heights. Jennifer smelled fresh enamel paint, which apparently had been spread economically thin on all the walls in a failed effort to destroy the sewer-like odor rising from the unsanitary floors. She was beginning to realize where the prison budget was being spent—and where it wasn't. Patching rotted sewer pipes wasn't the answer. She shook her head. *Short-term solutions for long-term problems; It never works.*

A smaller room was desired, which would've eliminated the echoing sound of voices that rumbled through as though everyone was speaking from the bottom of a deep deserted canyon. *This is just what I need. They might as well throw in a microphone and a couple of amps.* It never dawned on Jennifer that she needed to negotiate for a clean, quiet room too. But she was slowly learning not to take anything for granted when it came to operating the Homeward Bound Program.

Jennifer had thumbed quickly through Ronald Bookman's rap sheet: 180 pounds, 5 feet, 8 inches black man in his mid-fifties. She didn't take it too seriously. There was a lot more to people than their height, weight, and criminal records. Besides, stats were never updated after they came to prison unless it was because of negative behavior.

Ronald's short Afro hairstyle, fashionable in the late sixties, fit his personality in a way Jennifer couldn't quite describe. Maybe it was just that his long incarcerations had inhibited him from staying with the times. Or more than likely, it was so he wouldn't go unnoticed. Ron's predominate personality trait was unveiling his immaturity whenever he felt uncomfortable. He served time on two different robbery convictions before he was thirty years old. His third sentence was fifteen to thirty years for shooting a sales clerk in the process of holding up a convenience store although he always maintained he was not the one who pulled the trigger. He was convicted of first-degree murder and had completed twenty years on the last stint before volunteering for the Homeward Bound Program.

"Good afternoon, Ronald," Jennifer said, inviting him to have a seat next to her by removing six of the eight chairs before he came in. "What should we begin with today?" He slouched as she asked, folding his arms tight across his chest.

"I don't like Ronald," he said as though he was a child expressing a dislike for spinach.

"You don't like the name Ronald, or you don't like the person named Ronald?" she asked with a slight squint of one eye.

"People that like me just call me Ron," he said, focusing his eyes on the tabletop.

"May I also call you Ron?" Jennifer asked.

"Yeah," he said, nodding.

"The word is *yes*, and proper English is all I'm going to accept."

He nodded as Jennifer continued. "I wish you'd told me that you prefer to be called Ron. It's important for you to feel comfortable here. Anyway, Ron, do you have your short-term goals already written?" she asked, trying to make eye contact.

"I-I don't write so good," he said, shying eye contact.

"You don't write so *well*," she corrected. "That's okay. Write them the best you can, but you must write them. No one will ever see them but me."

"I-I don't think I can," he said, almost whispering.

"Yes, Ron, you can. You will. You knew the conditions of the Homeward Bound Program before you volunteered. Was there any part of the contract you didn't understand when you signed it?" she asked.

"I guess not," Ron said, shrugging, then he scanned the windows before standing to wander around the room. "Can he hear us?" Ron referred to the stationary guard posted just outside the closed door.

"I doubt he thinks you have anything so profound to say that he'd be willing to invest the necessary effort to eavesdrop," she said, irritated. This indicated that his attention was focused in the wrong direction.

"You know, you don't talk like anyone they ever fetched us before," he said, wearing a curious look while stuffing both hands into his front pockets. He continued to wander.

"Ron, can I have your undivided attention? Time probably doesn't mean much to you, but I—"

"Ha! That's a laugh! What the hell would you know about time?" he said, displaying a cocky smirk that she felt sure didn't fit the characteristics of his personality, but rather that of his fellow inmates. He liked copying the other prisoners. He liked the idea of fitting in with them, but at some level he knew he didn't.

"Well, silly me! I didn't know that the only way to understand time was to sit in this filthy mess and wallow in self-pity," she said, resting an elbow on the table. "See, I thought time went by at the same speed for those who actually got off their asses and turned their lives into something as it did for those who don't—or won't. Did time change for you when you got here or when you blew the head off the convenience store clerk for $127? That was the take on the

7-Eleven job, wasn't it, Ron?" Jennifer asked in an escalating tenor voice.

"All right already!" Ron said, eyeing the guard who'd turned to look through the window.

"Don't worry, Ron, he won't come in because of our loud voices," she said, almost chuckling.

"I guess the other guys was sure wrong about you," Ron said, sitting to comply with Jennifer's expectations. "Do you know what the other guys have been callin' you?"

"Does it have more than four letters?" she asked, squinting.

"Lily White," Ron said with candor. "That's what they been callin' you. And me too." Shrugging only one shoulder, Ron continued, "Well, you gotta admit that you don't exactly look like you belong carryin' your business into a prison. We all figured you for some Fifth Avenue shrink."

Now she understood why they'd all been so reluctant to openly share in a prior group session. "Well, I guess you better tell your buddies to be more careful about labeling, especially labeling people they don't know," she said, leaning back in the chair, fighting the broad dimpled grin that seemed determined to debut. "By the way, that's *Ms.* Lily White to you!" She allowed the smile full exposure.

"Got it!" Ron laughed, feeling vulnerable, the one thing he didn't want to feel. He knew now the others didn't have Ms. Lily White figured out quite as well as they thought.

"We got a long way to go, Ron," she said.

"I guess so." He looked down, rubbing both palms together between his knees.

Jennifer had surmised by the first group session that Ron probably had some mental issues and wondered why there hadn't been more follow-ups since he arrived. Whether they were innate or homegrown was yet to be determined. The head can take just so many hits before the brain gets irretrievably scrambled.

*****

Robert Henderson dashed to Jeff Hanes's office, hoping to catch his best friend still at work.

"Hi, Robert. It's good to see you," Jeff said, greeting him in the reception area. "Let's go in and take a seat." He led the way.

Jeff's office was modeled after the letter *L*, and the most private conversations took place in the bottom of the letter where the wall was uniquely papered in pictures of children playing. A small, round mahogany table accompanied four overstuffed chairs, creating a cove-like feeling inside the large light-paneled room. The larger part of the *L* was designed for anyone to feel like they were visiting "Grandma's living room" so that even the most timid stranger could feel at home. The space was often filled with the smell of freshly brewed coffee and a lingering aroma of peppermint, which drifted from the decorative candy-filled canister sitting on Jeff's desk. The long end of the *L* featured a huge bay window with baby blue vertical blinds, which exposed a view of the Clear Water Springs shopping district. A beige soft-leather couch by Jeff's desk looked inviting for the weary and troubled soul, comforting enough for a child to feel snug and secure. It was Jennifer's favorite spot.

Sitting in the privacy part of the *L*, Robert asked, "I suppose you've heard?"

"Who hasn't by now? How did Burt Walker manage an appeal for Charlie?" Jeff asked.

"Just a stroke of dumb luck on my part," Robert said, shaking his head, remembering the unexpected visitors who stormed his office late Tuesday afternoon. He breathed a sigh of relief before relating the story to Jeff.

*****

Phillip and Carol Amsbury had arrived at Robert's office unannounced, dressed casually in jeans and tees. They had convinced the receptionist that they had pertinent information concerning the night Stix was murdered and insisted on talking to Mr. Henderson.

"C'mon in. We can talk in here," Robert had said, showing them into his office. They appeared clean and friendly, but Robert picked up on their anxiousness to say what they had come to say.

"So you knew Charlie Bremmer?" Robert asked after they were seated.

"We knew everyone who hung out at the Brandy Snifter back in those days," Phillip said, who had wide dark eyes that complemented his curly black hair.

"See, Mr. Henderson, ten years ago, my husband and I were pretty heavy into the drinkin' and druggin' scene," Carol began. "We left Clear Water Springs the night of the murder for the sole purpose of checking into a rehab place out of state to get clean and sober. I used to be a freelance photographer, which is just another way of saying no one would hire me. But anyway, leaving town that night, we took pictures of everything—the school we both went to, our apartment, the library, and our favorite hangout, the Brandy Snifter." Carol said with sincerity. Her soft blue eyes appeared intelligent and paid tribute to her shoulder-length, soft-curled blond hair.

"Carol took a picture of what we thought were two men fist fighting in front of the Brandy Snifter at about midnight the night of the murder," Phillip said. "I can't tell you how many times that picture has become a topic of conversation. And we never knew what kept drawing us back to it. After all, we'd only seen Stix once, and that was in our stupor days."

"You were in the bar that night?" Robert asked.

"We were in that bar *every* night," Phillip said, not sounding ashamed or proud, just speaking candidly.

"Do you have those pictures with you?" Robert asked.

"I have all of them from that night, dated and timed," Carol said, pulling them from her purse. "Those two men fighting are Stix and Eddie Wallace. You can tell by their size that Charlie Bremmer isn't in the picture. See, he's much smaller than those men." She pointed to them while comparing another picture taken of Charlie that same night. She waited for Robert's response before continuing.

"Why did you wait so long to come forward with these?" Robert asked, his eyes focused on the faces in the picture.

"We had no idea that Charlie had been convicted or sent to death row. We were screwed-up druggies in our early twenties when we left here. It wasn't until I was transferred from the *Kansas City Chronicle* to the *Clear Water Springs Journal* that I started fishing through back issues, trying to fit the pieces together. And guess what? They *didn't* fit," Carol said, watching Robert's eyes zoning in on one picture and then another and another. He knew he was looking at the truth.

"What do you do, Phillip?" Robert asked.

"I've been a manager in retail for almost seven years, so when Carol got this job offer, I figured it wouldn't be too hard for me to find work here," Phillip said, glancing at his wife. "But, Mr. Henderson, there was no way for us to know about Charlie. Kansas City, Missouri, had bigger fish to fry on their ten o'clock news than filling airtime with a small-town murder in Colorado, and we were too busy getting ourselves straightened out to think about anything else." Phillip used a tone of unequivocal honesty that gripped Henderson's heart. *These people are on the level!* They knew Henderson could check into their stories in about ten minutes—and he did.

"Over the years, we've reminisced about the people and places in Clear Water Springs and all the other people who were just like us at the Brandy Snifter," Carol continued. "We kept pictures of them all and promised ourselves that we were going to look 'em up some-day, but we never seemed to get to it. I always thought it was odd that the memory of them stayed with us for so long."

"May I have the pictures long enough to duplicate them?" Robert asked. "I'll give them right back, I promise."

"Consider these yours. We have copies at home," Carol offered.

*****

When Robert finished talking about his visitors, Jeff asked, "Have you told Elizabeth about this?"

"No, I haven't had time. I've been up most of the night and all morning, trying to prevent an innocent man from being executed. I stopped by to see her this afternoon at the prison, but she apparently chose to take a week off," Robert said.

"Does she have any personal feelings tied up in this execution?" Jeff asked, wondering about the peculiar timing of her vacation.

"I don't know about that." Robert was feeling uncomfortable. "Well, I got to get going and find a way to let her know."

"If there's anything I can do . . . " Jeff said, then hearing his phone ring.

"I know. Thanks. I'll call you." Robert got up to leave as Jeff answered the phone.

Outside Jeff's office, Robert felt the shame of lying to his best friend, something he'd never done before and hoped he'd never have to do again. But he felt trapped between the truth he owed his best friend and the secret he promised to keep for the woman he loved. The fact was that he *did* know about Elizabeth's personal involvement with Charlie Bremmer.

Robert remembered sitting with Elizabeth in the green overstuffed chairs. She agonized over words, her pain so deep even tears couldn't surface to offer relief.

*****

"If executing a murderer is based on the premise that the act is justifiable, then why is this execution performed behind closed doors with only a few select people as witnesses? If it's justifiable, why are there so few qualified people willing to inject the lethal solution?" Her voice sank lower, and Robert felt the depth of her pain. "And what separates those people from any other random murderer?"

He guided her head gently to his shoulder, knowing no words would stop the suffering. Although Robert wasn't sure at the time Charlie didn't commit the murder, years of deep soul-searching had changed his feelings about the death penalty. Now the guilt of being the prosecuting attorney at Charlie's first trial felt like lye eating holes in the pit of his stomach. Because of this conflict of interest, Henderson had to take himself out of all the appeals for Charlie. He was no longer the DA but an attorney in private practice that had been called upon from time to time to be a public defender. The helpless, hopeless feeling of despair was only magnified by Elizabeth's soft sobs.

She sat straight in the chair, her face wrenched in pain, before Robert said, "I don't think you can ask me anything about capital punishment I haven't already asked myself—the uselessness of it all! What do we tell the next generation when they ask why we killed him? Are we going to say, or even think, Charlie was executed so he couldn't kill others? He wasn't being accused of being a mass murderer or serial killer. He hadn't beaten, tortured, and raped women and children. And he certainly wasn't a terrorist, domestic or foreign. Are we going to say it was to deter others from killing? Or we could say that we put him to death to show others how much we value life and hope they don't see the palpable convoluted logic!"

"It's like the mother who hits her son to teach him not to hit another child," Elizabeth said.

"People don't often see their illogical motives," Robert continued. "They're too blinded by their raging revenge. And if the death penalty was used on someone other than minorities and the poor, it might seem more applicable in heinous crimes. See, I don't think of the death penalty as being a punishment or a deterrent for crime. That much has been proven. But I do believe it should be used rarely, and never capriciously, and only for extreme situations, like the ones you just mentioned. That also goes for all extremist groups that terrorize and murder in the name of Allah or any other deity. These kinds of people can't help it. They do to others what has been done to them. They've been tortured somewhere along life's path, not necessarily physically. Their terminally damaged souls and minds have no way to heal—at least not on earth."

"But that's not how the death penalty is used. Too often it's used capriciously, and sometimes even with malice," Elizabeth said in a defeated tone and then confided, "I heard that one of the questions raised upon my appointment here was, 'How would a female warden handle an execution?' As if I wouldn't be tough enough just because I'm a woman. I no longer feel the need to prove myself to anyone in this system. The idea that executing a murderer takes a strong character is ridiculous. It takes a much stronger one *not* to execute," she said.

"Are you questioning Charlie's innocence?" he asked, eyes wide.

"No, he's innocent, that part I'm sure about. But I'm wondering how many other times we've sentenced an innocent person to death," she said, restraining the tears.

Robert was drawn to her piercing eyes, which showed her fear of executing the innocent. "What makes you so sure he's not guilty?" Robert asked.

Elizabeth got up to walk to the chair behind her desk and sat down. Observing his confused expression, she groped for the right words. She allowed her eyes to wander the room for a moment, and Robert intuitively knew that something was about to be revealed that, up until now, belonged only to Elizabeth.

"I talked with Charlie the night he came here to death row ten years ago," she said. Her penetrating green eyes changed from a sad blue to a shadowy hazel gray.

"And what? You believed his story about—"

"What I believe is that Charlie is incapable of lying now, just as he was incapable of killing then. I was married to him for seven years, Robert. He picked up a bad habit. I left him. He ended up in Cocaine Anonymous. He claimed it changed his life, and I believe him. It's that simple," she said, watching him shake his head in disbelief.

His eyes became fixed on Elizabeth's face as he waited for her to say this was some sort of a colossal joke, but he knew it wasn't. Her eyes always held chaste truth.

"I-I don't know what to say. I-I had no idea" was all he could manage to utter.

"No one does. I'd like to keep it that way," she said.

"No problem," he managed, attempting to absorb the shock. "But how many times have I heard you say that there are no secrets in prison?"

*****

Getting into his car, Robert could only feel relief after finding the memory of Elizabeth's words replaced by thoughts of how to contact her. Calling on his cell phone, he learned the prison wasn't releasing the warden's number. He thought of Perkins. *Maybe he'll help. He's one of her most trusted allies.* Driving to the prison's administration building, he saw most of the press had left, and only a few diehards remained, who were all too quick to ask, "Why are you trying to free a man that you helped send to death row? Now you're giving aid to the enemy! Would you like to comment?" Robert passed by them, ignoring their hounding questions. He knew all too well that the press wanted to remind him that he was the one who prosecuted Bremmer. What'd they think? He forgot?

"Well, Mr. Henderson, what brings you here?" Perkins asked, greeting him at the door. "Ms. Ellsworth's out of town."

"I need her number at the cabin," Robert said.

"Now you know I can't give out that kind of information even if I had it, and I'm not saying I do," Perkins said. "All I can tell you is that she's taken the phone off the hook so no one can talk to her right now."

"You mean she doesn't know?" Robert asked. "Can I wait in her office until someone is able to reach her?"

"Now *that* I can do for you," Perkins said, smiling. He led Robert down the long corridor where three staff members now had the warden on the phone, filling her in on Charlie's appeal.

"She wants to talk to you, in private," one said, handing Robert the phone and closing the door behind them.

"Why didn't you tell me about this before I left?" she asked as soon as they were alone.

"I wanted to tell you in person, privately, but by the time I could get to you, you were gone. Anyway, I got Charlie the best lawyer in town," Robert said.

"Burt Walker?" she asked, a quiver in her voice. "You're the best!"

"That's what I keep trying to tell you," he said with a chuckle. "I'll fill you in on everything when you get back here, but there's one thing you need to know," he said. Elizabeth tried to muffle her tears of joy.

"Are you okay?" Robert asked.

"Yeah. I'm okay," she said.

"Charlie's informed us that this will be his last appearance in court. He wants no more appeals, no more court dates," he said.

"Should I come back now?"

"No, you need the rest. Besides, there's really nothing you can do right now."

"You probably know this without me saying it, but you better be thick-skinned when the press gets hold of the fact that the same person who sent Charlie to death row has now secured him a high-profile defense lawyer," she said.

"They've already got hold of it, and I don't give a damn. If it hadn't been for a conflict of interest, I would've appealed it myself," Robert said.

"Good night, Robert," she said, sighing a smile before hanging up the phone.

After dropping the phone in its cradle, Robert whispered, "I love you." He felt a deep craving to hold Elizabeth close and forever even though he knew her heart didn't belong to him.

*****

Jeff knew he needed to tell Jennifer about Charlie's appeal in person, but as he pulled into her driveway, he saw Peter's car there. Thinking only for a brief moment as to whether he should go in or not, he found himself knocking on Jennifer's door.

"Hi, Jeff, come on in," Jennifer greeted him.

"I really don't want to intrude on the two of you, but there's something we need to talk about," he said, looking apologetically at Peter.

"No, that's okay, Jeff. I was getting ready to leave anyway," Peter said, kissing Jennifer goodbye.

They settled at the kitchen table. "I guess you already know about Charlie's appeal," Jeff said.

"Not the specifics. Does Elizabeth know?" she asked.

"I think she does by now. Robert feels he's found reliable witnesses. He persuaded Burt Walker to take the appeal," he said.

"You're kidding!" Jennifer squealed, showing surprise by lifting her eyebrows. "Charlie won't be able to claim incompetent defense *this* time."

"That's for sure," Jeff said, feeling happy to see her shoulders drop slightly and her wrinkled brows smooth out. "You look really tired tonight, Jen."

"Just a lot of stress," she said. "I feel like a balloon with a slow leak."

"That's good," he said, wanting to caress her head. "You won't have any problem sleeping, will you? In fact, Jen, why don't I sleep in your spare bedroom for tonight? It would make me feel better. *Really!* I know those calls have to be creating some sleepless nights."

"Well, maybe that wouldn't be such a bad idea. I'd probably sleep a little better. Tomorrow I'm going with Peter to Aspen for some skiing. I'm sure that'll help me get a better perspective on things," she said, trying to convince herself.

But she tossed and turned and slept restlessly while her mind played out hideous reruns of the monsterlike man and Doralee being shot. Each dream became more distorted, more violent, with visions of lethal weapons dancing around her face. She'd awake in cold sweaty chills, her heart racing as though it might just jump right out of her chest. Eventually, exhaustion persuaded her fearful mind to rest, and shallow slumber followed.

Jeff's sleep didn't come in the first few hours. He could hear intermittent, distressing sounds coming from Jennifer's room, bringing back feelings of helplessness. He wanted to rush into her room and hold her—all night if necessary—until she could feel safe. He knew underneath it all that she had been traumatized and would deal with it in her own way and in her own time. If he tried to help before he was invited, Jennifer would say, "Now don't try to catch me before I fall."

But what Jeff had no intention of sharing with Jennifer was the fact that he simply didn't trust Peter. He had no visible evidence to back those feelings, and until he did, he would keep quiet. She seemed to adore him, and Jeff was going to leave well enough alone—for now.

While Jeff and Jennifer struggled to fall asleep, Peter Winslow had some moonlighting to do. In a run-down area of Clear Water Springs where people no longer shopped or even wanted to be seen, Winslow entered through a back door of a small slum building that had long been boarded up and forgotten.

"Hi, Peter, take a seat," Lark said, pointing to the rickety table with four beat-up chairs.

"What he doing here?" Peter asked, looking at Hank Poovey.

"Breezy wants him here," Lark replied.

"Where's Breezy?" Peter asked.

"You know Breezy doesn't show for these kinds of meetings. When Breezy shows, heads roll!" Lark said with an ostentatious wicked grin. "Jennifer's been attending regular scheduled meetings for the Colorado Criminal Justice Commission, and because it's an open meeting, one of Breezy's men always attends. For each meeting, Breezy sends in a different man to keep any suspicion away from him. He isn't too concerned over HB 134 that would allow the convicts to vote while still in prison, but he is concerned about HB 135, which allows time to be taken off the inmates' sentence by staying clean and sober. That's way too much of an incentive not to drink and drug. That's the same thing as stealing from Breezy. Now look, Peter, you either take care of this or—"

"Consider it taken care of already," Peter interjected. "Tell Breezy that Jennifer's not going to do anything, okay? You got my word on it."

"Our informants say Jennifer hangs out with the spokesperson on the hill," Lark charged. "They are a little too chummy for Breezy's likings. Are you surprised by this, or did you already know?"

"No, I didn't know, and yes, I am surprised." Peter began to rub his forehead, trying to erase the confusion.

"This bill cannot pass! Period!" Lark said, slamming his fist on the ancient table.

"This could hit our bankbook pretty hard. Breezy won't stand for it. The merchandise has to keep moving as always. If this bill passes, Breezy says we'll lose at least 25 percent of our revenue, maybe more! You think he's going to stand still for that?"

"What? What do you want me to do?"

"She's your responsibility. We told you not to fall in love with her when we set her up as your girlfriend and began using her to get the drugs to the prison."

"Look! This bill is a long way from being passed. A lot can happen between now and then," Peter argued. "And I'm not in love with her." He barely squeaked by with that lie. He had tried so hard not to fall in love with Jennifer, but her warmth and kindness had crept up on him just like one of her dimpled smiles.

"They're getting close to going to the floor of the Colorado House of Representatives for a vote. You do realize that if it passes there, then it goes on to the Senate, and if it passes there, it goes on the governor's office to be signed?" Lark announced perturbed. "I'm telling you not to let Jennifer Collin become a problem, or the next time she has a car accident, it will be fatal! You got it!"

Peter fell back in his seat. Oh my God, Breezy did have a hand in Jennifer's car accident. What would I do without her? What if something happened to her because of the drug operation?

"Don't worry, I'll take care of everything," Peter mumbled. "But please don't arrange for any more accidents or leave any more threatening messages on her phone recorder."

"I don't know what you're talking when you say threatening messages. That's not Breezy's style. That's not how he operates. You should know that." Lark looked surprised. "He doesn't pussyfoot around when it comes to his bank account losing money."

"You know, Jennifer only has a few short months left at the prison so—"

"I don't care if she leaves tomorrow. She's still involved with HB 135, and that's what puts her life in jeopardy. You got it!" Lark warned.

"Like I said, it probably won't pass anyway. It's a long shot at best," Peter insisted.

"You see it stays that way," Lark demanded.

Chapter IV

"Good morning," Jeff said, emerging from the spare bedroom, tucking his shirt into tapered-legged trousers. "Hey, I was going to make breakfast for you this morning."

"That's okay. It's about ready now. Why don't you pour me some milk before you take a seat," she said, flipping the pancakes over and then pouring orange juice into flower-rimmed glasses. "As you know, I'm not big on breakfast unless I have company." She reached for the top of the corduroy robe, securing a tight closure around the neck. *Why am I feeling the need for modesty with Jeff? He'd seen me in my jammies before. For Pete's sake, he's seen me in my bathing suit.*

"Ah-h-h, I hear the coffee pot calling my name," Jeff said, reaching for mug before pouring the milk. He was amused by her inhibited gesture, which continued even after breakfast began.

Jeff waited until the pancakes had just about disappeared before saying, "Last night, you didn't want to talk about the obscene phone messages or the maniac, but I would like to ask you something now."

"Go ahead," she said, pouring extra syrup over the last two bites of her pancakes before devouring them.

"Could any of this tie in with your past clients or maybe spouses of past clients? We have to look at every avenue, Jen. How many abused women have you counseled?" he asked, finishing the last drop of orange juice.

"Too many to count."

"Exactly," he said. "How many recently? Let's say in the last year or so."

"Well, as you already know, by January I'd started to turn all my efforts toward initiating the HBP into the prison and began limiting my client intake. By July, I only had a handful of clients, so I closed my office and moved all my belongings here, like one day after I bought my house. I referred any clients that I felt needed more counseling to other colleagues," she said, gulping down the last swallow of milk.

"Were any of those last few clients women who had been abused by men?" he asked.

"Yeah, there was one. Lori Watkins. She worked through some boyfriend abuse problems," Jennifer said, patting a napkin on her milk-rimmed lips. "But the kind of retaliation you're inferring usually happens when the client is still in therapy, which, for Lori, was more than six months ago."

"I was just wondering," he said, resting an elbows upright on the table, laying his chin in a cupped hand.

"I know the feeling," she said, clearing the table.

"Jen, I'm having your neighbor, Angela, checked out by Detective Malloy."

"Jeff, I don't think—"

"Remember, every avenue."

"Okay, but as rotten as she has been to me, I believe she's nothing more than a pot stirrer who finds a way to get everyone all upset and then sits back and watches. I don't honestly think she has a police record."

"Maybe not here, yet. Well, thanks for breakfast, but I better get going," Jeff said abruptly, recognizing the doubt in her eyes. "You need to get ready for your trip." He headed for the door, Jennifer in tow. "Have you told Peter about your car accident?"

"Yeah, sort of. Actually, he got most of his information from the newspaper," she said. "He didn't ask for any additional info, so I let it go at that."

"Well, that's probably for the best," Jeff said.

"Thank you, Jeff, for everything. I don't know what I'd do without you. I feel bad that you have to be mixed up in this mess," she said.

"I don't *have* to be. I *want* to be," he said, kissing her forehead before leaving.

"Wait, Jeff, I forgot to wish you a happy Thanksgiving. By the way, what are you doing today?" she asked.

"I've been invited over to some friends' house," he said.

"Then you're not going to be alone?" she asked.

"No, I don't find it necessary to isolate myself on the holidays anymore," he said, smiling. He wished her a happy Thanksgiving and left.

*****

Throwing some things together for the trip, Jennifer was surprised to feel genuine excitement. Maybe it was because she knew being with Peter this weekend would kind of like being a teenager on a hayride. There would be stimulation. She could sure use the break—from everything.

For now, she could let go of the times hesitation about her relationship with Peter had caused confusion. The kind that had never been identified, but would sweep through like an unexpected gush of wind. Then a slow quiet would return, and the feeling would somehow become meaningless, almost imaginary. Today, she felt free to concentrate on the positive side of her emotions, which discreetly whispered dreams of Peter and her always being together. Peter was the only person to come around in a long time that gave her hope that she could comfortably keep Jeff in the "friendship column." Anything close to ambiguous feelings placed imbalance in her life, and for Jennifer, that was just unacceptable.

Peter Winslow was the picture of what contemporary society has described as the tall, dark, handsome type. Although his boyish face meshed well with his high energy level, neither characteristic confidently reflected the image of a man in his late forties. He had been a muscle-building enthusiast and went to the gym three or four times a week to work out, but lately he spent more time with Jennifer and a little less time at the gym. She couldn't help but marvel at Peter's impeccable taste in clothes and had yet to see him in anything as mundane as blue jeans. She found his idiosyncrasies humorous as well as refreshingly titillating. In some ways, he reminded her of a comical Ken doll, Barbie's partner—both fabrications of Madison Avenue. Peter was also the kind of guy whom Jennifer went out of her way to avoid—until now.

After only five months of dating, she couldn't justify any expectations, consciously or subconsciously. Thoughts of Peter's extravagant gift buying were shrugged off as "just being Peter's way." He enjoyed talking about almost anything except his past, which Jennifer thought was curious, but she saw no need to pursue a line of questioning that only seemed to make him feel uncomfortable. *So maybe he didn't have a nifty childhood. Maybe there was pain that he wasn't prepared to talk about yet.* Peter was a successful businessman and an attentive partner. Most of all, he possessed an animated sense of humor, which made her feel twenty years old again. For now, maybe that was all she needed to know.

Resting one hand on the phone, she rehearsed a couple of questions she had for him, but the phone rang before she could pick it up and dial.

"I was just going to call you," she said, surprised to hear Peter's voice.

"Is that anyway to answer the phone?" Peter chuckle. "How'd you know I wasn't Jack the Ripper or the Boston Strangler?"

"Because neither one of them ever calls me," she said.

"Yeah? And they better not," he laughed. "So what time will you be ready to hit the road?"

"Half hour ago," she said.

"Girlfriend, you *are* organized. How 'bout I pick you up at eight this morning?"

"You mean ten minutes after eight, don't you?" she said, ribbing him about his predictable tardiness.

"I'll be there at eight," Peter said. "By the way, your car will be ready in a week or two, but until then, I'm giving you a lender to get you by, another Subaru, if you don't mind. Your old Subaru will be getting a new hood, fender, and windshield. Plus, they'll knock the dents out and clean it up as good as new. Luckily, there wasn't a lot of damage."

"Thanks, Peter. See you soon." She hung up the phone, pleased her questions had been answered without having to ask.

Jennifer used the short wait to organize files. She settled in the third bedroom, which had been converted into an office before the ink had time to dry on the mortgage papers. To Jennifer, organization meant lessening the pressures of a chaotic world, which she had presumed the rest of society had merely learned to either accept or ignore.

Light-oak bookcases lined one entire wall and extended from the floor to the ceiling. The room escaped the overcrowded look with the depth created by sculptured beige carpet. On a shorter wall stood matching filing cabinets, providing ample room for past-client information, which she held for a minimum of four years on a thumb drive. Each file was coded by colors and numbers to protect client privacy, such as the color red with a number one identified first-time violence, the color blue with number two identified ongoing depression. The only uncoded words were the names on the filing tabs.

Pulling open the bottom drawer of a filing cabinet, her attention was drawn to a bent tab on a recently filed folder. A quizzical look swept over Jennifer's face after reading Lori Watkins's name. Sitting on the floor, file in hand, she thumbed through Lori's experience with her abusive boyfriend, still wondering how the file had become damaged. Her bewildered thoughts ended abruptly when Peter knocked on the front door. She ran down the hall to open the door.

"Hi, Peter," she said, suppressing any perplexing thoughts about the damaged file.

"Hi, babe." He entered with buoyant, carefree steps, holding a miniature clay turkey in the palm of his hand. "I know I'm a little late, but I forgot to gas up my Land Cruiser. Am I forgiven?" he asked, with the assurance of immediate clemency.

"You are too cute," she grinned, "and so is your friend." She held the ceramic turkey as if it was a valuable piece of jewelry. She envied Peter's exuberance, which went into high gear at the crack of dawn. She loved the way he always seemed to be thinking of her. "Let me put a couple of things in order and we can go."

Jennifer went back to the office alone and returned Lori's file to its original place before they headed out the front door. After locking the dead bolt, she forced all thoughts of Lori and the bent tab out of her mind.

The ride felt tranquil as Jennifer gazed at hundreds of shades of red, orange, and green adding to the sparkling hues of the mountains. It looked as if a painter came by and dripped watercolors by bucketfuls over the landscape. It had been one of those glorious Indian summers where hot days intruded into September and October, delaying fall's colorful arrival. Everything had escaped snow except the high country.

Peter talked and hand gestured, skipping harmoniously, as well as humorously, from one subject to another. Jennifer remained silent, mesmerized by the inexplicable strength one could absorb from the mountains. It was as if they had a personality of their own and were allowing her a humble insight into their complexity. Peter seemed almost oblivious to the sight of several herds of elk and deer, and even a buffalo ranch. Jennifer didn't miss the opportunity to enjoy nature at its finest. Her mind went into neutral, pondering such trivialities as what the deer thought when getting a glimpse of their own reflection as they drank from a crystal-clear mountain lake. Or what the sound of speeding tires snugly adhering to the pavement sounded like to the squirrels, rabbits, and chipmunks. And whether the birds just go their merry way undisturbed, no matter how many new freeways mutate their environment. Are they really as free as they look?

Peter broke her blissful thoughts by reaching into his pocket and pulling out a key. "Here. I'd like you to have this. It's to my house via the garage."

"Why?" she asked, taking the key with skepticism.

"I just thought if you ever wanted to come over when I wasn't home, you could just let yourself in," he said.

"Thanks, Peter. That was thoughtful of you." She dropped the key to the bottom of her purse, feeling unprepared for this step in their relationship. Maybe it was just Peter giving her reassurance that there were no other women in his life, but intuitively she already knew that from the beginning.

"You know, Jennifer, you don't talk very much about your work. How's it going at the prison?" he asked.

"It's too soon to tell, but I'm hopeful."

"I've never asked this, but do you deal with really hardened criminals?"

"You mean, as opposed to the softened criminals?" she asked, biting her bottom lip to prevent a grin.

"You know what I mean," he said, exposing his toothy grin.

"The men I counsel have all led very different lives from what you're used to. They aren't bad people. They're just people who have needed help for a long time," she explained.

"Well, do you go by the theory that they're sick or something? I mean, does the prison operate like a hospital or more like a warehouse?"

"I see the prison simply as a warehouse, not a place conducive to healing or wellness. For example, let's say you went into an emergency room at a hospital because your arm had been broken. Now let's say you sat there for days, or even weeks, but no one ever gave you medical treatment. So you leave the hospital with an arm that has mended itself incorrectly, leaving you crippled to some degree. You'd have the same problem you did when you went in, except now it'd be worse," she said.

"That's a scary antidote for our criminals," Peter said, pausing thoughtfully. "But see, the difference between them and me is that while I was in the emergency room, I'd be screaming for someone to fix my arm."

"The inmates scream too. It's just that they don't know what needs to be fixed," she said.

"Maybe not, but they know they're in pain."

"That's very insightful, Peter. And yeah, they do. But for most of them, pain, in one form or another, is all they've ever known. They think everyone is in that kind of pain, but it's just that the rest of the world hides it better," she said.

"And if the prison operated like a hospital?"

"Doctors don't treat your pain in a punitive manner, whether its cause is self-inflicted or a negligent accident. And they don't need to assign blame in order to help you heal," she said.

"Is that how psychologists think about emotional pain?"

"I don't know. I do," she said, reflecting.

"When I read about the Homeward Bound Program in the paper last July, I remembered something about the recidivism rate," he said.

"Yeah, I'm conducting research on why the recidivism rate is so high," she said, impressed that he remembered detailed information about her work. Most people sidestep discussing her chosen vocation. It's messy and uncomfortable.

"Well, Ms. Lily, are you getting hungry yet?" Peter asked. "There's a nice little restaurant up ahead."

"How'd you know about that name?" she asked, startled.

"I-I dunno. I guess I heard it somewhere," he murmured. "You want something to eat?"

"No thanks. I had a big breakfast, but let's stop anyway. I could make room for coffee," she said, still feeling bewildered about his knowledge of her prison moniker. The only one who knew about it, besides her men in the HBP, would probably be Mr. Perkins, but she was fairly certain that that kind of information wouldn't have been passed by Perkins or any other kind of information dealing with the prison.

"You had a big breakfast? The woman who can only manage juice and toast in the morning?" Peter asked with facetious surprise.

"Yeah, well, I guess I was hungry this morning," she said, seeing no reason to tell him Jeff had spent the night or why.

"Here it is," Peter said, pulling into a parking spot. He jumped out to open Jennifer's door, bowing at the waist with sheer whimsical graciousness. "Come with me to the Kasbah, my dear."

"You are too funny, Peter, and sweet too," she said with a cheerleader's smile, bouncing down from the Land Cruiser.

"But not as sweet as you," he rejoined, holding her hand.

They were still laughing and cooing at a table inside when, suddenly, the romantic mood was broken when Peter felt something warm streaming from his nostrils. He pulled a handkerchief from his pocket to absorb the blood that first had trickled, then gushed, from his nose.

"My gosh, Peter, does this happen often?" she asked, rummaging through her purse, looking for anything absorbent.

He rushed to the restroom, returning minutes later with an apology. "I'm really sorry about that. I'm sure it's just the high altitude."

"I hope so," she replied apprehensively.

Arriving at the rented chalet in Aspen, Jennifer said, "Oh, Peter! This place is gorgeous!"

"And this is just the foyer. Wait till you see the bedroom loft," he said playfully.

"But wait. Look at that moss-rock fireplace and the windows! Have you ever seen so many huge windows? It's like a glass house. Think of all the great plants you could grow here," she said, her big brown eyes seeking out every nook and cranny.

"Yeah, it's nice, but let's take our bags upstairs," he said. "Here, I'll help carry yours." He was trying to use his eyes to portray a slow seduction, but to Jennifer, he looked more like he was imitating Groucho Marx. She laughed at the ingenuity he used to amuse her.

As Peter carried the bags up the sharp-winding, wrought iron staircase, Jennifer followed in a deliberate slow pace, gaining different perspectives of the chalet with each turn. Reaching the open loft, Peter set the bags down before feeling disappointed that Jennifer wasn't at his heels.

"Oh my! You should see this view from the top step, Peter," she said, feeling like a proverbial mouse inspecting the floor plan.

Peter came over to her just long enough to take her hand and lead her to the loft, saying, "Uh-huh, it's nice. But this is nicer." He planted a long, passionate kiss on her moist lips and laid her down gently, slipping her sweater over her head. She helped free him of his trousers and then . . .

Jennifer's mind drifted back to the first time they had made love. It was Labor Day weekend and a bunch of her friends had asked her and Peter to go with them camping at the lake. She remembered how Peter jumped at the chance even before asking her if she wanted to go; he later apologized for the inconsideration. When the paired couples arrived at the lake, Peter immediately began setting up camp. Jennifer was better at taking direction on a camping trip while Peter pounded pegs into the ground for securing the tent and provided a large plastic throw-over for the top of the tent. This would allow the rain (if any fell) to run off the top of the tent, keeping both of them from getting wet. She collected rocks for later when they would want to secure a campfire and used two trees for anchors for a clothesline that would dry out wet bathing suits and towels.

After the wine had been imbibed, fresh fish were grilled and eaten, three salads were consumed, and pie was best decided for break-fast, everyone sleepily stumbled to their tents. Jennifer had a good idea why Peter was so anxious to go on this camping trip. It meant when they were alone together, things could become warm and fuzzy, maybe even intimate. But first they would lie on their backs in front of the tent on the cool ground, hands clutched together, listening to all the creatures—big and small—attempting to identify them by their vocal chords. They pinpointed the small and big dipper in the sky and marveled at the distinctly shaped half-moon.

As they lay down in their makeshift bed in the tent, Peter turned over and kissed her gently and seductively, pulling her night shirt off. After their lovemaking had been consummated, they fell asleep in each other's arms.

The following morning, while they were breaking camp, Jennifer couldn't shake the feeling that something had been missing in their night of passion. It wasn't as though she wasn't physically satisfied; it was more of an emotional absence. She just couldn't admit that Peter wasn't the only person on her mind last night. To admit that would be the same as admitting that she had two lovers, and that would be unacceptable—something insufferable. It would be the same as cheating. She didn't need any more self-loathing; she had all of that she could stand working through her issues in AA.

*****

After gearing up the next morning in skis and poles, Jennifer gave all the equipment a final visual inspection. "I sure hope I don't break anything today. Remember, I'm not exactly the skier that you are."

"You'll do fine. Just have fun. I'll meet you at five thirty this afternoon at the snack bar," he said, pulling small, chic goggles over his eyes.

The sunny day on the green beginners' slope offered perfect skiing conditions for Jennifer. She pushed off time after time down the snow-packed mountain, the terrain visible. She thought about Peter skiing the fresh-powdered black runs, the terrain steep and hazardous, and chills ran down her spine. But she envied her daredevil partner.

Hours later, she spied Peter's owl-eyed face caused by wearing goggles in the sun with no sunscreen. Jennifer joined him at the snack bar and covered her smile with her mitten.

"I'm pooped. How 'bout you?" she asked.

"We could go take a nap before dinner," he said.

"I'm afraid if I went to sleep now, I wouldn't wake up till morning."

"Who said anything about sleeping?"

"Where do you find your inexhaustible source of energy?"

"In my pocket," he said, patting his heart before standing. "C'mon, let's go."

Jennifer regained her strength by dinner and was delighted with the restaurant Peter had selected. Watching people chatting and the roaring fireplace made her feel warm and safe. She knew she would capture this precious moment, storing it neatly in her retrievable bank of memories. The flickering of the fire created an ornate glimmering on the hardwood floors and log walls, dancing as gracefully as two clandestine lovers.

When not another bite of the exquisite seafood could be eaten, Peter pulled a small gift-wrapped present from his pocket.

"This, my love, is for you," he said, bursting with pride.

"Oh, Peter, you shouldn't have," she whispered, exposing its contents. She anticipated another piece of expensive jewelry.

"Do you like it? Here, let me put it on you," he said, holding the ring between his thumb and index finger. "Jennifer Collins, will you marry me?"

Jennifer's body went numb, and her ability to articulate the English language failed. Peter placed the three-carat diamond engagement ring on her finger, leaving the unanswered question still at large.

*****

Monday morning came much too soon, at least in Jennifer's opinion. She stumbled out of bed to answer the aggressive knocking on the front door. The man from the repair shop had brought her a replacement car until hers could be fixed.

The cloud of confusion in her mind was a good indication that the reality of the weekend was struggling to register long after physical alertness had surfaced. An uneasy feeling that life was pushing her around without the benefit of direction felt like a Ferris wheel ride, the kind that doesn't pause for intermissions. With little cognition and no expressed consent, a hypnotic urge led her to call Jeff.

"Are you busy this morning?" she asked.

"Not too busy. What's up?" he asked.

"I was wondering if you could stop by."

"How about in an hour? By the way, how was your ski trip?"

"Oh, um . . . not a dull moment," she fumbled.

When Jeff arrived, a look of surprise showered his face. "Well, don't you look homey in your pink-flowered pair of flannel pajamas! Aren't you going to work?"

"Later. The men have to earn their keep in the morning, remember?" she asked, allowing her voice to border on sarcasm. Jeff smiled and requested coffee.

"Let's take it into my office. I want to show you something," she said, leading the way.

Lifting Lori Watkins's folder from the filing cabinet, she said, "Look at the tab on this file."

Not yet knowing the significance, Jeff asked, "Is this the file of the last abused woman you counseled?"

"Yeah, but it was filed under *Z*, not *W*, and the tab's been bent," she said.

"Hmmm, that *is* strange, considering how meticulous you are about your files. Someone's been in here."

"Yeah, well, the day you called to tell me about what Detective Malloy had found out, I came home to find my front door unlocked, and you know how security conscious I am. I didn't say anything to the police. I guess I forgot," she said. "I hadn't had a great day, by anyone's stretch of imagination."

"Whoever came in here might have left by the front door, but how do we know they didn't get in another way? But, they surely knew what they were looking for. " he said.

"Yeah, but they didn't take anything. Don't you think that's curious?" Jennifer asked.

"They tried to take information," Jeff said.

"But remember, I color-code everything to protect clients' privacy," she reminded.

"Yeah, that's true. I forgot. Can I take the file with me? Maybe there's a clue in here," he said.

"Sure. By the way, when I was away, I got two more of those messages," she said.

"And while you were away, I arranged for twenty-four-hour surveillance of your home. It's the van parked across the street," Jeff said, walking to the door. "If you can't play offense, then at least play defense."

"Pretty ironic, huh? I'm beginning to feel safer in the prison than I do in my own home," Jennifer said.

"You want to come and stay with me until this all blows over?" Jeff asked, knowing the answer before he asked it.

"I think staying here will bring things to a head quicker."

"God, you're tough!" he said, half kidding, half serious, then added with sarcasm, "Besides, what would the neighbors say?"

"Get outta here," she smiled, watching him walk to his car.

Jeff drove back to his office, mentally categorizing behavioral patterns from Peeping Toms to schizophrenics, until he narrowed some specific characteristics about Jennifer's menace. He only calls when he thinks Jennifer's not at home, symptomatic of feeling intimidated by confrontation. There are control issues since he wants to do all the talking, never giving Jennifer a chance for rebuttal. Narcissistic, can't take any form of criticism. Feels powerless, seeks gratification by terrorizing his victims. Needs to be drug—or alcohol—influenced to feel bravery. Has a heart that love has never touched. But all those symptoms also fit Angela, except maybe the drugs and alcohol. Jeff couldn't be sure of that either when it came to Angela. She certainly wouldn't be the first to be a closet alcoholic trying to blend into the background of the suburbs.

Jennifer dressed for work, feeling that Jeff's ability to grasp an ominous situation and push for resolution would end the nightmare soon. But starting out the door, arms full of books, she spotted the out-of-place, grayish blue van parked across the street, which only seemed to resume misgivings that maybe even Jeff couldn't conquer the devil that pursued her. The driver nodded inconspicuously as if to say, "I'm not your intruder, I'm on your side." Jennifer derived little security from the gesture.

Arriving at the prison, Perkins escorted her to Rec Room One. Jennifer was thankful she could show some restraint from asking questions that usually made him feel uncomfortable, but that didn't stop her craving to know more details about Charlie Bremmer's case. The truth was, she not only cared for Mr. Perkins, but she also respected his loyalty to Warden Ellsworth.

"Hi, Michael," Jennifer said, meeting her first client at the table. "I'll only be here in the afternoons from now on."

"So I've heard," Michael said as he watched her forehead grow small wrinkles. "Ms. Lily, there ain't no secrets in this place."

"*Isn't.* The word is *isn't.* Remember, the way you use the English language can make or break a job interview faster than your history will."

"Yeah, I know," he said, looking at the floor.

"Yes!" she snapped quickly. "The word is always *yes,* never *yeah.*"

Michael Bishop was a tall, husky black man in his late forties who stood 6 feet, 2 inches and weighed 220. He had short black hair and a shiny complexion with big round eyes that were set in just enough to realize that the windows to this soul had shut down more than once. Michael's size summoned images of intimidation, but his melodious voice contradicted that. An aura of style and grace covered up his surreptitious insecurities.

Michael had three felonies on his record, all drug related. On his first conviction, he served four years on a six-year sentence; on the second, he completed seven-and-a-half years on a ten-year sentence. But on this last conviction, second-degree murder in connection with a drug deal gone bad, he was sentenced to twenty years and had completed fifteen before volunteering for the HBP.

"Do you have your paper ready on long- or short-term goals?" Jennifer asked.

He handed her a paper that been erased a few times. She read, "When I git out of here I wanna go to work for a glass place."

"I know it isn't much of a paper, but I don't write so good," he said.

"So *well*, you don't write so *well*. That's fine, Michael, but can you elaborate a little bit more? Suppose you tell me what kind of glass place you mean," Jennifer requested.

"It's called glassblowing. I first saw it done when I was in Mexico," he said as she watched his eyes grow brighter. His face lit up like a Christmas tree, and she was sure that he was sharing with her his lost dream, and whether he knew it or not, he was also sharing some newfound self-esteem.

"Go on, I'd like to hear more," Jennifer said.

Excitement rose in Michael's expression as he explained glassblowing, using hand gestures with enthusiasm. "It's like a place where they melt down glass, and then they put a gob of it on the end of a blowpipe, and then air is blown through it to form the glass into a hollow sphere. The size, shape, and thickness of the glass are controlled by the pressure of the air and the angle at which the pipe is held and the speed at which the glass cools. It's formed into different shapes by the glassblower with tools, and then he twirls the pipe on a special bench. During this time, the glass is reheated so it can be formed easier."

"Have you ever actually done any glassblowing?" Jennifer asked.

"I have. It was a long time ago in a village in Mexico, in between jail times," he said with a quick grin. "A Mexican taught me. Somehow we overcame the communication problems. He was able to gesture enough, and I was able to read on the subject in English. We made out okay. Remember, you said we could be anything we wanted to be if we wanted it bad enough. You said we weren't any different from anyone else and not to put our goals too high or too low. You said to be realistic."

"Yes, I said that," Jennifer said. "Which do you think your ambition is?"

"Probably too unrealistic," he said, eyes dimming, indicating the admission of his dream had been an embarrassment.

"Why?" she asked.

"You mean, *you don't?*" Michael asked, a lilt in his voice.

"No, I don't," she assured him. "This is an achievable goal. Do what you would've done with your life if you could do it all over again."

"Ain't I . . . Aren't I . . . a little too old? I mean, isn't this something a kid on college break, would do?" he asked, observing her face attentively.

"Maybe, but don't compare yourself to others. Just follow your heart," she said.

"Yeah . . . I mean yes. I like that thought, but how would I find someone to teach me enough so that I could earn a living at it?" Michael asked.

"You can start by making inquiries into a college catalog or books in the library," she said, wondering which obstacle would come next.

"There's no privacy in a place like this. They'd call me fairy or wimp or, well, you know. You don't want to be known as a faggot in here, it ain't healthy . . . I mean, isn't healthy."

"Maybe I need to get out more because I don't see the correlation between glassblowing and homosexuality," she said. "How about if you practice saying, 'I need to do what's best for me, and I'm not going to wait for their permission.'"

"I guess I could do that," he smiled, feeling empowered by rehearsing it in his mind.

"I'm sure there were people who laughed at the Wright brothers, Thomas Edison, and Ben Franklin."

"But those were *white* men," he said.

"Your excuse list is growing longer and longer. Let's take a look at your self-made roadblocks: glassblowing is too unrealistic, I'm too old, other inmates might name-call. Yup! It's time to play the race card because you've used everything else," she said.

"It's not like that," he said, shaking his head in disagreement.

"Really?" she said, raising her eyebrows.

"I suppose this is where you're going to tell me I need to overcome how white people feel about the color of my skin," he said with a certain rehearsed sarcasm.

"No. This is where I tell you that not everyone *has feelings* about the color of your skin. You'll quit worrying about what other people think when you realize how seldom they do," she said, grinning.

"You mean, how seldom they think?" he asked.

"You got it," Jennifer said.

Michael paused to think, then laughed in his natural, tender voice. "Isn't that the truth, Ms. Lily? You know, you're nothin' like we thought you'd be."

"I'll take that as a compliment," she said with a quick wink.

Chapter V

Derek Coleman, a white male in his mid-forties, stood 5 feet, 5' inches, and weighed 155. Part of his straight light-brown hair flopped over a narrow forehead, touching the tips of his eyelashes. The intermittent whiplash movements of his head were an absolute annoyance to Jennifer. Derek's thin, even lips and round blue eyes contrasted nicely with the baby-clear complexion, giving the appearance of a much younger man.

The prison's psychological evaluation concluded Derek was narcissistic. Jennifer felt his symptom of outward self-centeredness could hardly qualify him for such a harsh label. In her opinion, it was a characteristic that only surfaced to protect a deep-rooted inferiority complex. Derek fought with tenacity against the "little guy" image he was sure others had of him. He'd use abrupt, callous language whenever he was being ignored or challenged or thought he was. In group sessions, he claimed the tallest chair was his, sitting a couple of heads higher than the rest of the group. That was his comfort zone.

Derek had two felonies of record: grand theft auto in which he served seven out of a ten-year sentence and possession and selling cocaine. He had served fifteen of his twenty-year sentence before volunteering for the HBP.

"Hi, Derek. Take a seat," Jennifer said on a cold December afternoon in Rec Room One.

"Hey, Ms. Lily," he said, grabbing the high-sitting yellow chair and pulling it next to her.

"Derek, how about using this chair for our one-on-one sessions?" she asked, pulling over a chair of equal height to her.

Reluctantly he obeyed but allowed "the attitude" to surface.

"I've had a chance to read your goals paper. You write very well," she said.

"For a convict, you mean," he muttered.

"I mean you write well. Period. Tell me why you chose to be a paramedic," she asked.

"What? You think I've set my goal too high?" he asked, challenging her from the corner of his eye. "That I'm not bright enough to be a paramedic, right?"

"Derek, settle down. No one's attacking you—or your goals. Paramedics are known for keeping a cool head in the midst of chaos," she said. "You know what *I* think, Derek? I think you want to use me to talk you out of this. You don't own the feeling of fear of failure. Many others possess it, others let it possess them," she said.

"I ain't afraid of nothin'," he said.

"I have a great idea. Let's start over again, but this time you play the part of a rational adult seeking career counseling. I'll play me," she said.

"Rational? Adult?" he smiled and snapped his head back, flipping the hair out of his face.

"Cute, Derek," she said with a smile. "You're quite a comedian when you're not trying to be difficult. Do you really want to be a paramedic?"

"It was all I ever wanted before trouble started knocking," he said.

"That's good, Derek, but you know it'll require special classes."

"I only had a year left of college when I got busted," he said, shrugging.

"You went to college? I didn't see that in your file." She looked perplexed. "It says you only finished high school."

"It's not going to make any difference what you tell them in here. The less they know about you, the better off you are. But it's not like it wasn't mentioned a few hundred times at my trial. Selling popular recreational drugs got me through school financially. Unfortunately, I started using the stuff, and that's when everything went to hell," he said, flipping a clump of intrusive hair back only to have it roll right down again. "But for awhile, it also kept me awake to study. Got a BA in biology."

"So all you'd need now are the paramedic classes, right?" she asked.

"Yeah, but because of the fact I have no income or, as the court would say, 'no visible means of support' and have a felony record, I doubt if I could get into school. And in case you haven't noticed, I'm not a kid anymore," he said, tossing his hair back.

"At least when you do an excuse list, you do it all in one breath. That's good, Derek. It saves time," Jennifer said.

"Those aren't excuses! You told us to be realistic, remember?" he said.

"Yes. Realistic, not fatalistic!" she snapped back. "Derek, when you were selling drugs to go to school, had you ever looked into grants, scholarships, or loans?"

"No. My dad taught me a long time ago that I needed to be self-sufficient. And that means never accepting charity," Derek said.

"Charity? C'mon, Derek, you're smarter than that," Jennifer said, noticing an inquisitive look in his eye movement, not a defensive look which is characteristic of a narcissistic person.

"What do you mean?" he asked.

"A government grant comes from taxes, which most of us feel is better spent on education than what the government usually uses our money for, like building more prisons. Scholarships are donated by people who would rather see you in college than selling drugs on the streets to their kids. A loan is paid back at a low interest rate, usually starting six months after graduation," she said.

He glanced into her eyes before steadying his sight on the chipped tile floor, biting his bottom lip with contemplation. "Well, I guess if I had it to do all over again." He breathed a long sigh.

"Which you do," Jennifer pointed out.

"Yeah, I guess I do," Derek said with an impish grin.

"The word is *yes*," she exclaimed. "Keep your eye on the ball. Picture yourself at an interview for a career as a paramedic. Most professionals are looking for articulate language. I think at one time you spoke well . . . before prison, right?"

"Right." Derek couldn't help but see himself as a professional, and a big grin was proof enough for Jennifer to see his goals were realistic.

*****

Kent Beasley, a black man who just turned sixty, stood 5 feet, 9 inches and weighed about 165. He had large, straight teeth that gleamed when he smiled—which wasn't too often, due to the dry sense of humor he used as emotional armor. Those big brown eyes scanned the surroundings of every situation to determine if he was on friendly ground even after familiarity with a known person had been established.

Prison records revealed Kent was a Vietnam hero and suggested his problem with drugs originated during the war, which sounded like an oversimplification to Jennifer. The key to Kent wouldn't be found by knowing what happened in Nam, but by uncovering the denial of what happened in Nam.

From the time Kent left Vietnam at the age of twenty-four, a record of domestic violence, alcohol abuse, and drug addiction followed him. He spent time in different county jails for small infractions of the law, i.e., trespassing, loitering, public drunkenness, street fighting. In between, there was a long procession of visits to sanitariums before an overworked, out-of-patience judge sentenced him to twenty-five years for habitual criminal activity. This is what the inmates call the small bitch. Presently, he'd served sixteen years before volunteering for the HBP.

Jennifer found Kent's psychological evaluations to be contradictory, evasive, and inconclusive. She tossed them aside. She wasn't impressed or enlightened by buzzwords used on psychiatric wards, which only produced labels without meanings. A family member gave Jennifer some insight in a letter, which read, "Our Kent died in Vietnam and a complete stranger returned to our lives."

"Now, Ms. Lily, tell me how you ended up in a place like this and how does that make you feel?" Kent asked after walking into Rec Room One and finding amusement in Jennifer's eye squint. "The game is called role reversal. It was a meaningless, psychological exercise forced upon me in the loony bin."

"I see," she said, smiling at his inventive way of letting her know that she couldn't say anything that he hadn't already heard. "Have a seat. I've read your goals, but I'm not sure which one is short-term and which one is long- term."

"I thought I could do carpentry work to support myself while I go to school for computer science. I hear they're doin' a lot of building just south of here," Kent said.

"That sounds well planned out. But didn't carpentry work cause you some problems in the past?" she asked.

"Now, Ms. Lily, you and I both know it wasn't carpentry work that caused my problems," he said. "Things were bad for me a long time before that."

"Are those times in the past?" she asked.

"I can only hope."

"Actually, we can do better than that. Should we try? What'd you think your problems were—I mean, in the past," she asked, hoping his dry wit wouldn't override the moment.

"I don't know exactly," he said, resting his folded hands on the table. "But I don't buy into any of the mumbo jumbo labeling or the psychobabble the sanitariums issued me in an effort to describe my behavior. I was paranoid because of self-medicating, so they took my drugs away and gave me psychotropic drugs. Then I was able to do the lithium shuffle. Either way was self-destructive," he said, surprising Jennifer by articulating his drug history.

"Tell me about you. Your life."

"Like, when I was a kid?" Kent asked.

"If you want to. It's not exactly what I meant. Suppose you divide your life into three separate parts: your life before the war, your life during the war, your life after the war. Which one can you talk about?" she asked.

"My life during and after the war seems to all run together. My life before was much different, but no more screwed up than anyone else's, I guess," he said.

"What about during the war?" she asked.

"I think there's some things in a person's life that should never be talked about, Ms. Lily. War is one of them. Now I know that psychologists, like yourself, think ya oughta talk about everything," Kent said.

"I'm not sure I agree that we have to talk about everything, just the parts you had the most difficulty with," she said.

"Well, okay, then that would be after Nam," he said in a slow manner, pausing to reflect. "My family said I was a different person when I came home, but hell, everyone's a different person after coming home from war."

"Probably, but not everyone begins a career of domestic violence and drug and alcohol abuse," she said.

"When I came home, I felt like a stranger in my own home. I thought *they* had changed, not me. My son didn't know me from Adam. I thought everyone was against me—even my mom and dad. That's the part of my past I hope is gone," he said.

"Do you still feel they're all against you?" she asked.

"No, I don't. But you have to understand what drugs can do to your mind no matter if you're self-medicating or if some quack gives them to you. Drugs seemed to be given to me to help the people around me—not to help me. When I landed here, I made up my mind to never do any drugs again, and I haven't. It took a long time to fight my way back from that dark abyss, Ms. Lily, but my head finally cleared. I began to understand why my wife divorced me, why I needed to get rid of the resentment of another man raising my son. I began to back away from fighting words," he said.

"Weren't you involved in some fights?" she asked, referring to his rap sheet.

"I used to get beat up pretty regular when I first got here, but one of the more humane guards caught on to what was really happening and put an end to it," he said.

"Were the men from the HBP involved?" she asked.

"Now, Ms. Lily, you know we don't snitch in here."

"Derek and/or Travis," she said without a moment's hesitation.

Kent smiled, showing his pearly white teeth. "You know, you're pretty good at this stuff."

"Just a lucky guess," she said, wrinkling her nose. "Our time's about up for today, but we'll talk a little more about Vietnam later."

"Ms. Lily, can I ask you something?"

"Anything!"

"Why would you want to help people like us?" he questioned.

"Everyone needs help from time to time, whether they know it or not," she told him. "No one ever really makes it on their own, Kent. I don't think it would work any other way. People helping people was the way the universe was meant to work."

*****

Perkins was waiting to escort Jennifer off the grounds when she stepped out of Building A. The December snow had stopped piling up, and bright sunlight was chasing water down the sidewalks and roads.

"How's it going, Ms. Collins?" he asked as they walked.

"We're getting there, slowly but surely," she said. "I want you to know I'm not going to ask you any more personal questions about Ms. Ellsworth and Mr. Henderson."

"If I do what?" he asked, snickering in a jovial voice.

"C'mon, I'm not that bad," Jennifer snorted a chuckle.

"Are you headed for your car or the administration building?" he asked as they made their turn.

"Oops, neither one. I think I forgot one of my files back there," she said, fumbling through the remaining ones to see if it could be found. "I can walk back and get it on my own, it's okay."

"Well, I dunno," Perkins said, rubbing his chin. "It's kinda frowned upon."

"Don't worry. I'll go back, pick up my file, and leave," she promised.

"Okay, but don't go anywhere else," he cautioned as he headed for the steps of the administration building. Jennifer started back, but when she turned to glance at Perkins going up the steps, a shadowy figure lurking around her car caught her eyes. Feeling her heartbeat accelerate and her breathing become labored, she started back toward her car. When a guard's uniform could be identified, she slowly strolled closer to him.

"Hank, what are you doing by my car?" She could tell Hank was thrown by her sudden and unexpected appearance.

"Nothing. I just bent over to pick up something I had dropped," he said unconvincingly, slightly winded.

Jennifer knew he was lying, but why? What was he trying to hide?

Later, Jennifer headed for Nino's Cafe for a working dinner. She postponed going home. She wasn't sure if it was because of the tiring phone threats or the outstanding doubts she had about the surveillance team's competence, but she reconciled that it was six of one, half a dozen of the other. The quiet drive down the mountain gave her the time to analyze her ongoing situation. *Playing defense just makes me feel more like a victim, so playing offense is the only way to stop this guy. But how?*

Unaware of Jennifer's plans for dinner, Jeff pulled into Nino's and found a parking spot in the last row. As he headed for the entrance, he spotted Peter standing by Jennifer's car and waved while walking toward him.

"Hi, Peter," Jeff called, looking around. "Where's Jennifer?"

"Uh . . . Hi, Jeff." Peter was obviously startled, standing behind Jennifer's car. "I guess she's inside. Do you two have an appointment tonight?"

"No, I didn't even know she was here," Jeff said, watching Peter's peculiar behavior. "Is there something wrong with her car? I saw you looking at her right rear wheel."

"Oh no, I was just checking her studded snow tires for safety," he said, fidgeting.

"Well, I hope they pass muster," Jeff said, carefully using a non-mocking tone. "I heard you had an exciting ski trip."

"Yeah, I suppose Jennifer's already told you the big news," Peter said, brushing loose dirt from his trousers. But watching Jeff's perplexed look, Peter continued, "You mean, she didn't tell you about the rock I bought her? You know, the three-carat diamond engagement ring?"

"N-o-o, she didn't," Jeff said in an almost inaudible voice. Quick composure allowed him to reach out a hand and say, "Well, then . . . um . . . I guess congrats are in order." He shook Peter's hand.

"Thanks," Peter said. "Let's go in and we can both surprise her."

"I wish I could." Jeff hurried to pull his car keys out. "But I'm running late."

"But you just got here," Peter said.

"Yeah . . . well, actually, I was just using Nino's parking lot. I have other business to attend to," he said, waving as he turned to leave.

Jeff drove back to his office, feeling like he'd swallowed something the size of a bowling ball that became stuck halfway down. His chest pounded. He wandered to his desk, hoping his body and mind would find acceptance in the news that shot like bullets out of Peter's mouth. He admonished himself for not being totally honest with Jennifer of his passionate feelings he had for her and it forced a distasteful discovery he hadn't been willing to admit, even to himself, until now. *I guess we all hide things from ourselves sometimes.* Twisting and turning a pencil that had been lying on his desk. *Maybe I just thought she wouldn't want to share her life with someone who had more of his behind him than what he had in front of him.* He laughed a little, thinking about how many times he'd warned others of the danger of projecting the outcome of any given situation.

Absorbing the shock, Jeff wondered why Jennifer hadn't told him about the engagement. And why wasn't she wearing the ring and jumping up and down with excitement? That would've been the Jennifer he knew. Or is it something she trying to hide from herself? Normally, I know about her hesitations and indecisions on any given subject. *Should I ask her about it? Maybe not.*

*****

After the unexpected dinner with Peter and listening to him repeat his version of the conversation with Jeff, Jennifer drove home. Thoughts of these two men discussing the skiing trip, the marriage proposal, and the three-carat diamond ring bounced around in her head uncomfortably. She preferred that they'd never had any time alone together. Jennifer tried comforting thoughts, projecting a sane scenario. *Yes, Peter probably portrayed a lot of drama. That's just Peter. Jeff took the news in stride because that's Jeff. Besides, what difference does it make now?*

She should've been the one to tell Jeff about the ring. All that was needed was more time. "But time will only ask for more time," an uninvited voice echoed. Chuckling, she thought of Scarlett O'Hara in *Gone with the Wind*. "I can't think about this now. I'll go crazy if I do. I'll think about it tomorrow." Good ol' Scarlett! Now there was a woman with a clue.

Snow fell on and off throughout the evening, spreading a thin coat of clean white powder on the grass, dampening the roads and leaving the air smelling crisp. Jennifer pulled into the driveway, feeling as uneasy about the surveillance team parked across the street as she was about the stranger who threatened her world.

Reaching the front door, a strange feeling swept through her as she focused on the large footprints in the snow leading to the side of the house. The outside lights gave her courage to follow them to the backyard. Suddenly, she heard the sound of heavy footsteps, like stampeding elk. Then an unrecognizable voice screamed, "Who's there?" It was hers.

"It's just us," Jubal Tanner called as he rounded the corner of Jennifer's house. He pulled his identification card out of his pocket as he shined a flashlight on Jennifer.

"Get that friggin' light out of my face, you idiot! You scared the hell out of me! You know that?" she shouted rhetorically, on the verge of tears, while holding one hand over her heart.

"We're sorry, Ms. Collins, but when you disappeared from the front of your house, it was our job to find out why," Jubal said, hoping the explanation would calm her.

"I can tell you why!" she screamed, fear now turning to anger. "See those footprints? They lead to my back door. Where were you when those were made!"

"Here. They were made by the meterman soon after the snow started falling," Jubal calmly replied.

"I followed him for two hours just to make sure he was legit," Ethan Waters added, trying to console her.

Jennifer sighed long and hard, teetering between tears and further venting before apologizing. "I'm sorry . . . I've just been a little jumpy lately."

"We understand, Ms. Collins," Ethan said.

As they walked her to the front door, she asked if they had seen any of the neighbors that day acting furtively.

"Not really. Just the neighbor who lives in the green house walked by. She and her husband are retired so they can take walks anytime," they told her.

Jennifer wasn't too worried about LeAnn Stout. She might be passive-aggressive to the hilt but not a prime suspect for conspiracy to murder. She was more of a whiner than a doer and usually set Jennifer's teeth on edge if a conversation over two minutes took place. "Anyone else?"

"Angela's husband is back in town," Ethan remembered. "We saw him unpacking his car and going in the house."

She wasn't too worried about ol' Mica. She could only imagine what life would be like trying to survive with Angela under one roof. Luckily, he was gone most of the time—working somewhere. Angela would have had to approve, or even arranged, for him to be gone ten months out of the year because there's no way this type of marriage would work for most couples. Even though it was hard to picture them as a couple, they both seemed satisfied with the little time they spent together, Angela scrutinizing his every move at home. Since Mica's two months at home was spread out through the year, he could manage quite well. But everyone wondered where his brilliant smile came from—at least until he opened his front door and then it dissipated as though someone came by and with one fell swoop, brushed it right off his face. And *someone* did.

*****

It was a quiet morning just before Christmas, long before the sun was ready to announce another day. Jennifer thumbed through stacks of notes and files lying open on her desk. She wondered how she'd ever completely deprogram Ron Bookman and Michael Bishop from prison life. Because of their ages, statistics showed they'd have the lowest rate of recidivism. But was that enough? She wanted so much more for them. Unfortunately, it was a fact that institutional dependency would set in after living in a controlled environment for more than half their adult lives. It prevented them from making the simplest of everyday decisions about bathing, brushing their teeth, what clothes to wear. They simply went with the flow, like cattle being herded from one pasture to the next. It forced them to fall into one extreme category or the other: emotionally hibernating from the general public, as she suspected of Michael, or becoming an emotional parasite for any group who'd have them, as she suspected of Ron.

Kent Beasley and Derek Coleman were, by far, the brightest intellectually of the six. But was that enough? Kent's outer composure led one to believe the absence of drug use and some deep soul-searching was the path used to achieve emotional stability. But he was still hiding something from himself that could be potentially destructive to long-lasting freedom. The answer was to either detonate or disarm the unknown before parole was granted.

Even though research confirmed only 17 percent of the recidivism rate was due to violent crimes, it didn't minimize Derek Coleman's aggravated capabilities. Constant overt reactions in an attempt to convince the world he was invincible would land him back in prison quicker than any drug problem. He wasn't nearly as close to emotional stability as Kent, but the cause of his self-made roadblock was obvious: anger. It was somehow linked with the relationship he had—or didn't have—with his father.

*****

Jennifer felt unusual reluctance while dressing for the monthly meeting with Jeff, a stipulation of the HBP. *Maybe he won't mention my engagement.* Warden Ellsworth wanted to make sure she had someone to lean on who understood what any psychologist would be up against in this state prison. Slipping on gray slacks and a white cotton blouse, she paused before adding the pearl earrings Peter had given her. Eyes scanning the dressing table, she picked up the engagement ring and embraced it close to her heart, thinking back to the first time she met Peter Winslow:

"Ms. Collins, I'm Peter Winslow from Winslow Insurance," the voice said on the other end of the phone. "How are you?"

"Fine. Thanks for calling so soon after my disaster this morning," she said, wondering why the owner was calling and not the regular insurance agent who serviced the policy.

"I wouldn't call the small dent in your car a disaster, Ms. Collins. And remember, the other car hit *you, you* didn't hit them," he said.

"Aren't the results the same?" she asked, chuckling.

"Not really," he said, enjoying her humor. "I'm calling to let you know your rates will remain the same and to tell you I want to expedite the repairs."

"That's very generous of you. What do I do next?" Jennifer asked.

"Not a thing. I'll send my adjuster out to your house immediately to get an estimate, and we'll have your Subaru in the repair shop this afternoon. You'll have it back in about two days. I'm lending you a new car in the meantime," he said.

"That's great. Thanks again."

"No problem. Glad I could help," Peter said.

They continued with small talk every day after that because Peter found a reason to call, come rain or shine. Their conversations became longer and more personal until they agreed to meet at Nino's Cafe. Peter was ten minutes late, which set the stage for his notorious tardiness. But as their relationship grew, she felt the patience shown for his lack of punctuality was a small compromise.

Jennifer came back to reality. She didn't want to be late, so she laid the ring back down on the dresser and scurried out the door. She ignored the ringing phone. By now, it only echoed threatening overtones.

*****

"Well, don't you look nice today, Ms. Collins," Jeff said, using an out-of-character emphasis as Jennifer entered the office.

"Um . . . Thank you," she said, taking a seat on the white leather couch, feeling some skepticism.

"You're in rare form today," she said, shifting the conversation away from her appearance while studying his facial expressions for clues.

Sitting behind the desk, he folded his hands loosely and leaned back. "Yeah, I guess I am. I was just thinking about when I went through some pretty bad times after my wife died. There were months where I don't recall what happened or what I did—or even if I ate or not. I wouldn't have made it without you. Did I ever thank you for all the support you gave me?"

"Many times." She remembered feeling helpless in an effort to console him, witnessing his hair turning gray almost overnight and the loss of appetite that worried her to no end. But eventually, he started to stand taller, the ocean-blue eyes returned to a soft but bright hue, and a gentle facial expression replaced the ashen look.

"Just remember, Jeff, you helped me through ninety miles of bad road at one time. And we both know I wouldn't have made it through if it hadn't been for you—and someone upstairs who must love me very much," she said, watching a sweet compassionate smile broaden across his face.

Comfortable silence fell, then Jeff said, "Okay! Enough of all that miserable history. Tell me how things are going in the HBP. Has anyone asked you out yet?" He teased her, something he hadn't done since before his wife died.

This is not Jeff! Who is this person in masquerade? Maybe I like this one better. She smiled and a nervous chuckle followed. "No, not yet. I keep them too busy for that."

She felt hot blushes rush to both cheeks that laughter couldn't camouflage. The warmth melted in the pit of her stomach and the nervous energy began to play out the Mexican hat dance, making it convenient to ignore the eerie buzzing sound in her head—the one that warned her that something was happening or about to happen.

She never grew to understand why these sensations came and went in nanoseconds, only that later the meaning would become clear.

"So anyway, what's happening with your men in the HBP? Have you gained any insight to explain the high recidivism rate?" Jeff asked.

With strict attentiveness, he listened to the progress of the inmates and the prolific and resourceful techniques used in an attempt to deprogram them from prison life before their release. He loved watching the show of passion Jennifer demonstrated in her work. Her eyes, soft but firm, related the insight developed for governing sympathy versus empathy, always coupled with a professional attitude. It tickled him the way she tossed her head back laughing when repeating an insensible answer from an inmate. He'd heard others describe her as a bleeding-heart liberal, but he could only think of her as a liberal in the sense that she was progressive, tolerant, and generous. She brightened his office—and secretly, his life.

"Ms. Ellsworth isn't the same as she was during the negotiations," Jennifer said.

"I've known her a long time since her early days as warden when I used to be the prison psychiatrist before all the cutbacks," he said, twisting a yellow pencil. "I agree, she's not the same anymore. I suspect she's found the responsibilities of a warden disillusioning."

"Well, anyway, I haven't uncovered all the reasons for the high recidivism rate. The problem is far too complex and individual for me to know it all right now," she said. "I better get going if I plan on having lunch with Peter. Well, it's okay, he's always ten minutes late anyway." She smiled.

"For lunch?" Jeff asked.

"For everything," she said, curling a grin and shrugging.

"By the way, Jeff, Peter knows about the threatening phone messages," Jennifer told him. "He was at the house one day when the phone rang, and I didn't answer it, so the recorder came on. It's no deal. I told him I get those kinds of calls from time to time."

"Did he believe you?"

"Seemed to."

*****

Arriving at Nino's, Jennifer spotted three connected empty parking spaces in front. "Ah, serendipity," she said, ignoring the fact that Peter preferred she park in the back instead of on the street. *Oh well, it's easier to ask for forgiveness than permission.* She parked in front.

Nino's Cafe was snuggled in between a mass of old-town retail shops and had a steady business from open to close. Small but clean, their red-checkered tablecloths and wax-dripped candles stuffed in empty wine bottles expressed an unhurried era filled with simplicity. Taking a seat in a booth, Jennifer thumbed through the menu that had long ago been memorized.

Peter slid in the booth close to her. "Hi, babe. What'd you order?" he asked, flashing seductive dark eyes and long lashes ostentatiously before kissing her cheek.

"That's impossible. Your ten minutes aren't up yet," she said, grinning flirtatiously.

"What are you talking about?" he asked with unconvincing innocence.

Chuckling, Jennifer said, "Peter, you know you're always ten minutes late. Even when I'm late, you manage to be ten minutes later. It's so spooky."

"Why did you park on the street?" he asked, knowing he'd never gain the winning edge about tardiness.

"Stop that. You're just trying to change the subject," she giggled and then nudged him.

"Maybe, but as an insurance broker, I know street parking is more dangerous because you and/or your car are more apt to get hit," Peter said, using his familiar protective voice.

"I'll be more careful next time," she smiled coyly.

After salads and sandwiches were devoured and the bill was paid, they lingered at the table to whisper and laugh at Peter's jokes. Finally, Jennifer said, "I've got to get going."

"I'll walk you to your car."

Driving to the prison, Jennifer marveled at the way Peter showed concern for her safety and how he tried to protect her from all the rough edges of life. She just didn't have the heart to tell him that she'd already been cut on some of those edges. Besides, it would spoil the fun. To him, it seemed as though she hadn't experienced any tornadoes, let alone hurricanes, and he was going to make sure she never had to. Peter made her feel cherished.

Chapter VI

T ravis walked into Rec Room One like a Monday morning full-back who lost Sunday's game.

"Hi, Travis," she grinned, watching him portray the only image he wanted people to see.

Travis Talltree, a name he insisted on being called, was a towering, bulky Native American Indian in his early forties. Travis had a long face, initially because of genetics, but today it served as emotional armor. He wore a disgruntled facial expression regardless of any inner, upbeat private mood he may be experiencing. Jennifer surmised that the look of discontent was planted to keep others at arm's length. His shiny black hair had been recently cropped unfashionably short in a flat top for reasons unknown.

Travis started fighting about the same time he learned how to walk, and he remained combative throughout a series of foster homes and schools until he finally graduated into barroom brawls. This career criminal began as a penny-ante thief, bouncing in and out of juvenile homes and county jails until the age of twenty-five. The life took him into burglary, where he shot a man in the process of burglarizing his home. The charge can become first-degree murder when someone is killed during an act of a felony. Instead, Travis was sentenced to twenty years for first-degree assault and had completed fourteen before volunteering for the Homeward Bound Program.

"We need to talk about your goals," Jennifer prompted.

"Now what? You don't like 'em, right?" Travis challenged. "Well, I'd be an awesome furniture maker." He leaned back far in the chair until the front legs lifted.

"Where'd you get your experience?" she asked.

"During my tour of duty through foster homes, I'd get lucky sometimes and land back on my people's reservation in Arizona with real family. They've been making furniture for generations," he said, trying to look and sound prideful, but coming across as snobbish. "It's much better quality than you'd find here."

"Excuse me," she said, reaching to brush something off his shoulder.

"So what's that? A cockroach or something?" Travis flinched.

"No, I was just trying to remove the chip on your shoulder, you know, the one you seem so determined to hang on to," she said. "Get rid of it, Travis. I'm not the enemy."

"I-I was afraid you'd object to me making furniture," he said, dropping his gaze along with his emotional armor to test the water. "Do you?" He avoided eye contact.

"If you're thinking about going back to the reservation, well, you have a lot of bad history there," she said.

He started to chuckle. "Ms. Lily, I have a lot of bad history *everywhere*! But I'd like to see my uncles and cousins again. I haven't seen 'em since I was a kid."

"I know, Travis, but I understand they're pretty heavy drinkers. Can you afford to be living and working with them?" Jennifer asked.

"I haven't drunk in almost fourteen years," he stated with pride.

"That's because you've been *in here*," she said, snorting a chuckle that led them both to laugh out loud.

"You and I know that I could've gotten it in here if that's what I wanted," he said.

"Yeah, I know."

"I only want to go back long enough to relearn the finer points," he said, almost pleading.

"Why not enroll in a community college or trade school instead?" she asked.

"I hadn't thought of that."

"Please do. But anyway, I want you to know I'm going to be discussing verbal abuse in our next group session. Do you have any thoughts on that?" she asked.

"I don't put up with nothin' from those low-life son of a—"

"Whoa! Wait a minute. Are you going on the assumption, based solely on the nature of your offense, that you're somehow better than the other inmates in this prison?"

"At least I'm no baby fondler or rapist!" he said.

"No, but you managed to terrorize every foster family you lived with. Think how you hurt those people, not to mention the other children living there. What about all the pain you caused when you chose to instigate barroom brawls?" she questioned. "Think of the wives and mothers who had *that* mess to clean up. And what about the man you shot while burglarizing his home? Just because he's physically recovered doesn't mean you haven't caused permanent damage." She felt he needed the reminder. "If he would've died, they could've convicted you on first-degree murder, and even though he lived, they still could've convicted you on attempted murder, but they cut you a break. I suggest you make good use of that."

"I still think inmates or anyone that hurts children like *that* deserves to die," he said softly, staring at the floor.

"Are they the only ones you have verbally abused?" she asked.

"No, but they're the only ones I'd like to see dead." He spoke with an uneasiness that showed a side that Jennifer hadn't seen. His angry, tormented eyes bulged as though he was being electrocuted.

Jennifer glanced at her watch, took a deep breath, and leaned back in her chair. "You know, Travis, I think we better stay and talk about sexual abuse."

"Yeah? Why?" Balancing the chair on two back legs, Travis folded both arms tight across his chest.

"It won't just go away by itself, you know," she said, feeling her suspicions had been confirmed.

Setting the chair down on all fours, rubbing the back of his neck, he hoped the pain would soon cease. The inference hit him like a Kansas tornado as he began to feel a spinning sensation. "I-I don't know what you're talking about. You think I'd let somethin' like that happen to me?"

"*Let?* Do you think children who have been molested *let* it happen?" she asked, sensing it was time for the push.

Travis began sweating, his eyes darting about until the only words uttered were "Why we talkin' about this dumb stuff anyhow?"

"I want you to listen to me," Jennifer began softly. "Children are precious gifts from God on loan to us for a very short period of time. *No one* has the right to touch them in inappropriate places or force them to perform in ways unfit for a child. It's the child's inherent right to expect us, as a society, to protect and cherish him. When we fail to do this, we've failed the child."

Travis stood and almost started to speak, but a tear ran down his face and he couldn't. So he left the room without a word, leaving Jennifer to wonder if her reliable intuition was enough. Her knowing what happened didn't keep Travis in his chair. Her expectation was for him to vehemently deny any such thing ever happened.

Walking back to his cell, Travis felt everything had come crashing down again. His stomach was tied in knots, and the only way to keep from pounding a wall was to clench and unclench his white-knuckled fists. Shame replaced anger after realizing he had revealed the one crucial secret stored in a remote corner of his mind—the secret that had refused to disappear. It was the only thing he thought he'd be taking to his grave.

Jennifer made a note to schedule their next session in three days. With Travis's quick temper and with no tools to deal with the pain, she worried about consequential behavior—the kind that helped land him here.

Private practice educated Jennifer about the length of time spent building trust with a client before they would reveal a well-kept, but detrimental, secret. Travis was devastated by his personal disclosure. But the fact was that many victims had great difficulty in overcoming their shame, guilt, and anger. Travis disguised his feelings by trying to overwhelm the world with anger; today he only overwhelmed himself.

*****

Tomas Lopez Gonzales was a small-built Mexican is his late thirties. In the beginning of the HBP, he took pride in a head with no hair, but now it was beginning to show signs of a dark shadowy growth. Much to Jennifer's surprise, his face seldom wore anything but a contagious smile—plus a goatee he was sure added a touch of class. There was innocence to his immaturity, a novelty in the prison system, except for the mentally ill inmates. And the only other exception was the kind of immaturity that stemmed from long-term incarcerations, beginning at an early age. Tomas didn't walk. He bopped along with a swinging movement that could've been set to music.

The state's crackdown concerning driving under the influence bought Tomas his first sentence of five years in prison. He completed two and a half years before going to a rehabilitation center for the treatment of alcoholism. He was sober only six months before he found himself behind bars again; only this time, the charge was vehicular homicide while under the influence. He completed seventeen years of a twenty-year sentence before volunteering for the HBP, becoming Ted Hatter's replacement. Ted had dropped a *hot* urine analysis, which eliminated him from participating in the HBP.

"Well, hey, Ms. Lily," Tomas said, rubbing the new growth on the top of his head.

"Hi, Tomas," she grinned. "I know you haven't had time to write about your goals, so we'll just talk about your ambitions for now, but later I'll expect a written outline."

"I'm an excellent bricklayer," he said with the exuberance of a kid describing skills he possessed on a skateboard.

"Is that what you really want to do when you get out of here? Or is it just something that's familiar and comfortable?" she asked.

"Well, if you're asking me if bricklaying is my life's dream, I'd say no. But I *am* good at it, and we both know a job will be necessary for me to leave this joint," Tomas said.

"What was your life's dream? Before prison, before drinking?" she asked, tilting her head up a notch.

"When I was a kid—and that's how far we'd have to go back—I wanted to be a fireman. But it's kinda too late for that now," Tomas said, shrugging.

"Why? What time is it?" she grinned and glanced at her watch. Could he realize the irrelevancy of time and age when actualizing a dream?

"I'm thirty-nine years old, Ms. Lily. I doubt if I could hack it as a fireman," he said, wondering why he needed to point out the obvious.

"And . . . um lifting, toting, and laying bricks in the hot sun all day is what? A cool breeze?" she asked. "If you knew for sure that you could still be a fireman, how hard would you be willing to work toward that goal?"

"You really think I could be a fireman?" Tomas asked with a dumbfounded look.

"If that's what you really want and if you're willing to work hard enough to place yourself in a position for an interview," she said.

"What would I have to do, exactly?" he asked.

"Schooling," she said.

"I wasn't never any good at school," Tomas said, his head hanging.

"Or English, but you haven't been in school for over twenty years, and you didn't attend much then. Give yourself a chance," she said. "Start with some fire science books here in the library, and then you can take classes when you get out."

"You know, the other guys will probably laugh at me," he said.

"Why? Are you funny?" Jennifer asked. "Besides, why do you care what they think? Try and remember it was their *best* thinking that got them in here." She held back a grin.

Tomas started giggling until it turned into laughter. "I wish I could be more like you, Ms. Lily," he said with young admiration.

"Yeah? Well, it's not as easy as it looks," she said, emitting a dry sense of humor one seldom saw.

*****

Jennifer dreaded another meeting with the review board, which was scheduled for after the new year. She had already started to occupy precious minutes thinking about it on her way home. *If I could only convince Tuttle that in the long run, punishment costs more than reha-bilitation.* Research made her realize that the recidivism rate is the most costly expense for the taxpayer—and the most preventable.

She wondered what approaches could be used to help create a shift in Tuttle's perception—a way in which he could view things from more than one angle. But she knew he was set in his ways, and an act of congress probably wouldn't change that. The public's obsessive-compulsive methods of handling any collective problems have always been to overtip the scales to the right as far as what they had already been tipped to the left. This appeared to be true whether the issue was gun control, discrimination—age, sex, color, creed, religion, abortion, or the death penalty. Overcompensating like that just leads us back to the same problems, only in reverse. When it comes to criminals, society seems to be either bloodthirsty or apathetic—no middle ground. She wished leaders could see that these more difficult decisions may not need to be decided by the majority. It's not as though the U.S. government had never enacted laws without allowing its citizens to vote on it.

All thoughts dissipated when her cell phone started ringing.

"Hi, Ms. Lily," said the voice on the other end.

"What? Where did you hear that name?" she asked, recognizing Jeff's voice.

"From Robert, who heard it from Elizabeth, who always says there are no secrets in prison," both said in harmony while laughing.

"Want to meet me at Raghetti's? They're having a special on seafood linguini," Jeff invited.

"Ah-h-h, that's my favorite. I'll be there. And, Jeff, there's something I want to tell you tonight," she said.

"Okay, see you in a few." *It's about time*, he thought, hanging up the phone.

Raghetti's, known as a fine dining establishment, used valet parking, and a large green-and-white-striped awning covered the entrance, making it look chic and elegant. The doorman only made it look expensive. Six massive chandeliers emitted a soft glimmering glow, providing an atmosphere that imitated London's fog. A steady parade of customers, dressed in a talented diversity, occupied the floor, where cheek-to-cheek dancing was the norm, even among the young.

"Are you ready to be seated?" the college-age hostess asked Jennifer.

"No. I'm waiting for my date—my friend," Jennifer said.

"Dr. Hanes?" the coed asked.

"Y-Yeah, how'd you know?" Jennifer asked.

"I just had a hunch you were the one he's been waiting for," she said, leading Jennifer to the table.

"It's good to see you," Jeff said, standing to seat her.

"You too." She smiled as she sat down. "Jeff, I wanted to be the one to tell you about my engagement ring," she said in one breathless gasp of air the second the hostess left.

"So why weren't you?" he asked, but he thought, *She never ceases to amaze me. Just when I think I know what she's going to do or say.*

"I wasn't sure how I felt about it," she said, sliding a white linen napkin onto her lap.

"I'm a little confused, so help me here. You don't know how you feel about being engaged?" Jeff asked, reaching for the other napkin and gently pulling it over his lap.

"I-It all happened so fast. One minute we were skiing, and the next, Peter puts a diamond ring on my finger," she said.

"It's pretty simple, Jen. Do you love him? Enough to marry him?" Jeff asked, wondering if he was really ready to hear the answer.

"I don't know . . . maybe. Can we talk about something else?" she asked, pleading.

"Okay," he said. "Let's talk about Charlie Bremmer or Lori Watkins."

"I don't need a menu. I'll have the seafood linguini," Jennifer told the waiter, who seemed to appear out of nowhere.

"Me too," Jeff said.

Jeff knew from reading the file that Lori became a shrinking violet around her boyfriend, Sol, because it pleased him. Otherwise, she was an outspoken, competent banker in charge of large investments. Going into therapy when Sol's physical abuse began forced Lori to come to terms with the devastating affects her father's barbaric domination had caused. She'd moved away from her father without dealing with her feelings of incompetence and uselessness; those feelings continued to imprison her when becoming involved with an overbearing man. When Sol came along, Lori was an easy target. During a year of therapy, she visited her father several times, came to terms with their relationship, and moved on with her life, which now didn't include Sol.

"Where's Sol now?" Jeff asked.

"I don't know. What difference does it make? Unless you think he's the pest in my life," she said.

"Detective Malloy and I are not ruling anyone out right now. I think it's worth looking into. It's just that I'm not convinced the bent tab was an accident or oversight. If someone was able to break into your house, leaving no other traces, then they are certainly capable of either refiling correctly or taking the file with them. It could've been months—even years—before you would've noticed if it was missing. He wanted you to think he found valuable information," Jeff said.

"What information? I code everything, even addresses and phone numbers," she said, fidgeting with her napkin. "You're the only one that knows the code."

"I'm sure he didn't know that. But if he thinks Lori left him because of you—and trust me, that's how he sees it—then you become the enemy. If it wasn't for you, they'd still be together, and on *his* terms," Jeff said. He plunged his fork into fresh garden salad that the waiter had set down. "I love these crisp salads, don't you?"

"The best," she said, eating a little faster than usual. "I'll call Lori tomorrow and see if she knows where Sol is."

"You skipped lunch again, didn't you?" he asked.

"You know me too well."

Between bites, Jennifer related the mix-up with the meterman, realizing for the first time how humorous the situation really was. She covered her mouth to tame the roar of laughter.

"I can just picture your temper flashing. I'll bet that was a real photo op!" Jeff said with a contagious, zealous laugh. "You don't like those surveillance guys, do you?"

"Who? You mean Starsky and Hutch?" she snickered.

"Are they really that bad?"

"I guess not. It's just that they're a constant reminder that I'm not safe."

Jeff nodded with a smile before telling her about Burt Walker trying to buy more time before submitting the new proof. "It was Burt's intention to look for more substantial evidence than just ten-year-old snapshots even though they are timed and dated. But he hasn't been successful in finding any."

"I would think that the photos alone would free ol' Charlie?" Jennifer said as the waiter set down the seafood platters. "That alone represents reasonable doubt. Remember, there was someone behind that camera who saw everything. Drunk, drugged, shouldn't matter. If that doesn't fly then Charlie should at least get a commuted sentence from death to a life sentence. "It'll probably get him a commuted sentence from death to life in prison."

"But Burt's looking to exonerated him completely. It gets tough finding that one piece of evidence that would set Charlie free, mostly because the tracks of a ten-year-old murder case fade. People's memories and stories start to change," Jeff explained. Then he took his first bite of the linguini. "It's like when you ask three eyewitnesses at a car wreck, 'What happened?' You get three similar but different answers. Ask them ten years later and not only will you get three different stories about what happened, but the makes and models of the cars have changed too."

"Oh, this is heavenly!" Jennifer exclaimed, taking another bite and then another. "Burt will get him off."

"You *are* the optimist."

"That's better than being called the lib-er-al," Jennifer said, taking a large swig of lemonade.

"Who called you that?" Jeff asked jokingly.

"No one. Everyone. Never mind, let's just eat," Jennifer said. "If you promise to behave, maybe I'll let you dance with me after dinner." She smiled her triple-dimple smile that verged on flirtation—or at least it seemed that way to Jeff.

After dinner, they danced. He thought the highlight of the night for Jennifer was the seafood linguini, but for him, it was this moment—holding her close and smelling her hair. His only wish was that the song would last hours, not minutes. He knew she had to be feeling something.

"Look who's standing right behind you," Jennifer said as they sat down at their table.

"Can I turn around or will you kick me?" he whispered.

"Hi, Jeff, Jennifer," Robert Henderson said, seeing the pair heading for their table.

"How you two doing?" asked Jeff, noticing Robert holding Elizabeth Ellsworth's hand. "We just finished dinner. Sorry we didn't see you sooner."

Jeff invited them to join their table for coffee and dessert, and the two men began a rapid, controversial debate about Charlie's case. Jennifer listened but secretly hoped Elizabeth would want to discuss the HBP. Instead, she said nothing. The warden's face only displayed discomfort in her squinted eyes and furrowed brows. *Does she object to the present conversation only because of my presence?* Jennifer wondered. *Will I ever become her confidante?* Feeling like an out-of-town stranger in Elizabeth's presence always brought the same feelings to the surface; something hidden deep inside this woman's heart wasn't going to allow any luxury of intimacy—with anyone. *Poor Robert. I don't have to be a psychic to see how in love he is with her.*

"Isn't the food great here?" Jennifer asked Elizabeth, offering a diversion from discussing Charlie Bremmer's appeal.

"Yes, it is," she smiled a protected smile. "I shouldn't indulge in the dessert if I expect to wear the same size clothes," she added, relaxing her tight smile only slightly.

"I know what you mean," Jennifer nodded, finishing the last bite of cheesecake.

"I don't know why either one of you worry about your weight. You both look great," Robert said, now joining their conversation.

"Are you kidding? Worrying about it isn't just our constitutional right but our obligation as women," Jennifer said, watching a little more tension vanish from Elizabeth's face.

"Men don't worry about such trivial matters," Jeff said before realizing his foot went in his mouth.

"Oh! Really? What about cars?" Jennifer asked. She watched a knowing grin spread across Elizabeth's face. "Am I supposed to believe that when men are at a stoplight, they don't compare their car to the car next to them to see how it fairs? Is it as fast as mine? Is it as new? Is it as expensive?"

"Well, I'd really love to continue this delightful conversation, but since Jeff's put us men in a 'can't win' situation, I think we'll be going," Robert said, laughing. He helped Elizabeth from her chair.

"Now don't let me chase you off. We can handle this, Robert," Jeff said, giving Jennifer a nudge.

"Well, it *is* getting late, and I have an early-morning conference," Elizabeth said.

"Tomorrow's Saturday," Jennifer said.

"Yes, but I'm the warden *every* day," she said with a quick smile as she put her arm in Robert's.

As Jeff and Jennifer strolled out to their cars, Jeff couldn't help notice how the moonlight danced off the tips of Jennifer's brown curls. Her eyes reminded him of pools of spring water that had a hint of light sweeping across them. The night out had helped erase the tense look she'd been wearing, but the natural, easy gait hadn't returned, and a watchful eye scanned the area around her car as he opened the door. Both sets of eyes discreetly darted to the back seat. Once burned . . .

"You know, it's not really all that late. We could go to your house and give Lori a call yet tonight," he said, wishing she could feel safe for no other reason except that they were together.

"Great idea. See you there," she said, locking her car door before fastening the seat belt.

Jeff decided not to inform Jennifer that Malloy ran a background check on Angela Colder and didn't find anything that would link her to wanting Jennifer dead, but a few peculiarities did show up, and the rest of the details Jeff chased down until he got the correct answers from the right people.

Angela Colder's platinum-colored hair was natural, buttery blond when she cheered for All Saints High School in North Dakota in her junior and senior years. After the head cheerleader broke her wrist in three places—needing pins and plates and a promise of never cheerleading again—in an attempt to try out a new pyramid scheme of Angeles's, Angela let the other girls know that *now* she would be head cheerleader. This would continue to be her claim to fame for the rest of her days. The others wouldn't say a word. They were too scared; everyone was. Angela announced that she wanted to be the lead in the drama club's spring play *The Miracle Worker*, knowing that Daisy Kindle had been chosen, hands down, to play Helen Keller. Daisy actually bore a striking resemblance to the young Miss Patty Duke; it was uncanny how she fit the role the way no one else could! The director, Mr. McClure, was almost smug about what was really kismet—fate, if you will. He didn't discover her; she already knew who she was.

The teachers and the rest of the school faculty tried to convince Angela that there were still a lot good opportunities for roles in the play. But Angela insisted that she wanted to be Daisy's understudy, claiming she wanted to do whatever she could to help Daisy learn her lines, bring her to fittings on time, help with makeup, rehearsals, and, in general, be at Daisy's beck and call. Daisy begged off many times, but Angela triumphed. If Daisy got off early from class to meet the other actors in the auditorium, Angela was already there. There was no getting away from her. Daisy was innately shy and very sweet, not at all outspoken like Angela, but onstage she shined! Angela saw this as a threat.

The day before Daisy's debut was the dress rehearsal. Mr. McClure asked the maintenance crew to block off the stairs leading left off stage until the damaged to two of the steps could be repaired. But Jeff could only assume that poor Daisy couldn't read or was a well-known rule-breaker at her school because she was found unconscious at the bottom of the stairs with a broken leg. He pressed the people he could find for answers about the accident. Today, none of Angela's classmates thought that it was an accident, but none would speak up at the time. Angela, of course, slid right into Daisy's role as Helen Keller. To say she didn't bring the house down would be an understatement. The play had been sold-out for weeks, but when Angela took to the stage, it was painfully clear to see there was only about a 50 percent turnout in the audience, mostly faculty that wasn't allowed to beg off and parents of the other actors.

Afterward, Angela continued to say that she didn't get the praise that was due her. Never mind that Daisy spend her last summer before college in a leg cast and wasn't able to enjoy any of the festivities with the rest of her classmates. Angela hadn't been invited to any of these outings but usually showed up anyway.

Jeff found it amusing that Angela's classmates still referred to her as the princess, but not with a civil tongue. It would serve no purpose at the moment to tell Jennifer any of this. Her plate was already full.

He drove into Jennifer's driveway, attentive of the surveillance team. They didn't bring Jennifer the comfort they brought to Jeff.

Chapter VII

Jennifer promptly retrieved Lori Watkins's file from her office and brought it to the kitchen table while Jeff made coffee. Sitting to dial the number, she realized it might be outdated and that the possibility of Lori knowing where Sol hung out these days was remote.

When a woman answered, Jennifer said, "I'd like to speak with Lori Watkins please."

"You must have the wrong number. There's no one here by that name," said the elderly female voice.

Jennifer apologized and hung up. "Now what?" she asked Jeff.

"What about calling Lori's mother?" he asked, sitting down at the kitchen table with two cups of coffee.

"Yeah, that's an idea, but I wonder what condition she'll be in after living with that brute of a husband for this long. It's worth a try, I guess," Jennifer said, flipping through the file until she found the emergency slip with Lori's mother's name and number.

"Could I speak with Amanda Watkins please?" she asked when the soft-spoken lady answered.

"Who is this?" the timid voice asked.

"I'm Jennifer Collins, and I'm trying to get ahold of Lori Watkins," she said.

"Your name sounds familiar, but I can't quite place you," the woman answered.

"I used to be Lori's therapist, and I was wondering—"

"Oh yeah! I remember you now. You saved my little girl from that awful man. What can I do for you, dear?" she asked candidly.

"I was wondering if you have Lori's new number."

"Well, yes, I do, but I can't give it out to anyone. Lori said so," Amanda said. "Besides, Lori's found herself a good man and is happy now. I don't think she needs your help anymore, dear."

"I think it's great that Lori found a good man, but I need *her* help with something. Maybe you could give her my number and ask her to call me."

"Sure, I can do that," Amanda wrote down the number.

After hanging up, Jennifer leaned back in her chair, biting her bottom lip. She wondered if Amanda would remember to call Lori.

Jeff patted her hand as if he heard her thoughts. "She'll call, don't worry. If nothing else, your clients are faithful," Jeff said.

The knock on the front door was startling, and the two swapped questioning looks. "Relax, few maniacs knock on their victim's door. I'll get it," Jeff said as he opened the door.

"Well, h-hi, Jeff," Peter said with a surprised look.

"Jennifer and I were going through some old files," Jeff assured him. "I guess we didn't realize how late it was getting, but we're done now." Peter stepped in and threw a wave to Jennifer.

"Come on in, Peter," Jennifer said, closing Lori's file and slipping it into a kitchen drawer. "What brings you by at this hour?"

"I was working late and wanted to see you before I headed home. Besides, we need to firm up our plans for New Year's Eve," he said, walking to the kitchen, with Jeff following.

"Would you like some coffee?" she asked.

"Sounds good." Peter took a seat next to her at the table.

"Well, I'll leave the two of you alone," Jeff said, throwing his coat over both shoulders and heading for the door.

"Thanks, Jeff," Jennifer said, "for everything."

Peter wondered what the meaning was in Jennifer's cryptic gratitude. He used to venture a guess or two about the intricacies of their relationship, but after the first few months of watching them communicate, he settled on the word *platonic*. Jennifer never offered any explanations about Jeff's place in her life other than professional reasons, so Peter saw no purpose in letting it become an issue.

Jeff clenched his teeth as he stepped out into the chilly night and headed for his car. *Is she really going to marry that goof?* he reflected.

The mere thought of them being alone together caused an irritation worse than a poison ivy itch in the groin, but he knew it was something he was going to have to live with—sooner or later. Opening his car door, Jeff glanced over at the surveillance team, noticing a hand subtly motioning him to come closer.

Jubal Tanner and Ethan Waters had worked as investigators for years but never in surveillance, a small detail Jeff chose not to share with Jennifer. Perhaps the odd couple did look a little like Laurel and Hardy dressed up like Starsky and Hutch, and they sometimes acted like Joe Friday and Bill Gannon on the 1960s TV series *Dragnet*. But if there were ever two investigators Jeff could rely on, it was Tanner & Waters Inc. Jubal and Ethan joked around a lot, but when it came to competency, no one could touch them. Jeff kept in mind that surveillance wasn't the easiest job. It was boring, tedious work with long hours that sometimes led nowhere. Up until now, the most exciting aspect of their surveillance had been watching the ladies walk four or five time a week after supper. They'd eavesdrop on their gossiping. Whoever didn't show up that day to walk got blasted the most. The ladies might run out of steam, but they never ran out of gossip—even in church. Jubal once told Jeff that he and Ethan always hoped that they'd pick up a good recipe or two, but the ladies never seemed to have time for such trivialities.

Jubal lived to eat; Ethan ate to live. And although it'd been said that Jubal wasn't a man who carried an extra thirty pounds with grace and style, his integrity and well-thought-out plans made him indispensable. Ethan's energetic style often caused conclusion jumping, but it ironically complemented the duo's efforts.

"What's up?" Jeff asked, piling into the back of the van.

"This guy, Peter, you know, the one that dates Ms. Collins—"

"Actually, they're engaged," Jeff interjected, feeling more irritated.

"Whatever. He's always inspecting her car. I mean, every time he visits her, the guy checks out her car. What's that all about? Does he know the situation now about the phone calls?" Jubal asked, chomping down on an egg roll and squirting some of the contents onto his lap.

"No, no way. Peter's just sort of . . . " Jeff said, stumbling for an accurate description.

"An idiot?" Ethan Waters interjected with a sardonic snicker.

"He's not really an idiot, he just seems like that," Jeff said, adding further irritation by finding himself in a position of defending Peter.

"Well, we'd like to follow him for a while," Jubal said, brushing crumbs off his lap as Ethan winced.

"Are you kidding?" Jeff asked, beginning to doubt their capability. "I mean, I know the guy's a little peculiar, not your average run-of-the-mill—"

"You gotta admit that whoever's terrorizing Ms. Collins knows an awful lot about her business," Ethan interrupted. "Look! He knows where she works. He probably even knows how to get past the guard gate, info he could've gotten by merely engaging in idle conversation with her."

'No! She's very careful about such things." Jeff leapt to Jennifer's defense.

"But at least take a look at this—in reality, not personally."

"Well, yeah. But Peter? All hepped up, toothy-grinned Peter?" Jeff asked. He was on the brink of bursting out in laughter. "I see the means, but not the motive."

"Whatta ya say? Can we tail him?" Jubal asked.

"Well, I suppose," Jeff said with a short sigh. "But while you're tailing him, I want you to hire someone to do nothing but watch Jennifer's house. And don't tell Jennifer. She already thinks this surveillance stuff is useless."

"Yeah, we got that," Jubal said.

*****

The following morning, Jennifer lay on the sofa with both legs propped up, resting in the sway of the camel's back as she twirled the three-carat diamond ring around her pinkie finger. Sipping coffee and admiring the plush growth of the philodendron family, she pushed esoteric thoughts and feelings about Peter aside and invited theoretical thoughts to surface about Travis Talltree and Tomas Gonzales, providing the perfect escape.

Their age, as well as their attitudes, placed them in a high recidivism group, and Tuttle would view their failure as the HBP's failure. During negotiations, the prison board estimated a 75 percent recidivism rate for the men in the HBP, which was the same recidivism rate without the HBP. Jennifer promised no more than 20 percent, which meant only one of her six men could fail to keep his freedom for a year after being released. None of the men had been able to do so yet.

Bringing Travis to terms with past sexual abuse was imperative if any healing was to take place. She had to find a way to help him get beyond the anger, his favorite emotional armor that was also a potential weapon.

Tomas's friendliness with the entire prison population was an effort to hide excess baggage he'd swept under the carpet long ago. In all likelihood, he had no desire to examine it, especially since ignoring it was easier and much less painful. The awareness that emotional armor could be made of smiles, as well as disgruntled looks, couldn't be denied.

Jennifer knew why the men had initially volunteered for the HBP: they wanted something positive to fill their resume for the parole board. But what they really needed was to work as hard at *staying out of prison* as they did at *getting out of prison* for their own good as well as for the good of the HBP.

*****

Later in the day, Lori Watkins called. She had the voice of an angel, if angels have voices. Jennifer remembered Lori had a slim-petite frame, and she always used to fold her tiny hands loosely on her lap during therapy. That she was clear and concise about feelings was what Jennifer remembered most about their sessions. She filled Lori in on the telephone threats, car accident, and bent tab on her file. After explaining that all her files are coded by colors and numbers, Lori's voice became less guarded.

"I've just been going through past clients' names that had trouble with abusive mates. You're the only one in the six months previous to me leaving private practice who was in that situation, which brings me to my first question. Do you remember what Sol's last name was?" Jennifer asked.

"Who knows? I mean, he lied so much, even the police weren't sure. He'd given them three or four different aliases," she said.

"Do you have any idea where he is now?"

"I'd wager one of three places: in prison, in a mental institution, or buried," Lori said with absolute confidence.

"Do you think he's ever been arrested?" Jennifer asked.

"I think Sol's one of those people who always manages to leave town quickly enough to avoid the trouble he instigated," she said, "even if his leave is temporary."

"Well, it's probably not him anyway, but I thought I'd check it out," Jennifer said.

"Good luck, Jennifer, and be careful. If it's Sol, well, he's a mean one," Lori said before they hung up.

*****

On New Year's Eve, Jennifer was wearing a pearl white, sleeveless floor-length evening gown. The garment's chest area was floral embroidered in pastels of blues, yellows, and greens. Made mostly of silk, it wrapped her body snugly enough to stimulate the imagination but hung free enough for inhalation to occur without discomfort. The plunging neckline gave ample space for the string of pearls that Peter had given her; the slit on the side stopped modestly just above the knee.

Tonight, they would dine leisurely and dance till the wee hours of the morning. Standing in front of the full-length mirror, Jennifer turned this way then that way, making sure everything fit just right. The hair piled upon her head, topped with soft small curls, needed only one more mist of spray for hold. Then she reached for the matching pearl earrings and the engagement ring, adding the final touches to a well-planned ensemble. She grabbed the small-beaded evening bag that was just big enough for the bare essentials a girl needs for a night out on the town. Slipping on a pearl wristwatch, which fit her wrist elegantly, she hoped he wouldn't be late.

"God, you look drop-dead gorgeous," Peter said, stepping into the house with the kind of grace that even Richard Gere would envy in his earlier days. Peter stared amorously into her eyes, pulling her close enough to kiss.

"You don't look so bad yourself," Jennifer said in a whimsical voice, a tone used only when hiding a matrix of feelings. She felt his slender, taut body press against her. He was wearing a new tux that most assuredly was neither a rental or bought off the rack.

"You're a very complex young lady," Peter said as she tilted her chin up slightly, leaving one arm wrapped around her waist like a belt. He kissed her and kissed her again.

"Complex? Maybe. Young? No," she grinned.

"Come to think of it, I've never asked how old you are," he said, kissing her lips softly so he wouldn't smear her rose-crimson lipstick.

"That's because you're a gentleman," she whispered after enjoying the kiss.

"I think we'd better get going." But Peter still held her warm, alluring body tightly.

"Good idea," she cooed, gently pulling away from his firm hold.

He'd made reservations at The Talk of the Town, a new exclusive restaurant that was celebrating its grand opening by serving free champagne and hors d'oeuvres. Afterward, they would stay for dinner, which would consist of whole Maine lobster, fresh Caesar salad, new potatoes, and garden-fresh baby peas. Peter had everything arranged: the best table, best waiters, and Cherries Jubilee. Nothing less than a flaming dessert would be magnificent enough.

Jennifer's eyes swam in the atmosphere, observing every piece of sterling silverware placed meticulously on white linen-covered tables, accompanied by fine china. The exquisite glass stemware was designed for elegance but multishaped for the purpose of identifying each exotic drink. The red-velvet cushioned chairs were created for comfort, their ornate arms were crafted for grace, beauty, and distinction. Patrons were talking in whispers as if they were in church while the orchestra played soft, romantic music.

"You look good enough to eat," Peter said after they had been seated and drinks had been served.

"Personally, *I'd* rather have lobster," she teased.

"And you tell me that *I'm* the one who doesn't know how to be serious," he smiled.

"You don't," she grinned back.

"Is that why you love me? You *do* love me, right?" he asked flirtingly.

"No, *that's* why I go out with you," she giggled.

"You want to dance?"

"With whom?" she said, looking around the room, camouflaging her grin with her left hand.

"Very funny," he said, leaning forward while wrinkling his nose.

Dinner was served by three waiters whose job it was to provide impeccable service, leaving the customers nothing to be desired. Salads were brought in pewter bowls on silver trays. Broiled lobster followed, sprawled across huge platters trimmed in romaine lettuce, lemon wedges, and boiled new potatoes. More side dishes were offered but declined.

Jennifer longed for and appreciated the light conversation during dinner before Peter insisted they dance. Three cheek-to-cheek numbers followed, then Peter escorted her back to their table, holding the chair until she was seated. "What would you say if I asked for a definite date?" he asked, cooing in a soft, romantic voice.

"I would say that this *is* definitely a date," she laughed, wishing their light conversation would continue.

"No, I mean a *wedding* date," Peter said.

"O-o-o-h! *That* kind of date," Jennifer said, watching the evening mood swing 180 degrees—south.

"Well?" he asked.

"Did you ever have the feeling that everything is happening too fast?" she asked.

"Yeah, I guess . . . But this isn't one of those times," he said. "Are we moving too fast?"

"*I* am," she said.

"Why did you accept my marriage proposal?" Peter asked.

"If you remember, I didn't," she said, watching his animated face turn into a frown. His brows crunched together and she added, "What I mean is, I was overwhelmed, even flattered, I guess. But I haven't given the idea of marriage the thought it deserves. There's just so much going on right now."

"You mean at work?" Peter asked.

"Yes, that's one." Then she added, "Look, we haven't really known each other all that long."

"Since July," he said, emphasizing the longevity. "Where are you from . . . Minnesota?"

"Where are you from, Kentucky?" she asked with a coy grin, wondering why the evening couldn't remain easy. But any hope of that was dashed as she watched Peter's head droop. His fingers fidgeted with the edge of the napkin while his lips shrunk to a pout.

"Aren't you in love with me, Jennifer?" he asked.

"It's not that easy, Peter."

"Really?" he asked, looking into her eyes.

"I think being in love comes in degrees. It's not like being pregnant, where you either are or you're not. Besides, even pregnancy comes in degrees—well, stages anyway. Love's not that black or white," Jennifer said, trying to get him to understand how she feels.

"Yeah, but you see, it is for me," he said. "What will it take? A year? Two years?"

"It takes what it takes," Jennifer said, watching his face twist and his eyebrows pull together. "Maybe we could set a tentative date, like the Fourth of July."

His eyes brightened once more, "All right! That's my girl! And, Jen, maybe after we're married, you could choose a line of work less dangerous. You're so talented and have so many choices."

Jennifer never saw that coming, not really. She thought Peter knew how important her work was to her. It wasn't even work to Jennifer; it was more of a mission that she felt determined to not just finish but win. What could he be thinking? She thought back on their many conversations about the significance of what she was trying to accomplish. He seemed to understand at the time, but now everything appeared to be about what he wanted.

"I don't think we should talk about this anymore tonight." Peter could hear her disappointment.

"I'm so sorry that I've upset you," he apologized. "It's just that I love you so much."

The ride home felt uncomfortable. Jennifer wished that there had never been a discussion about marriage or Peter wanting her to change careers. It certainly took the edge off a perfectly romantic evening. Peter was a wonderful guy, but tonight, his timing was far removed from his character of suave and debonair. She could only hope that Peter wouldn't want to spend the night as they pulled into the driveway. The mood had been lost. As they lay motionless side by side in bed, Jennifer was trying to justify what she was beginning to perceive as stubbornness and selfishness on Peter's part.

Peter felt he needed a new plan to keep her out of the prison system. He couldn't bear the thought of her ending up dead. It caused him more anguish to know that he could be the cause of it. He just wanted to be out of the drug business and to live his life clean and sober as an insurance broker married to Jennifer. The problem was that Breezy doesn't let people go once they are his. He had to find a way out of this because he couldn't live without Jennifer. If only he hadn't started using.

*****

The new workweek began by changing schedules to fit an extra session in for Travis Talltree, whether he thought it was needed or not.

Now over halfway through the Homeward Bound Program, Jennifer pondered the changes each inmate was willing to make and outlined each step yet needed. They were more open with her—and to one another. They participated in building their chosen career for when they were released, they'd made a start on curbing verbal abuse, which usually amounted to slinging profanity at other inmates. But now, detailed planning and critical questions asked precisely at the right moment were needed if these men were ever to be free—*really* free. She arrived at the prison for the afternoon sessions at 1:00 p.m. and requested to see Travis Talltree.

"Hi, Travis," Jennifer said, watching him take a seat at the table.

"Hi, Ms. Lily." He wore his usual disgruntled look, staring at the glass windows. "The guards told me you changed our schedule today."

"Yeah, I thought we should talk alone before our group session begins," she said. "In our last session—"

"I don't know what you thought, but you were wrong," he said, glancing at her before fixing both eyes on the blank television set.

"Is that how you want to deal with it, Travis?" she asked. "I think we both know you were sexually abused as a child."

"Even if it's true, you can't change it." He now focused on the floor.

"No, no one can do that. But by discussing it, we may be able to relieve you of the burden of carrying it," Jennifer said.

"Do we have to talk about this?" Travis asked, feeling agitated.

"You know, Travis, when you were a foster kid, you probably feared no one would believe you or that they just wouldn't have cared. As a man, it's probably become a source of deep shame."

He shuffled his feet on the floor, staring at both as though inspecting his shoes. Jennifer wasn't going to speak until he did no matter how long it took.

"If I only *think* about it, I can pretend it never really happened, that somehow I just dreamed it up," he said after about forty seconds. He threw his head back and rubbed his forehead.

"But it doesn't lessen the pain, does it?" Jennifer asked.

"No, but if I talk about it, I'm afraid it'll be more real than I can handle," Travis said, feeling anguish rip through his body as he cupped his hands over his face.

"It won't be. I promise. We'll work through it together," she said, laying one hand on his upper arm, breaking a stipulation in the HBP that prohibits physical contact. Hearing the guard's stick tap on the window, she removed her hand. "Together we can disarm the power that it holds over you."

With a head full of thoughts and feelings that were all mixed together, Travis began to tell the horror about the first sexual encounter while in foster care. At times he became overwhelmed, describing the helplessness of a five- year-old at the hands of a monster. First he would cry, then quickly utter a senseless joke to force a laugh, hoping to alleviate the pain. Although no one told him, Travis was sure that anal sex was a form of punishment for acts committed in foster care, which, in the beginning, amounted to cookie stealing. He spoke of the efforts made to be a good boy, but the punishment didn't stop. He relished the times when he was thrown out of a foster home and returned to the reservation, even if it was temporary. The daily drunken brawls on the reservation were what he was used to, and no one ever felt the need to assign blame. In his late teens and early twenties, he struggled to understand why problems with women seemed endless and why there were no male friends in his life.

Travis sighed before elaborating about a safe, secure place he'd visit when the pain became too great. It was a private place filled with utopia, a colorful world that protected him against the evils of reality and invited him to stay longer with each visit. Even now it continued to give comfort. Knowing that the fictitious place where Travis's mind escaped to for long periods of time was dangerous, Jennifer also knew it was what saved his sanity and probably his life. But what she wanted to help him do was to live in reality and to be comfortable with it.

Their session was far from a quick fix, but the wounds could start to heal now. Travis wasn't that helpless child any longer; he was a man who began taking steps into forgiving the injustices the world dealt him. There'd be other days then conversation would drift back to these torturous events, and Jennifer would point out the correlation between his anger and past sexual abuse. The optimum hope was that the imaginary place would become less necessary to visit as reality became more tolerable until enjoyment of life would fill that vacancy.

Jennifer took a day off to drive to Denver for another meeting concerning House Bills 134 and 135. She saw no need to involve

Peter—at least not now. She started to feel as though she was being followed but felt some sense of security driving the busy freeway instead of the back roads she sometimes used. Glancing at the rearview mirror made her wonder if she was just imaging the silver Cadillac slowing down and then accelerating whenever she did. *Am I being followed?* The caddy's dark, tinted windows made it impossible to know if a man or a woman was driving. Jennifer told herself that she was probably just letting her imagination run rampant. By the time she pulled into the parking lot at the state building, the Cadillac was nowhere to be seen. She looked around after getting out of her car and locking it. No Cadillac. She went in and took care of business and, afterward, drove home without incident.

*****

Marching down the long corridor that led to the warden's office, Jennifer hoped the meeting with the review board wouldn't turn into another "dueling pistols" exhibition. After making unrealistic promises to show more restraint, she entered Elizabeth's office.

"Hi, Jennifer," Warden Ellsworth said, looking up from the paperwork strewn across the oak desk.

"Are we meeting across the hall today?" Jennifer asked, noticing Charlie Bremmer's name on a file lying open on top of papers. She knew there was some other connection between the warden and Charlie, but she knew better than to ask.

"Yeah, if you want to go over now, I'll be there in a minute," Elizabeth said.

"What will I be up against today—questions or complaints?" Jennifer asked.

"Probably both," Elizabeth said candidly.

"Do you have any complaints about the program?" Jennifer asked, surprised that the gnawing, overdue question flowed out into audible words.

"No, my questions will be confined to a general progress report," the warden responded.

What Jennifer really wanted to know was if she could count on the warden's support, but she stopped short of asking. She'd always wondered which way Ms. Ellsworth voted—for or against the HBP. Knowing that a secret ballot was cast and victory was won by a slim margin didn't satisfy Jennifer's curiosity.

As the board members filed in one by one and gathered around the long oval table, Jennifer saw them as jurors preparing to give their verdict. Tuttle was engaged in reading his notebook as though it held all the secrets of the universe while he twisted the ends of his mustache. Elizabeth soon arrived and sat in the only vacant chair, which was next to Jennifer.

"Shall we begin?" the warden asked, opening a small notebook. "Jennifer, can you give us an update, who's going to make it and who's not?"

"It's not that simple," Jennifer responded, eyeing all the board members' faces. "Look, we all want the men to become responsible adults, get jobs, and pay taxes, but that's not going to happen overnight. They have a few handicaps, some stemming from spending too much time in captivity."

"What does being imprisoned have to do with them having handicaps?" Gordon Fairchild asked, the same board member who wore pinstripe suits and who was in constant pursuit of Tuttle's approval.

"The stagnation of their maturity is in direct correlation with the length of their incarceration. They haven't made even the simplest of decisions for most of their adult lives nor do they have the self-confidence to do so—anymore," Jennifer added.

"I'm sorry, Ms. Collins, but how much maturity did they have in order to land here?" Tuttle asked with a smirk.

"About as much as the guards," she said, shrugging with nonchalance, jabbing back. "Nutritionists say, 'You are what you eat.' But I believe that you are what your environment is. Their environment wasn't suitable for emotional growth before they landed here, and it still isn't." She timed Tuttle's explosion down to the second.

"Well, gentlemen, it seems that our prison Freud wants you to believe it's the guard's fault that the inmates are immature," he laughed flamboyantly, twisting one side of the handlebar mustache.

Jennifer glanced at Elizabeth's face, looking for signs of a rebuttal concerning Tuttle's sexist address of "gentlemen." The warden either didn't catch it, didn't want to catch it, or had grown immune to Tuttle's chauvinistic remarks.

"Look, it's this easy," Jennifer attempted to explain. "A small child raised exclusively by adults never experiences a childhood in the traditional sense, just as a young adult who consistently hangs around a much younger crowd misses the necessary challenges to meet adulthood." She kept her voice calm.

"So! What's your point?" the tyrannical voice bellowed.

"My point *is* you are what your environment is. *You* know how the guards talk to the inmates—like they're subhuman," she said, looking to the warden for support that never came.

"Are the guards supposed to mollycoddle the cons too? Hell, I thought poor treatment of the con was just all part of their punishment for being here," Tuttle said with a laugh, looking around the table and nodding to gain consensus.

"*Legally*, confinement is the *punishment*, not poor treatment," Jennifer said. "Treating the inmate in a subhuman manner is simply a 'perk' you give the guards to make them feel better about themselves for working here."

Tuttle burst into anger, hitting a fist on the table. "Do you have any idea how difficult it is to be a guard? Or does your all-consuming liberalism for the con not allow you to have compassion for those who *haven't* broken the law?"

"Do you have any idea how difficult it is to be an inmate? Or does that absolute world you live in not allow you to see things as anything but black or white? Guards aren't always right, and inmates aren't always wrong!" Jennifer retorted, immediately regretting raising her voice to match Tuttle's in volume.

"I think we're getting a little sidetracked here," the warden interjected.

Frustration filled Jennifer, knowing her words were falling on the deaf ears of well-meaning people who'd had their heads stuck into political grooves for so long that the word *change* had become blasphemy. *I can't alter the mind-set of a hundred generations by myself.*

"Fine!" Tuttle exclaimed. He remained irritated but used a calmer voice. "Let's talk about Ted Hatter."

"What's there to talk about?" Jennifer asked. "He dropped a hot UA and I kicked him out of the program."

"And how do you explain the escalation of the drug infiltration since the HBP came into effect?" Tuttle asked, leaning back in the chair, twisting the ends of his mustache.

"*Don't* even go there! First of all, it's not my job to explain it. And second, the men in the HBP are obligated to drop UAs every three days. They've stayed clean," Jennifer said, watching him seethe.

"That doesn't mean they aren't selling the stuff," he said, using a contemptible smirk. He knew the accusation hit below the belt.

"You got proof of that allegation? Then do something about it," Jennifer said. "Until then, I have work to do." She started to get up to leave.

Tuttle stood, yelling out one last criticism before Jennifer slammed the door on the way out. "And what about you being seen walking alone to Building A? If you don't mind the rules, how do you expect the cons to?"

Elizabeth's anger would no longer remain repressed.

"Sit down and shut up!" she said, watching the stunned look on Tuttle's face. "We have tried twice to get a progress report from Ms. Collins, and both times you've—"

"I was only—" Tuttle started to rebuttal.

"*And both times* you've acted like an ass, totally unprofessional. I refuse to continue to attend these meetings involving the progress report of the Homeward Bound Program. And I'll have no problem telling the right people why. *That* you can count on."

"I was only—" he started again.

"You have belittled and bullied every person in this room for your own personal gain for years. But you'll no longer bully me! I'll be obtaining my own progress reports in private meetings with Ms.

Collins. The rest of you can do whatever you want," the warden said, slamming her notebook shut and marching out of the room.

"Who in the hell does she think she is?" Tuttle asked, ego in full charge.

"I suspect that she thinks she's the warden," the newest and youngest board member answered softly.

Chapter VIII

Before the next group session began, Jennifer sat on the cement-block steps of the administration building, attempting to cool the red rage that burned to the core of her soul. After feeling her stomach muscles tighten and a spinning sensation interfere with her equilibrium, a voice from within muttered the unspoken resentments aimed at Tuttle. Did his wrath stem from his narrow-mindedness or from the obtuse, outdated barbarism to which he clung? A sarcastic thought erupted, Why split hairs?

Not all of Jennifer's antagonism had been born of Tuttle's narcissism. It had spread out, covering the other board members as well, up to and including Elizabeth. The warden's attitude seemed mystifying. *What could that woman be thinking? Why does she put up with such convoluted logic and ineptness?*

Sitting and fuming, Jeff popped into Jennifer's mind. At first she wasn't sure if it was just a knee-jerk reaction because she was feeling so low. But that thought was ruled out when she realized that Jeff held the utmost respect for Elizabeth Ellsworth—a respect that Jennifer wasn't even close to sharing, let alone understanding. She felt guilty about her hard feelings, but she simply had no patience with any warden who had allowed the prison system to be identified by the brick walls and not by the people who lived there and needed help. Jennifer saw the situation one way: Elizabeth Ellsworth *was* the warden. It was her responsibility to change things that didn't work. Well, at least when she wasn't knee-deep in budget meetings.

Perkins spotted Jennifer's forlorn look and buoyantly walked down to where she was perched on the cement steps of the administration building.

"You okay?" he asked. He sat down beside her and rested his bent elbows on both knees.

"I guess I'm just not ever going to understand that woman, am I?" Jennifer asked, feeling perturbed.

"Ms. Ellsworth?" he asked.

"That's the one," she said.

"You will—someday," he said, patting her shoulder and standing.

"Really?" Jennifer asked dubiously. She got up with him and they started their walk to Building A, trying to shed the feelings of retaliation that stubbornly lingered. "The thirst for revenge." Jennifer shook her head.

"Huh?" Perkins asked, mentally scrambling through a list of choices to decipher the topic.

"It's the culprit causing the revolving-door effect," Jennifer said. "The thirst for revenge. I can explain it, but I can't excuse it, Mr. Perkins. It goes something like this: Society locks up the criminal and treats them with hostile contempt for years. The criminal's hostility lashes out on society when they're released. Of course, the criminal returns to prison, and the vicious cycle of the revolving door is developed. I'm not the brightest person on earth, but even I can see revenge doesn't produce well-adjusted citizens capable of holding a job down and paying taxes."

"You blame the prison for the high recidivism rate, don't you?" Perkins asked, catching the hint of her cryptic beginning.

"You're damn right I do," Jennifer said. "The prison is either part of the solution or part of the problem, but it can't be neutral because of its power and influence over the inmates' lives."

"But they're here to be punished for what they did," Perkins said.

"We're punished *by* what we do, not *for* what we do," Jennifer said.

"And there's a difference?"

"Yeah, there is. If a mom asks her child not to touch the iron because it's hot, but the child touches it anyway, what happens?" Jennifer asked.

"The child gets burned," said Perkins.

"Right, so the mom doesn't need to spank the child *for* what he did because the child has already been punished *by* what he did," Jennifer said.

"So how do the inmates get punished *by* what they do when they rob, kill, or rape?" Perkins asked.

"The inmates need a consciousness-raising in order to cooperate with the rules of the universe. For example, when a mother punishes her two-year-old for hurting another child, the kid doesn't know why it's wrong, only that mom doesn't want him doing it. Normally, that's enough of a reason at that age. But long before we hit adulthood, we normally feel bad when we hurt someone because we can relate it to the pain we've had in our life," she said as they arrived at Building A.

"So you're saying if the inmates could feel the pain that they have caused others, then—"

"No, they need to first quit denying the pain that they've experienced," she interjected. "Then we can work together so that they know the wounds and scars they are carrying around don't have to cripple them forever."

"But first?" he asked.

"They work very hard on forgiveness, starting with forgiving others who have trespassed against them," she said. "By the time that they are that far along, it starts occurring to them how the world was meant to work."

"Does it always work that way?" he asked.

"Anyone can heal if they're willing to work at it."

"Then will their anger go away?"

"That's the part we're working on," she said. "Everyone has anger sometimes and there's nothing wrong with that. It's how you handle it that matters, and it makes the difference between being in prison *or* being free. It's important for them to want more than just survival skills. They could have so much more!"

"Have a good day, Ms. Collins," Perkins said as Jennifer walked inside.

*****

As the men gathered around the table, Jennifer spied Travis Talltree and Michael Bishop engaged in a private conversation. She wondered if meaningful sharing was happening or if they were just catching up on the latest Bronco scores. But either way, at least they were communicating and felt free to be friendly.

"What are we doing?" Ron Bookman asked, staying close to Jennifer's heels like an anxious puppy as she passed out reading books ranging from a fifth-to-twelfth-grade level.

"Okay, let's all take a seat," Jennifer said. "We're going to do some reading today."

"Why?" Ron asked, but he quickly rescinded the question after seeing an authoritarian look drilled his way. "I wasn't being disrespectful. I was just wondering."

Jennifer understood the whys and hows of Ron's low maturity level, but the rest of the world wouldn't—and the need was growing stronger for her to start seeing more maturity if he was ever going to make it on the outside. She knew that was probably not going to happen. Ron had no business living in a prison, just like he had no business living on the outside with no supervision. He needed to be in a mental health facility, at least to be diagnosed by a doctor. Maybe meds would matter. But there was no way the prison board would ever listen to her. Later, she would get their attention.

"Because she said so, dummy," replied Derek Coleman, flipping his hair out of his eyes.

Another piercing look from Jennifer brought a "Sorry, Ron" from Derek.

"Don't you think reading is a pretty important skill to have?" Jennifer asked the group. She needed to know what level of reading they were at and who needed the most help.

"We already know how to read, Ms. Lily," Kent Beasley said.

"Good, then you can start now," she said.

Opening a book, Kent began reading silently. He looked around the table at the men snickering. Ah! The pursued response! A feeling of nirvana flowed through his veins.

"Out loud please," said Jennifer, cocking her head with a smile.

Kent read first and then the others. Neither giggling nor snickering could be heard when Tomas Gonzales and Travis Talltree tripped on words such as *antique, superlative, enigma, continuity, gnaw,* and *unique.* Instead, Derek Coleman and Kent Beasley helped them with words that couldn't be sounded out, explaining which letters were silent and what the words meant.

"I'm proud of the maturity you've shown," Jennifer said after everyone had read.

The men looked puzzled. "I don't think we know what you mean, Ms. Lily," Derek said.

"Yes, what does reading have to do with maturity?" Michael asked.

"If you read well, that means you have academic maturity, but if you can listen with patience, it tells me you have emotional maturity, which will serve you far better than a formal education," Jennifer said.

"I don't know what you mean," Tomas said.

"Well, Tomas, there's a lot of financially triumphant people who are incapable of sustaining meaningful relationships or simply keeping their lives together. They lack the emotional maturity it takes to be successful," she said.

Kent noticed the questioning faces surrounding the table and said, "I think she's saying it wasn't only our deviate, criminal behavior that landed us here but also our lack of maturity."

Jennifer nodded. "You got it,"

"So you want us to act better here so when we're set free, we won't mess up again, right?" Ron asked. "Is that what you mean, Ms. Lily?"

"Nothing gets past him, does it?" Derek asked facetiously, feeling the disapproving eyes of Ms. Lily fall upon him. "Sorry, Ron."

"No one wants to hear apologies for your behavior or excuses for what you allow to come out of your mouth. They want to see changes," she said. "And in the absence of that, this will be your forever home."

"You know, Ms. Lily, it's not as easy as you think to be nice all the time in a place like this," Travis said.

"Most inmates go out of their way to piss you off," Tomas said.

"A lot of them do it so we'll take a poke at them, knowing we'll get kicked out of the program," Ron said while the others nodded.

"This is where emotional maturity comes into play," Jennifer said.

"How?" Ron asked.

"It takes two to tango. If you don't participate by blasting your opponent with every conceivable bad word you know, the harassing will stop," she said. "Just ignore them."

"What about the guards? Can we ignore them too?" asked Derek.

"They harass us more about being here than the inmates do," Kent said.

"You can't ignore a direct order by a guard, but you can refuse to show anger," she said.

"But it's hard," Ron said.

"I know," replied Jennifer.

*****

Jennifer saw the time tick by as Valentine's Day appeared and left. There were now only two months left of the HBP, and there was no way to fight the enemy: time. Neither the constant stream of expensive gifts Peter lavished on her nor could the incessant harassing phone calls deter her from yearning for her morning sessions back with the men.

But now an idea was born of necessity: it wasn't enough that the men just earn their parole; her involvement went much deeper than that. But she needed Jeff's help if the idea was ever to be actualized.

*****

Meanwhile, Jeff got a call from Tanner & Waters Inc., which had no intention of discussing their findings over the phone. A compromise was struck for a meeting place: a small coffee shop on the west side of town—a little dumpy but no heavy traffic. Jeff's car wouldn't be recognized.

"So what'd you find out?" Jeff asked, watching them both squirm.

"You're not going to like it," responded Jubal.

"Don't *even* tell me Peter Winslow's the one making those obscene phone calls," he said, feeling a wave of nausea.

"No, actually, that's the good news. We don't think he is," Ethan said.

"Thank God! Then why the troubled look?" Jeff asked. "Now wait a minute. If you two have information about his personal life, I don't want—"

"You'll want to know this," Ethan interrupted.

"Oh no! Does it involve another woman?" Jeff asked.

"It's a little more sinister than that," Jubal said. "You know, we've always thought Winslow's behavior was bizarre. Well, one night he came to Ms. Collins's house and headed straight for her car, like he always does. Only this time we used a pair of binoculars to watch. He was getting something out from behind the right wheel base."

"Dirt, mud, snow? What?" Jeff asked apprehensively.

"No! It was some object he put in his coat pocket. And then he just left, never went inside the house," Jubal said.

"Is that it?" Jeff asked, dismissing any evil connection.

"No. We've seen him do the same thing in parking lots of restaurants, concert halls, movie theaters, wherever they meet," Ethan said.

"I'll admit that's peculiar, but I don't know what it has to do with—"

"Curiosity got the best of us," interrupted Ethan. "So one night, we used a flashlight to examine Ms. Collins's car and found a black metal box, about four inches square, bolted underneath. It had a key lock."

"Maybe it was some expensive gift he was holding for her," Jeff said.

Jubal and Ethan looked dubious. "We think he's running drugs out to the prison via Ms. Collins," Ethan blurted out.

"What are you talking about? That's a quantum leap, don't you think?" Jeff asked, outraged by the mere thought.

"Try and remember this ain't our first rodeo. But putting that aside, every time Winslow 'inspects' Ms. Collins's car, he either is putting something in the black box or taking something out," Jubal said.

"And who is it that always insists on taking Ms. Collins's car in for repairs, whether it needs it or not? Winslow. We figure it gives him time to remove the black box before some mechanic puts it up on a hoist and starts asking too many questions," Ethan said.

"We started to get really suspicious when we heard on the police scanner about the drug influx out at the prison. That started in November, the same month Ms. Collins started working there, right?" Ethan asked.

Jeff felt stunned but managed to ask, "Why does this necessarily eliminate Peter as a suspect for the threatening phone messages?"

"Because he wouldn't want to do anything that would draw attention to Ms. Collins or her house," Ethan said. "He's got a good thing going on. Quite lucrative."

"I can't go to Jennifer with these suspicions unless I can find a way to confirm them. It's just too little to move on," Jeff said.

"Well, if you care for her, you better do something quick before she loses her job," Jubal said.

"Her job? What about her life?" Jeff asked, thinking about the consequences if Jubal and Ethan were right.

"What's next?" Jubal asked.

"Just keep your eyes open and your mouths shut. I sure hope you've documented everything," Jeff said.

"We have," Ethan said.

"I'll make a list of the things I want you to check on. Be thorough, but be discreet," Jeff said. "What do you know about Angela Colder?"

"Nothing, really. Just that we saw her husband come home but we haven't seen him outside since."

"You won't, at least not without a leash," Jeff said with a snicker. "Now get to work."

Jeff hoped the brisk walk to his car would wear down the agitation swimming through his head, but the chilly air filling his lungs only made it increase. He tried to make sense of everything or even something. As he arrived at his office, he casually thought, *Maybe they've watched a few too many cop shows.* But deep down, he knew what Jubal and Ethan had told him couldn't be shrugged off that easily.

Moments passed before a conversation he had with Jennifer about Peter's consistent tardiness replayed as though it had been safely stored for this moment. "Ten minutes late," he said out loud, remembering Jennifer's words verbatim. *No wonder Peter didn't want her parking on the street and why such a fuss was made when she parked in the driveway instead of the garage,* he thought, feeling his limbs go numb. *Peter's not in love with Jennifer. I bet he learned what she could do for him in the local newspaper that reported the proposal for the Homeward Bound Program.*

A flood of incidents gushed through his mind, like the time he saw Peter in the parking lot of Nino's Café, claiming to be checking Jennifer's tires.

Jeff called Robert Henderson on his cell. "I could sure use a friend about now," Jeff said.

"No problem, I'm already in the neighborhood. See you in a few," Robert said.

*****

Jennifer grabbed her briefcase out of the locker, left the prison, and headed for Jeff's office to fly her idea past him. Reaching the reception area of his office, Jeff's door was closed, and the receptionist had stepped out to run errands. She heard muffled voices coming from inside the room.

Jeff opened the door slightly while the men chatted a few parting words, and she felt the reception area grow eerily quiet as the voices became more audible and identifiable.

"How are you dealing with her engagement?" Robert inquired.

"How do you think?" Jeff said.

"Why don't you just tell her how you feel?" Robert asked.

"You mean, why *didn't* I tell her a long time ago?" Jeff posed.

"Well, it's not too late, you know."

"She's engaged now. I don't want to confuse her."

"Confusion's a good thing sometimes," said Robert. "Or are you afraid of rejection, just like the rest of us?"

"There's probably a little of that in there too," Jeff smiled.

"Someday, the two of you are going to say exactly what you mean—to each other," Robert said.

Embarrassment swept through Jennifer as though the eavesdropping had been intentional. She felt as though hot-pink liquid blush was filling all the veins in her body. She scampered unseen for the restroom down the hall and then wondered if the now crimson-colored cheeks reflected in the mirror were a result of mortification over hearing a private conversation, or was it because she heard the truth? She wished the words had never been said, just as much as she wished she hadn't heard them. Turning the water on with one quick twist, she splashed cool water on her burning face, looking closer at the person in the mirror. "You didn't see *that* one coming, did you?" she said, reaching for paper towels.

Self-control surfaced once again until a gush of tears flowed without permission. When the flood was restrained, Jennifer freshened the streaked makeup and wiped the smeared lipstick before applying fresh. Thoughts went back to the earlier days of their relationship, when she'd chastise herself for being so in love with Jeff. It was brutal to fill herself with shame over feelings that no one has ever had any control over and never will. It'd been wrong to ache for him, but she finally got over it, or so she thought. Jennifer bit the red lips to keep the tears from falling. Long-ago feelings had been rationalized into a transference type of love, the kind that a patient develops for their doctor. Besides, Jeff was married then and even though his wife was dying, no one had the right to mess with that. She rationalized that Jeff was in her life, but only as a friend. There was no guilt to bear for that.

4Jeff's door was closed now, and no voices could be heard when she tapped gently, "Anyone in there?"

He opened the door wearing a bright smile. "Hi, Jen, what brings you by?" he asked, leading her toward the place she always called hers on the leather sofa.

"Things," she said, getting comfy. *If I get through the next half hour, I deserve no less than an Oscar.*

Jeff sat at the desk and leaned back in the swivel chair. "What kind of things?" he asked, teasing.

"Well, I think I'll just skip over the dueling-pistols session with Tuttle and tell you that the men have suitable work goals now. Ronald Bookman was the only one who picked an unobtainable goal," she said.

"I already heard about the dueling pistols. So what's Ron's work goal?" Jeff asked, using a hand to cover the grin.

"I figured you heard about Tuttle. Anyway, Ron wanted to be a policeman," she said as they both started giggling.

"What'd you tell him?" Jeff asked.

"That it wasn't very realistic to pursue a career in law enforcement with three felonies on your record." She wore a mock smile. He always liked her animations and the enthusiasm she showed.

"What about the other problem? Any progress?"

"Ah! Their maturity level. It's okay, I guess, for inside prison walls."

"And when they get out?"

"That's what I really came here to talk about. They need a stepping-stone, some kind of halfway house for when they're released. Ronald Bookman and Michael Bishop have spent over half of their adult lives in prison. We can't just set them free," she said, "especially knowing about Ron's mental illness."

"Do you want me to check on what's available in the community?" Jeff asked.

"I already have. Unfortunately, the halfway houses here don't accept anyone with a violent background."

"That'll keep the population down," he joked. "What about out of state?"

"I don't want them out of state. I want them here," she said, watching Jeff raise his eyebrows. "I want to open a halfway house for newly released inmates right here in Clear Water Springs."

"Okay then. What do you have to do?" Jeff asked.

"I was hoping you'd be able to help with that small detail," she said coyly.

"You did, huh?" he smiled. "Well, I'll see what I can find out for you. We don't have much time."

"Time," she said, shaking her head. "There's that word again. It's my worst enemy. Almost. My whole approach to counseling has been altered uncomfortably because of time. Sometimes I border on preaching, lecturing, moralizing—all the things I hate —but always in the interest of time."

"Have any of the men really opened up to you?" asked Jeff.

"Yeah, Travis Talltree had a breakdown-breakthrough experience."

"Then it really doesn't matter how unconventional you think you are because at least one of them trusts Ms. Lily White," Jeff said, grinning. "The others will too."

"It's late, and I need to get going," she said, walking to the door. She felt Jeff at her heels. Resting a hand on the doorknob, she turned to him. "Robert and Elizabeth must be getting pretty close for her to have told him about the dueling-pistols scene at our board meeting. That's how you knew, right?"

The two stood toe to toe when Jeff whispered, "Yeah, they are, and yes, it is."

Jennifer stood motionless, looking into Jeff's eyes, thinking, *I've seen that lovesick puppy dog look a hundred times. And now it hits me like a Mac truck? Am I so preoccupied with everything going on around me that I didn't take the time to read my best friend's body language?* Her knees felt weak and she could barely breathe.

Jeff leaned over and kissed her lips. His ocean-blue eyes gleamed when he came up for air, causing her bottom lip to quiver in the excitement of his touch. He kissed her again, long and passionately, pulling her body close. Surprised at her encouraging response, he couldn't let go.

"Jeff, I've got to go," she said, pulling slowly away from the embrace.

"Why?" he whispered, aching for more.

"You *know* why," she said, opening the door to the reception area. "I'm engaged to another." She scurried to the outside door, leaving Jeff behind.

Jumping into the car, she felt her emotions going in more directions than what Rand McNally's knew existed. Taking the downtown route for expedience at this time of night with no one around sounded ideal. *Only six intersections with traffic lights to get through*, she thought. She passed a late model Ford pickup truck in the left lane to keep pace with the synchronized traffic lights. Hitting one yellow light after another forced her to accelerate, with the hope that the next light would be as green as grass. But it suddenly changed red, and the sound of her screeching brakes could be heard for blocks, just seconds before the pickup truck jolted into her bumper. Hands gripped around the steering wheel, she murmured, "Why didn't he stay in the other lane?"

By the time the police report was taken and names were exchanged, she drove home feeling exhausted, dragging herself in the front door. She counted her blessings: she wasn't injured and didn't get the ticket.

"I can't do this tonight," she said, looking at the blinking message light on the phone and scanning caller ID. It exhibited two anonymous callers with different numbers and two calls from Jeff Hanes.

All she really wanted—actually needed—was a good night's sleep without any interruptions. Jennifer lay there with her eyes closed, hoping sleep would drift her into utopia. She changed positions frequently, assured sleep would come each time she rotated her body. She clung to the pillow beside her, burying her face and loathing herself for having romantic thoughts of Jeff. Was she really in love with him, or did Peter fill that space sufficiently? *This is such bad timing*. She and Jeff had so much in common and mostly agreed on everything—just not always at the same time; it was partly what attracted them to each other. Was she really satisfied with Jeff as her best friend *without benefits?* Peter made her feel light and breezy—young again. "Oh God! Just shoot me!" were the last words she remembered saying before falling asleep.

"Jennifer, if you're there, please pick up," Jeff's voice said on the answering machine at 8:00 a.m. the following morning.

"Hi, Jeff," she said after picking up the phone.

"Don't you think we should talk?" he asked, listening to silence fill the time and space between them. "I-I owe you an apology. I was way out of line. It won't happen again. I know you're in love with Peter. I can accept that." Another long silence filled their time. "Are you still there?"

"Yes, I'm still here," she said with a long soft sigh. "I just want things the way they used to be."

"They already are. I promise."

"That's good enough for me." She knew deep in her heart that the only way to get past anything, especially if it's messy, is to face it. It's what she always preached to the men she was counseling, wasn't it? Before leaving for work, she remembered to report the accident to Peter, who said, "I'll take care of it. Both of you are insured by us. It won't be a problem."

Jennifer was glad to be greeted by Perkins as she parked in front of the administration building.

"You look tired today, Ms. Collins," Perkins said, opening the car door. "Rough night?" He grinned.

"Who taught you how to talk like that?" she asked, smiling while closing her car door. "You've been hanging around me too long."

"I've been hanging around *here* too long," he snickered. "By the way, Ms. Ellsworth wants to see you."

"I bet she does," said Jennifer.

"Excuse me?" Perkins said.

"Never mind, you'll hear about it soon enough, I suspect," she said. "I've been wanting to ask you something."

"Now, Ms. Collins—"

"No, it's not about them," Jennifer explained. "I was wondering how often you see the men from the Homeward Bound Program."

"You must know that the reality of my situation is I'm actually more of a security guard for the administration building than an officer in the units. But I see them from time to time when I have business in the other buildings," he said. "Why do you ask?"

"I wanted to know if you've seen any changes in their attitudes since I first came here. I want to know what they're like when I'm not around."

"Well, Ms. Collins," he said, scratching his head and pausing, "I could ask around for you, but the guards will probably give me a jaundiced view of any inmate. But let me see what I can do, okay?" He walked her to Warden Ellsworth's office.

Jennifer's slow, dawdling steps indicated there was no hurry to meet with the warden, especially because she had no intention of apologizing for walking out on Tuttle before the meeting had been officially closed. She was sure of two things: that she would walk out again under the same circumstances and that she was sure that there would be a lesson from the warden about patience, a short paragraph about respect, and a word to the wise, then she'd be out of there. Jennifer felt that she wouldn't ever understand why the warden couldn't see what's actually happening and everything that Jennifer was up against—alone. *There's got to be some reasoning with the warden. She's an intelligent woman. Tuttle's an ass. What part of that doesn't she get?*

Chapter IX

The warden's door was open when Jennifer popped her head in to ask, "You want to see me?"

Elizabeth Ellsworth had been sitting quietly at her desk, allowing the unknown about Charlie Bremmer's future to occupy much of a twenty-four-hour day. Thoughts of Charlie's appeal were always paramount compared to the dissension with the board concerning the HBP or even the rest of the truth she owed Robert.

"Yeah, I do," Warden Ellsworth said, rising to close the door and offering Jennifer a seat.

"Thank you." Jennifer sat in one of the overstuffed green corduroy chairs that faced the warden's desk.

"Because I derive so little information from our progress meetings, I was wondering if you could brief me on what's happening in the program," Elizabeth said, assuming a businesslike manner that matched her facial expression.

Jennifer felt confused. Instead of being placed in a situation of having to defend herself or the men in the HBP, she was actually being asked about the men's growth. Or was she? "The men have made progress, Ms. Ellsworth." Jennifer was prepared to choose words with care until she knew exactly what the warden really wanted.

"In what ways?" Elizabeth asked with sincerity.

"Well, let's see. They've all chosen obtainable career goals," Jennifer said, not comfortable with divulging any personal specifics that the warden didn't really need to know.

"Career goals?" Elizabeth asked, her face wearing a dubious expression.

"What? Cons can't have careers?" Jennifer asked. "They're supposed to be short-order cooks, janitors, and toilet scrubbers?"

"I was thinking of their ages," Elizabeth said with candor.

"Age has nothing to do with a career. It's simply a tiring excuse for not trying," Jennifer said. Elizabeth squinted before the piercing eyes all but swallowed Jennifer.

"Have I done something to you for which I should be apologizing?" Elizabeth asked, remaining eerily calm and maintaining strict eye contact.

"No, Ms. Ellsworth. I'm sorry I sound a little rough around the edges. I've gotten so used to defending the men in the HBP that . . . " she trailed off.

"I understand," Elizabeth said. The warden relaxed her tone and allowed her eyes to soften. "What other progress have they made?"

"They're learning how to bond," Jennifer said and then paused to wait for a reply similar to "skip the warm and fuzzy stuff," but it never came.

"To each other or to you?" the warden asked, looking intrigued.

"Both, really." Jennifer explained about connection and attachment, two social aspects that hadn't been implemented into the men's lives before the HBP.

"How'd you accomplish that?" Elizabeth asked.

"I demanded it. They do what I tell them because they want to get out," Jennifer said. "I figure if they no more than go through the motions of bonding, some of it has to stay with them when they're released."

"That's good, Jennifer," Elizabeth nodded. "But when they're released, they'll no longer have one another. Will that cause them to feel abandoned?"

"When that time comes, the men are going to have to learn how to live life on someone else's terms other than the prison's," Jennifer said candidly.

"Do they *really* want that?" Elizabeth questioned. "Are they ready, Jennifer?"

"Not quite yet," Jennifer said, "but they get closer every day."

"I want to thank you for the update," the warden said, taking a seat behind the desk. "I'd like you to keep me personally informed of the men's progress on a monthly basis. I won't ask any hard questions, okay?"

"Why? I mean, what about the board meetings?" Jennifer asked as she got up to head for the door.

"I don't have time to attend them anymore," Elizabeth responded. "One more thing, Jennifer." Elizabeth twisted a pencil that lay on her desk. "I'm sorry but I have to ask . . . The drug influx here, do you know anything?"

"No, and contrary to someone else's opinion, it's not very likely my guys are pushers either. I mean, they're probably all going to be released in the next couple of months or so. They're not going to jeopardize that. Remember, they know what it takes to *get out*. It's *staying out* that seems to be the problem."

"That doesn't mean they don't know about it."

"I can't believe you'd say something like that! So you're really no different from Tuttle! This meeting wasn't because you cared about the inmates in the HBP. Do you know so little about the way things work behind bars that you can pretend that nothing would happen to my men if they talked? Their lives wouldn't be worth a thin dime in here," Jennifer said. "Oh yeah, that's right. You don't set them up to fail."

"I'm sorry, Jennifer," the warden said with true regret. "I should've known better."

"Besides, drug use in this prison is hardly a novelty," Jennifer said. "No disrespect intended."

"None taken, I assure you," Elizabeth said. "But it's never been this bad for this long. Everyone can tell when a shipment comes in, but then things die down again, usually for months. But not this time. I'm looking for the one main source."

"Well, *look* somewhere else," Jennifer demanded. She then pulled the office door open and saw Robert Henderson's surprised face.

"Excuse me, Robert," she said with equal surprise.

"I was just about to knock," he said with a smile, stepping into the office. "Elizabeth tells me you're doing a great job here, Jennifer."

"Really?" she said with an incredulous look, bidding them both a goodbye.

After the door closed, Robert turned his gaze to the warden. "You know, Elizabeth, that girl has no idea how you really feel about her," he said, sitting in Jennifer's empty seat.

"I know," she said, rubbing the back of her neck.

"And I seem to keep running into people who don't want her to know how they really feel about her," he chuckled.

"Been talking with Jeff?" Elizabeth grinned.

"How'd you know?" he asked, puzzled.

"I've known how they feel about each other since the first day I saw them together. It was last July during the negotiations for the HBP," she smiled, her mind recalling them clearly.

Jeff and Jennifer were standing in the foyer of the administration building, sharing what Jennifer must've perceived as imperative information on how to negotiate for the program. Jeff's attention never waned, wearing an isn't-she-wonderful look. Her voice was like music to his ears, and he stood taller and talked quieter as she looked to him for answers. Jennifer could've asked for no more than directions to the restroom, and his attention wouldn't have wandered. Whatever advice he gave, Elizabeth was sure it was etched in stone in Jennifer's mind. From a distance, they could've been a married couple, a client and lawyer, or a doctor and patient. But a closer look would reveal the man thought the lady hung the moon; the lady thought the man walked on water.

"What I don't understand is why they both fight it," Elizabeth queried.

"She's engaged to someone else, you know," Robert said. "Some guy named Peter Winslow."

Elizabeth strolled over to take a seat next to him. "What's Jeff going to do about it?" she asked.

He turned to her, a shy look replaced the confident one usually worn. "I don't know. What *does* a guy do when the woman he's in love with wants someone else? What's your suggestion? For Jeff, I mean," Robert said.

She leaned a little closer to say, "It might not be very original, but I'd tell him that honesty's the best policy. What does he have to lose?"

"His pride, if she rejects him," Robert said, wading deep into her eyes.

"She won't," Elizabeth grinned before standing to move to her desk. "Besides, I doubt if Jeff's self-esteem is that fragile. But what I'm more interested in is if Burt got another date set for Charlie."

"No, but he ought to be grateful for the two extensions the judge has already granted." Robert noticed how she changed the subject in one fell swoop and why.

"Do you want to talk about this?"

"Not really."

"Good. In that case, would it be too bold of me to ask you out for tonight?" Elizabeth asked with a suspicious grin.

"No," Robert answered immediately. "Pick you up at seven."

*****

Jennifer and Michael Bishop had settled into a comfortable counseling session, reading excerpts from *The Art of Glassblowing*, a book ordered when none could be found on the subject in the prison library. Michael eagerly shared every new detail learned, secretly hoping her continued support and encouragement wouldn't cease.

Michael was a loner, that much was certain. Whether or not he came that way to the prison hadn't been determined. But what had been determined was that his personality and gentle mannerisms would serve him well in this chosen career. They'd provide a way for him to find himself through individual self-expression. Michael's tenderness, the most protected hidden emotion, would flourish in any environment that provided an opportunity for independence and anonymity. Jennifer had grown to understand why the men held a certain kind of respect for Michael, often confiding in him.

But she was curious to know what lay beneath the seemingly sedate personality.

"You know, Michael, I don't really know very much about your life before prison," Jennifer said in a queried tone, cocking her head.

"There was so little of it," he said, snorting a chuckle.

"Were you happy?"

"I suppose I was when all us kids were little, before Dad left," Michael said.

"How many were in your family?"

"There were five kids, all boys. But later, Mom had another kid, a girl, I was told."

"Why do think you were happy as a kid?"

"Ya see, Ms. Lily, when you're little, you don't know the meaning of words like *poverty, food stamps, welfare, three-room flats*. It was really a pretty carefree time. I didn't even know people came in different colors until I was about five or so," he said, laughing aloud. "We only lived and shopped around people whose skin was the same as mine. *Colored* was the term used then. Later I somehow became a Negro, and of course I became a black man, but that was before I became African-American," he said facetiously, as he rubbed his chin. "It only took about sixty years for everyone to agree to call us what we already were."

"You didn't know you were black? How'd you find out?" Jennifer grinned at the choice of spin placed on his childhood.

"I overheard Mom and Dad talking about Dad losing his job because he was colored and wasn't needed anymore now that they found a white man to take the job. I asked my oldest brother what that meant. He thought I was trying to be funny, you know, like I already knew. But how could I? It wasn't as if there were white people in my neighborhood," he chuckled.

"You are too funny!" she laughed. "How'd you feel after you knew?"

"Oh, I guess 'bout like I do now. I mean, I never understood why such a fuss was made over the color of one's skin until I was told to make a fuss," he said, shaking his head. "You know, Ms. Lily, you were right about me. I had used the color of my skin as an excuse for many failures and, I guess, for lots of things. It became easy, even expected of me, by both blacks and whites."

A short, comfortable pause proceeded as Jennifer nodded slowly. "Were you and your brothers close?"

"I guess so, for a while anyway. But after Dad walked out and my oldest brother went to prison, I was left raising the other kids," he said with a detected calmness, a quiet place he found out of necessity.

"Where was your mother?"

"She worked the first two years we were on our own, but after that, she just hardly ever came home," he shrugged, implying the small significance given to the situation.

"How'd you manage?" Jennifer was intrigued.

"I didn't because she kept staying away longer and longer. Social Services took the kids away one day when I was out scavenging for food. They came back for me, but by then I'd hit the road," Michael said.

"How old were you?"

"Ten, 'leven, something like that."

"What'd you do? Where'd you go?" Jennifer asked, wondering if he'd ever told this to anyone before.

"I lived with prostitutes for a while. They fed me, gave me a place to stay, even sent me to school. I stayed with them till I was fourteen or fifteen. It was the last real home I ever had," Michael said. "I really loved those ladies, and they loved me. So for a brief time in my life, I did everything that kids do."

"Why'd you leave?"

"Because, one day, I came home from school and learned they had taken on a new 'partner,'" he said, accenting the word by drawing imaginary quotation marks in the air.

"And what? You didn't like her?" she asked.

"It was Mom," he said, without a trace of emotion. "She didn't even know who I was, but I knew her."

"I don't remember any of this from your file." Jennifer looked puzzled.

"The only other people that know about this are the others in the program," Michael said. "We talk a lot more now to one another. I mean, *really* talk."

"I'm glad," she said.

It wasn't hard for Jennifer to deduce why drugs became such an integral part of Michael's life. And the question of whether he'd become a loner before or after prison had now been answered. No wonder he was sedate! Everything after puberty must have seemed damn uneventful!

It was more than a pulse that kept Michael alive. The eyes to the soul might've shut down once or twice, but this private world filled with thoughts and memories had been well protected. His future had been put on hold for three decades. Was he ready to live it now? Forgiving the people who'd abandoned him was one thing—he'd probably already done that—but there was a bit left to go before complete healing could take place. Just a few more steps would be all that were needed. But would their limited time together rob him of the opportunity?

*****

Jennifer reviewed notes about Derek Coleman as she waited in Rec Room One for their one-on-one session. Derek's father worked for the FBI and his mother stayed at home—incessantly. He idolized his father, a man who built expectations for his son from his own inadequacies.

Often, Jennifer and Derek's time together was enlightening, but sometimes he would take a severe spin into hostility, becoming defensive without provocation. Together they had shared laughter, ideas, and the knowledge of philosophers. But like the rest of the men, Derek had also invented his own private world. The problem was it hadn't been invented to keep others out but as a place to hide the truth from himself.

"Hi, Ms. Lily," Derek said, taking a seat at the table.

"Hi, Derek," she responded, closing the notebook. "I brought you a catalog and schedule from the university so you could still apply for summer session. Maybe just a couple of classes to start if you want. I'd be happy to help you fill out the forms."

"I'm sure I can do it myself," he said. "I *do* know how to read, you know."

"Derek, even the most self-sufficient person needs help sometimes," Jennifer reminded.

"Well, then they aren't really self-sufficient, are they?" Derek asked, tossing the hair from his face.

"This kind of brings us back to your creative financing methods for college, doesn't it? You know, where you'd rather break the law by selling drugs than ask for financial help," she said. "Remember?"

"But I don't believe in asking for help when I can take care of myself. My dad taught me that a long time ago."

"Really? How'd he do that?"

"The first time he saw me back away from a fight, well, I learned right then," he nodded as though the memory was always current and readily retrievable.

"What happened?" she asked, tilting her head.

"I was about four, no, five, because I remember being old enough for school," Derek started. "Well, anyway, me and my dad was waiting in line one day to buy advance tickets to a football game. This big kid pushed me. It wasn't hard enough to knock me down, but I stepped back to be closer to my dad, thinking the kid would leave me alone, and he did. After we bought our tickets and walked back to the car, he really let me have it. He shoved me to the ground and yelled that if I was ever going to be a man, I better start learning how to stick up for myself. I lost a tooth and sprained an ankle that day, but I learned never to take any crap off anyone again. From then on, if anyone messed with me, I made them sorry."

"How'd your mother feel about this?" she asked.

"We didn't tell her. Me and my dad were good buddies, and we never told her when he had to hu—I mean, hit me," Derek said.

"Do you think what he did was okay? I mean, for parents to batter their children?" she asked.

"He didn't batter me!" Derek exclaimed. "That's a gross exaggeration. He used firm steps in teaching valuable lessons. There *is* a difference, you know. He was actually quite noble." Derek felt the record had been set straight as he flipped the hair from his eyes.

"How old were you when he stopped bat—I mean, using firm steps to teach valuable lessons?" she asked.

"I guess when I was about seventeen. That's when he died."

Any attempt to tell Derek what his father did was nothing short of child abuse would push him further into that comfortable world that allowed him to live in full-blown denial. The same would be true in trying to convince him of the probability that his mother knew about the abuse but was simply too scared to do anything, possibly fearing retaliation. But all wasn't lost. Derek had tied some pieces together that confirmed at least half of her suspicions. If only he would've brought this episode up in the appropriate role of a victim, not as a son determined to convince himself of his father's love through an epic of heroism. The effects of child abuse could be treated much easier than the effects of denial, partly due to certain elements in healing that have to come from the victim's efforts. But how could Derek help himself if he refused to acknowledge that shoving a five-year-old to the ground with enough force to break a tooth and sprain an ankle was, in fact, criminal assault on a child?

*****

"I've found some information about your men," Perkins said as he walked with Jennifer.

"Is it something I want to hear?" she asked skeptically.

"Yeah, I think you do," he nodded. "Most of the guards hate your men."

"Well, *now* I feel better," she said facetiously.

"Do you know why the guards feel that way?" he asked, without waiting for an answer. "Because they say your men act like they're better than the rest."

"And I'm supposed to be happy about this?" Jennifer squinted her eyes.

"You don't get it, do you, Ms. Collins?"

"Obviously not."

"You gotta think like a guard."

"No, thanks!"

"See, what's happenin' is your men are refusing to participate in the badgerin' and bickerin'. They don't stare the guards down when they're being pushed around anymore. And the other day, one of the guards told Travis Talltree what a worthless piece of you-know-what he was, and do you know what Talltree said? 'You have a nice day, sir.' It was great! I wished you could've been there," Perkins said, laughing so hard he stopped to catch his breath.

"*My* Travis said that? You *go*, Travis!" Jennifer said, laughing. "What about the rest of them?"

"From what I've been told, Michael has set the pace, and now they all follow," he said. "I don't think you have anything to worry about."

"This *is* good news," she said, knowing Travis was learning how to deal with life's little inflictions without having to go berserk and rip someone's head off in a heat of uncontrollable anger.

*****

The take-charge side of Elizabeth Ellsworth chose a quiet Mexican restaurant in a small bedroom community of Clear Water Springs. It would provide the perfect atmosphere for the words that always seemed to get stuck in her throat, words that had been purposely omitted in all of her conversations with Robert Henderson. The female side of her remembered Mexican food was Robert's favorite, the perfect path to a man's heart. The logical side of her selected a place that couldn't be confused with a bustling fast-food outlet and where Robert could hear what he had the right to know—and escape gracefully, if needed. She'd never meant for their relationship to go this far; it just happened. But now was the time for truth. For years, the only way Robert played a part in Elizabeth's life was from newspaper articles that hyperventilated over high-profile cases that the district attorney's office tried. But a year ago, when Robert's belief system changed about the use of the death penalty, he resigned as prosecuting attorney and went into private practice. Elizabeth read with admiration his humble apology three years after the execution of an innocent man. Robert had been convinced of the man's guilt from day one and fought tenaciously to have him put to death. When the man's relatives won a court order to have the body exhumed and tested for DNA, Robert's self-esteem came crashing down after learning the man couldn't have been at the murder scene. Afterward, he reexamined all past cases where expert prosecuting skills helped sentence someone to death and Elizabeth admired him for this. When he came across Charlie Bremmer's case and realized there hadn't been an execution yet, Robert worked hard to find a way to commute Charlie's sentence to life. He started with a knock on the warden's office door upon the advice of his best friend, Jeff Hanes.

*****

"Did you have something on your mind when you invited me here, or are you simply charmed by my winning ways?" Robert asked, showing a broad smile as they lingered over cocktails before ordering dinner.

"We need to talk," she said.

Robert's smile dissipated. It was as though the sun had just set in the ocean, swallowing the rest of the day's light. *This can't be good. Anytime a woman says "we need to talk," well, it's usually goodbye time.* "Yeah? What about?" he answered as casually as he could, and braced himself for the worst.

"There's a misunderstanding between us concerning Charlie and it's my fault," she said, looking down in the blue salt-rimmed margarita glass.

"There's no misunderstanding. I know how you feel about Charlie," he said, feeling the bite of the words sting as he sipped his Johnnie Walker and soda.

"That's just it, I don't think you do."

"Well, I know you were once married to him and still have a lot of feelings for him," he said, gulping down the drink. He hoped for a quick, anesthetic effect. "You're waiting for the day the man's free and the two of you can be together." He quickly set his glass down with a thud. "End of story."

"No, that's not the end of the story. Sure, I hope Charlie's set free because he's not guilty of the crime. But he's not the man I once was so in love with," she said, looking into Robert's confused eyes.

"Because he's on death row?" Robert asked, somehow knowing that couldn't be it.

"If we shared the same kind of love that once blessed us, death row wouldn't matter," she began. "But we're not the same people anymore. He went one way and I went another, opposite directions at equal speeds in the criminal justice system. Today, we're just good friends. How could we be anything else?"

"And Charlie feels this way too?" Robert wanted so much to remove any doubt.

"Yeah, *now*. I'll be perfectly honest, Robert. Charlie told me he still loved me when he first came to death row. And maybe I needed to hear that then. But since then, and before you came into my life, we agreed no one could turn back the hands of a clock and save what was lost."

Robert reached out to squeeze her hand. "You don't know how many times I prayed you'd come to that conclusion. You know I'm in love with you, right?" he asked with a perpetual boyish grin.

Elizabeth's smile revealed she knew, but she didn't announce a mutual feeling. "Should we order?" she asked, picking up the menu.

"What do you want for dinner?" He tried to act as though he was focusing on the menu, but what he really wanted to know was why the words *I love you* weren't reciprocated or at least drew some kind of comment.

"I'm not sure," she said, in a nonchalant manner before grinning. "What would you like for breakfast?"

His head popped up, and a wide-eyed Robert began to glow.

Chapter X

Kent Beasley waited patiently for his session to begin even though he was thinking of clever distraction tactics. Although it was assumed that he hid his deepest, most inner thoughts and feelings behind facetious humor, the truth was that daily jesting made them bearable.

Growing up, Kent was a quiet, unassuming sort of kid who preferred being alone. But after Nam and a trail of visits to sanitariums, his reserved tongue went into overload after discovering speech and communication weren't synonymous by nature or definition. Speech was simply an inalienable right and could produce flare without meaning, but communication was based on trust.

If he learned nothing more from the war, Kent learned that today's problems were frivolous, at least compared to the reoccurring nightmares robbing him of sleep and eroding his mind. They always began in slow motion, flashing silent snapshots of body dismemberment and the bloodstained faces of unknown soldiers. But as their speed accelerated, the volume grew to a din and his head throbbed with the sounds of M16s blasting inches away from his pounding ears. He witnessed hundreds of helpless, injured souls who scrambled aimlessly and screamed incessantly, always with the expectation that he would find them refuge. Then an array of smells filtered through his nostrils, including burnt flesh and hair and acrid gunpowder. But the stench of fear would invariably be what choked him awake.

"Hi, Kent. Sorry I'm late," Jennifer said, laying her files on the table.

"No problem. You got a note from home?" he asked with a quirky grin.

"Let's see, I have it here somewhere." She fumbled through the files in pseudo pursuit. After tossing him a get-down-to-business look, she asked, "So you got any questions before we start?"

"Yeah. What's a nice girl like you doing in a place like this?" He used the mannerisms and voice of a pick-up artist in a singles bar on a Saturday night.

"I enjoy a captive audience." She grinned.

"That's a good one, Ms. Lily." Kent tilted back on the legs of his chair and nodded.

"Now the last time we met, I asked you to divide your life into three stages. Before, during, and after Nam," she said, paving the way for a session. "Why don't we talk about your life *during* Nam."

A weary look swept over his face and he folded his limp hands. They sat motionless on the table as he wondered, *Why now? After all, there was no memory of anyone ever taking this much interest in my life when the bombs were bursting in air. But now they want to know? I could tell them what I felt: helpless. Is that what everyone wants to hear?*

While Kent was in Vietnam, his childhood memories dissipated much like a puff of smoke disappeared into thin air from the pipe his father occasionally lit. All thoughts concerning the carefree days of childhood evaporated: the taste of an ice-cream cone on a hot summer day as it dripped down both hands faster than he could lick it off, the red bike with the broken seat and missing handlebar grip, and learning how to ride with no hands. Faraway recollections of his family begged to surface but never actually did, at least not enough to project an accurate imagery. The fun days of skipping school in his senior year seemed as remote as the first day of kindergarten and as uneventful as toilet training. Life was lived in the moment and staying alive to see another day of senseless killings would complete his young biography.

"You know what, Ms. Lily? The war's over. It went into overtime, and no one won—not even the politicians."

Using a sigh and a smile, Jennifer asked, "How 'bout you give me a quick rundown on your background then? Things about your childhood, parents, siblings."

"My mother and father, those two were quite a pair! Dad was a big-time drinker, used to hit Mom and us around. Of course, she doesn't remember that now. But like I said before, our family probably wasn't any more screwed up than anyone else's, at least not in our 'hood," he said before chuckling. "I was always grateful we didn't own any guns. Seriously!"

"Siblings?" she asked.

"Six. We don't see much of one another. I guess everyone assumes that big families are happy families, like the Waltons or something. We never learned the art of closeness."

"Where would you have learned it from?"

"Right," Kent agreed. "I wish the folks could've done a little better, then maybe I could've handled Nam a little better." He paused before continuing, "Maybe I wouldn't have been so scared all my life, an emotional bomb always imploding."

"You mean *exploding*, don't you?"

"No, I didn't explode until later, after Nam. I imploded mentally and emotionally long before that. Everything inside just broke down, but no one knew because the shell was still intact."

"How did you get into the service?"

"Well, first I lied about my age by two years and had false documentation to back it up. But basically, no one cared," he said. "Basic training was no more than breaking you down to rebuild you their way to be a killer. Suicide crossed my mind every day."

"Did you tell anyone?" she asked.

"Paranoia was my only friend. Who was I going to tell?" he asked. "My drill sergeant recommended me for my first promotion from an E-2 to a PFC at the end of basic training. He held me up as a shining example of someone who really had it together." He shook his head in disbelief. "By the time I left Advanced Individual Training, I was a corporal on my way to Vietnam."

"Did thoughts of suicide fade in Nam?" she asked, wondering if survival instincts prevailed.

"Oh yeah, and I was looking forward to Nam. I was sure I'd die, and then I'd finally know peace. I didn't die, obviously, but I found a comfortable self-sedation zone."

"Yet you were a hero in Nam, a few medals, I understand," said Jennifer.

"No, Ms. Lily. The reds, whites, crystal, and smack—*they* were the heroes. It was their life now. I was just passing through. I had no idea who was inside that army uniform, and I didn't want to know. After my second tour of duty, several more promotions came my way on the battlefield. The last one was master sergeant. Yeah, I got the Bronze Star, two Silver Stars, a Purple Heart, and a bunch of other junk. Big deal."

"So drugs were working for you? They eased the inner pain?" she asked.

"Yeah, and I would've done anything to keep it that way," he said before grinning and shaking his head. "It was certainly better than the lithium shuffle that was forced on me in the loony bins."

"The fear you talked about, did it cling to you in Vietnam?"

"No, like you said, the drugs eased the inner pain. Besides, by this time, life was just one big game. Actually, it was a dream about a game and somehow I was winning," Kent said.

"Your family told your doctors that the root of your problem stemmed from watching your best friend die at the end of your second tour of duty," said Jennifer. "They say you were suffering from survivor's guilt."

"I heard that same psycho mumbo jumbo, Ms. Lily. I wasn't one of those guys who said, 'I wonder why he died and I didn't.' I was the guy who said, 'I've killed 'em. All of 'em.'"

"Why?" she asked.

"I had a battlefield decision to make after my company commander was fatally hit. I made it and my best friend died, along with dozens of others I didn't even know," he said in a tone as serious as she had ever heard from him. "We all called him Spuds because of his love affair with potatoes."

"What was the battlefield decision?"

"To withhold Spuds's request for an air strike. I knew that his platoon was getting hit pretty hard, but my three other platoons were in close range, so I felt sure we could reinforce and relieve. Besides, I'd called for air strikes before and they either never arrived or arrived too late. He tried to tell me how bad things were, but I thought he was just panicking," Kent said.

"Then what else could you have done?"

"A question I've asked myself a thousand times. Maybe if I hadn't been on drugs, he'd still be alive," he added with remorse. His throat was tightening, and all the indecisiveness and second-guessing was surfacing, just like in the nightmares.

"You're not on drugs now. What would you have done today in the same situation?" she asked.

"I honestly believe," he said, choking on the words, "I would've done the same thing based on the information I had at the time." Tears filled his eyes.

"There was nothing else you could've done."

*****

That evening, lying on the hard cot, Kent listened to the sounds of prison life as the day closed: steel doors slamming in unison, lights flickering out one by one, a guard's reprimand of an inmate who was playing music past curfew, a toilet flushing in the next cell. He looked up at the cement ceiling where others before him wrote catchy prison poetry in verses not spoken in mixed company. A relief came that had long been waiting to be owned. Maybe what he did in the war was all he could do; maybe it was all anyone could do. Finally, the words coming from Ms. Lily confirmed that. It was the first time he'd heard his voice speak of what happened, not omitting the final scene. Thoughts of past decades flashed through an open memory bank, making him wonder at how life would've been without the willingness to allow the poisonous venom of guilt to run through his veins. Before falling asleep, he repeated a quiet prayer for himself, as well as for the son he never knew.

*****

Jubal Tanner and Ethan Waters came unannounced to Jeff Hanes's office on a sunny March day, just as he was leaving. He invited them in, hoping they weren't the harbingers of bad news, but he braced himself for the worst anyway.

"Did you investigate everything on my list?" Jeff asked.

"And then some," Jubal said.

"Tell me everything," said Jeff.

"We got into the black box and took samples to the lab, the one you told us to use. They identified the drugs as cocaine, methamphetamines, and marijuana," Ethan said.

"How'd you get into the black box?" Jeff asked, feeling his worst nightmare becoming a reality.

"I have a friend in the locksmith business," Jubal said, shrugging to emphasize the simplicity of the accomplishment.

"What else?" Jeff asked.

"Peter Winslow doesn't have a thriving insurance business, but oddly enough, he does have a thriving personal bank account not attached to the business," Jubal said. "I have a friend who works in Winslow's bank who loves free tickets to the Avalanche games." He grinned.

"What about money? Did you actually see any money in that black box?" Jeff asked.

"Yes, and per your instructions, we didn't touch it," Ethan said.

"H-He . . . um . . . " Jubal started.

"What!" Jeff said. "I want to know everything."

"Winslow isn't just selling. He's using too," Ethan said.

"How can you tell?" Jeff asked, looking puzzled.

"How can you *not* tell? I mean, no disrespect, Dr. Hanes, but the man's pupils, his constant runny nose that bleeds more than occasionally, his energy level that supersedes a high school senior playing sports, his sleep deficit, I mean, it's right there for anyone to see," Ethan said. "Ask Ms. Collins about his lack of appetite and his—"

"Okay already! I get the message!" Jeff said.

"You still want us to keep the surveillance on her house?" Jubal asked.

"Yeah, apparently we're dealing with two separate things here," Jeff said. "And she's still getting phone threats."

"One other thing, Mr. Hanes," Jubal started. "That neighbor you're suspicious of . . . um . . . "

"Angela Colder?"

"Yeah, that's the one. Sometimes she goes through Jennifer's mail and once she stole her newspaper," Jubal said. "You know, Jeff, Angela was pretty friendly with a stranger and not a well-kept stranger either. I guess she was giving him directions, but he got away from us, so we don't know for sure what was going on. But it was hard to imagine her talking to someone like that. Know what I mean?"

"Let it slide for now, but document everything," Jeff warned. "It's odd though."

"In what way?"

"Because Angela usually gets the kid to do that kind of work."

"You mean Helen? The short one that dresses like an adult but hasn't quite made the grade?"

"Yeah."

Jeff found it interesting that Angela was getting more daring— or more careless. What was her agenda really? It's clear she doesn't like Jennifer; her overly sweet smile can't hide that. But does she actually hate Jen? There's only one step from jealousy to hate. But would she actually risk her freedom just to injure her. How much further would she be willing to go? What is she hiding about the stranger who showed up in the neighborhood?

*****

Later, Jeff leaned back in the swivel chair after Jubal and Ethan left. Turning around to the window to get a better outside view, he randomly gazed at pedestrian traffic hounding the shopping district.

His mind floated in and out of reality, searching frantically for a solution that would spare Jennifer's livelihood and, maybe, her life. And then it hit him.

"Robert?" Jeff said after dialing Robert Henderson.

"What's up?" Robert asked.

"You got some time tomorrow to stop by?"

"What time?"

"'About noon."

"I'll be there."

*****

The following afternoon, while driving out to the prison for a group session, Jennifer practiced the well-rehearsed role, hoping the words would sound more authentic than they did in a week's worth of verbal preparation. Giving personal information in a prison environment was a taboo and could be a deficit to any credible psychologist, which, by itself, was a stigma among the general population. Would her intuition affirm her timeliness? How would the men react? Maybe they already knew. *There are no secrets in prison*, she thought with a smile, parking in front of the administration building.

"Are we ready to start?" she asked, folding both hands on the table after taking a seat with the men in Rec Room One.

"I am," Ron Bookman said.

"Okay," she paused, then, "I'm Ms. Lily and I'm an alcoholic." She systematically looked at each individual expression at the table.

"Oh, I get it," Ron said. "We're having an AA meeting for our group session today."

"One small problem," Derek Coleman said. "Ms. Lily can't chair, only someone with a desire to quit drinking can."

"She can't even be here if it's a closed meeting," Ron said, priding himself on the understanding of the traditions of Alcoholics Anonymous.

"Pick me, Ms. Lily. I'll chair the meeting," Tomas Gonzales said, waving a hand in the air.

"No, pick me," Derek said, waving a hand higher and shaking it harder.

"I think she can chair this meeting, can't you?" Michael asked softly.

"I qualify," she said, watching looks that ranged from shocked to befuddled.

"No way! How could you be—" Ron started.

"An alcoholic?" she interjected.

"You don't look—" Tomas started but stopped.

"Like an alcoholic," she said, finishing his question. She recollected the clichés about alcoholism. "Michael, how long have you known?"

"Kent and I suspected from our first session," Michael said.

"And you didn't tell the others?" she asked.

"It wasn't ours to tell," Kent said.

"So you're all saying she *is* an alcoholic?" Ron asked.

The men chuckled before Derek asked, "So, Ms. Lily, how long?"

"Ten years ago," Jennifer said.

"Thinking back on it though, you talk just like the people in our meetings," Derek said.

"Let's begin," she said, initially reciting from memory the preamble to Alcoholics Anonymous, which begins every meeting from the Big Book.

An hour later, Jennifer breathed a sigh of relief. If she'd had any doubts, they all melted away, and a new connection formed among them. She thought the men had found a remarkable way to communicate and suspected that they probably held their own AA meetings other than the one the prison allowed—once or twice a month. She still had some concerns if each of these men could live a productive life and never return to prison again. She'd grown close to them and wished she had an additional six months before they were set free. *But maybe*, she thought, *the halfway house idea would fly, and somehow they wouldn't have to be free and all alone.* Jennifer had heard some grapevine talk about some of the men wanting to share an apartment together when they get out. If the men did this without any help, they would be back.

*****

Insecurities and inadequacies floated like a dark cloud over Ronald Bookman as he remained in Rec Room One for a one-on-one counseling session. He wondered why the others always poked fun at him and yet befriended him too. What was he? Just a mascot for the group? Would he ever really fit in anywhere?

Ron was more adolescent than adult, and Jennifer hadn't figured out why yet. Was he born that way? Or, as Jennifer suspected, did he just get hit too many times on his head? His prison psychological evaluation wasn't cluttered with useless labels like many of the others in the HBP. This amazed Jennifer because she knew they could've had a field day in analyzing Ron's behavior. It didn't take a psychologist to figure out that Ron suffered from a diminished mental capacity. No one thought it was important enough to find out why. But Jennifer was determined to know the whole story before the Homeward Bound Program ended.

Ron possessed a sort of innocent beauty, and had his life not taken a criminal career path, he might've been able to receive proper treatment. Others may never perceive him as he wished they would, but in many ways, his adaptation to the world, and prison, was nothing less than incredible. What many failed to realize was that his adolescent behavior didn't reflect the innate insight he used to evaluate his environment or the people in it.

"Why do those guys always treat me like I'm stupid or something?" Ron asked.

"I don't know, Ron," she said, sympathizing. "Some do so to make themselves look smarter. Why do *you* think they do it?"

"I think it's really because they're as scared as I am," Ron said. "It's just that I don't hide it as well."

"That's pretty perceptive, Ron," Jennifer said, smiling.

"Is that good, Ms. Lily?" He waited for approval.

"That's *very* good, Ron," Jennifer smiled while nodding. "I was wondering if you'd be willing to talk about your artwork."

"My artwork?" he asked as if it had never been brought up before.

"Yeah, I was wondering if you'd ever thought about illustrating books," she said.

"N-No, Ms. Lily. I don't think I'm good enough," said Ron.

"Why do say that? Have you ever submitted anything?"

"Well, no, but . . . "

"Would you be willing to submit some of your drawings to a publisher?" Jennifer needed to know how brave he was and how far was he willing to go.

"W-Will you be disappointed if they don't like 'em?"

"I could never be disappointed in anyone who was trying to improve themselves," she said. "But why are you assuming they wouldn't like them?"

"Are you serious?" Ron looked confused, but he sat straighter in his chair.

"Of course. Hasn't anyone ever shown an interest in your drawings?" Jennifer wondered if she was the only one who saw his talent.

"I guess my mom did."

"And your dad?"

"No way! He wanted me to be playing ball when all I really wanted to do was draw," said Ron. "He thought I was a sissy."

"Do you *know* that's what he thought?" she asked.

"It was his favorite nickname for me," he said. "If he caught me drawing, he'd break every one of my crayons. One day he burnt my easel and paint pallet out on our front lawn."

"Why?" she asked, narrowing her eyes.

"Because he hated me and my mom."

"I doubt that," she said, watching him nod to correct the disbelief. "Okay, for a moment, let's pretend he didn't hate you or your mom, but only himself. How would he have treated the two of you then?"

"I don't know," he said after a long deliberation.

"Think about it."

"The same. He would've acted the same. But why would he hate himself?" Ron asked.

"I don't know, I didn't know the man," Jennifer said. "There could've been many reasons."

"Well, I guess it doesn't matter now. He's dead." Ron shrugged. "Besides, I can't change it."

"Him dying doesn't invalidate your need to know, nor does the fact that you can't change it."

"How would I find out why he felt the way he did?"

"Think about his life. When and where did he grow up? What was his relationship with his parents? Did he choose work that brought joy to his life?" She paused, then continued, "When we get together next time, you'll have some answers, I'm sure."

"The *right* answers?" he asked, questioning his ability.

"Yeah, Ron," Jennifer smiled. "The answers are inside of you, not me."

*****

In the meantime, critical thinking spun a web of options for Robert Henderson as he drove to Jeff's office, preparing for the inevitable debate. Reason suggested that Jeff wouldn't have wanted to see him alone had the surveillance team not found anything of interest in the black box. Robert was determined to assure Jeff that Jennifer would be okay. But how could he? There was no way to turn Peter in without implicating her. And there was no way Peter could be allowed to continue drug trafficking. He'd suggest to Jeff that the black box could be removed first before calling the police, but he wasn't willing to wait until Jennifer's program ended. Too much could happen to too many people. Surely his friend would not only understand but also agree.

"Glad you could come by, Robert," Jeff said, offering him a seat close to his desk.

"I can tell by the look on your face that the surveillance team confirmed their suspicions," Robert said.

"Yeah, they did," Jeff said and filled him in on the particulars.

"We've got to turn him in. You know that, don't you?" Robert asked as he prepared for Jeff's rebuttal. "I know how you feel about Jennifer, but we can't just let a drug dealer operate at will."

"I think I've found a way to get Peter and not involve Jennifer," Jeff said, tapping the eraser end of a yellow pencil on the table.

"I'm all ears."

"What if Jennifer didn't own her Subaru anymore? Let's say she bought a different car, one that sits too low for the convenience of the black box," Jeff said, grinning just enough to let Robert know there was more to the plan.

"But just removing the vehicle won't stop Peter. He'll just find another way. Count on it."

"I am," Jeff said, "but it'll only help to convict him when the time comes."

"How sure are you that Jennifer will be ready to trade her car in?" Robert asked.

"I can find a way for it to break down one more time. I'll suggest it's time for another one. She's mentioned it herself a couple of times," said Jeff.

"Well, that's true. She does hold a lot of stock in what you say. She'd probably go for it." Robert continued, "But how are you going to remove the black box before she trades it in?"

"I'm not," Jeff said, watching Robert's face ashen. "The minute she makes the trade, I'll buy it before the dealer has a chance to clean it up."

"Oh, okay! And Peter's fingerprints are probably all over that black box, aren't they?" Robert started to grin. "What'll you do with it?"

"I'm going to keep it in my garage until the IIDP ends, then I'll tell the police everything. If she's questioned about Peter's dealings, at least she won't own any of the physical evidence," said Jeff, looking like the proverbial cat that ate the canary.

"There could be legal ties. I mean, if she's married to him by then," Robert said. Seeing Jeff's eyes dart south, he wished he could retrieve what was said so pragmatically.

"I don't have any power over that," Robert knew better.

*****

Tomas Gonzales remained Jennifer's going concern despite the contagious smile and the bop in his gait. If anyone had adjusted to prison life, it was Tomas, or so it seemed. He had a hard, fine-tuned body from working out with barbells with the other inmates. The prison hadn't supplied her with anything but his rap sheet. They must have thought that that was all there was to Tomas. But what lurked behind the lively eyes, gregarious smile, and jovial mannerisms? All anyone knew was that his devoted, hardworking father raised Tomas alone in the United States after leaving Mexico. So how does a kid like that end up juggling a lawless career?

"Hey! Ms. Lily," Tomas said, taking a seat in the counseling room. "How's it going?" He filled the room with a sense of nirvana.

"Hey, Tomas," she said, intercepting the contagious smile.

"What's our plans for today?" he asked as though the choice was between a Sunday picnic or an overnight camping trip.

"Let's talk about your background. We haven't ever really done that," she said, watching the elation drop from his face.

"Well, I already told you what I wanted to be since I was a kid—a fireman," he said as though his smile and fast talking could hide the apprehension. "And I've already checked out some fire science books," he added quickly, hoping to deter the inevitable direction of their conversation.

"Yeah, I know. That's good," she said. "But we haven't talked about your upbringing. Is there any reason we shouldn't?"

"Is there any reason we should?" he asked, realizing nothing was going to impede her path.

"How old were you when you came to the United States?" She knew these were the questions he'd always been able to avoid answering.

"I was two when my father moved me here."

"And your mother?"

"*Mi madre quedarse en Mexico para cinco anos.*"

"English please!" she said.

"It doesn't sound as bad in Spanish." He showed a slight impish grin that vanished after realizing Ms. Lily remained relentless. "My mother, she stayed in Mexico for five years while Dad found work in the United States. Their plan was to buy a home when he returned."

"And did they buy a home?"

"No," he said, wishing that was the end of the story.

"Why not?"

"Because when we got back to Mexico, my mom had other children."

"You have other brothers and sisters?"

"*Half* brothers and sisters," Tomas said, emphasizing his mother's infidelity.

"I see. Your father then apparently brought you back here," Jennifer said. "When did you see your mother again?"

"Two weeks later. I was sent to live with her after my father died." His voice barely audible.

"Your father died two weeks later!" she exclaimed.

"He took a powder, a gunshot blast through his head," he said, imitating his father's actions by using a hand and a finger to simulate a gun, aiming it at his head. "I was seven years old the night he put me to bed for the last time." Tomas watched the compassionate look grow in Jennifer's eyes. "I went to his room and sat beside the bed until the cops came. I never cried. A few days later, I was sent to live with my mother, whom I grew to hate by the time I knew the facts of life. I used to hit her." He lowered his head. "She sent me back to the United States to live with family friends. I've never been back. That's what you wanted to know, isn't it?"

"What I want to know is how you're resolving the hatred you feel for your mother," she said.

"Well, I can't tell you that I have yet. If I did, you'd know I was lying," he admitted with an impish grin. "But since I started the HBP, I've been going to all the mandatory twelve-step meetings and domestic violence classes."

"And?"

"Well, I've spent the last three months in denial about my drinking, but I'm finally over that. Maybe now I can move on—as they say."

"Have you written or talked with your mother?"

"No, I'm not ready yet, Ms. Lily."

"Okay, just keep working at it," she said. "Let me know what I can do to help."

Chapter XI

On a sunny Sunday in March, Jeff Hanes drove to Jennifer's house under the pretense of a lunch date. But what was neatly hidden was his aspiration to save her from Peter's illegal activities and an indisputable desire to spend time with her. Guilt trickled slowly through his veins; he saw it as the gradual drip of icicles melting from house eaves on a warm spring day. But it didn't deter him from what needed to be done. If anything, it rationalized itself into a sort of benevolence. The only real danger was playing the knight in shining armor role with a woman who detested such things. Eventually, an adventurous feeling took control as he rehearsed the covert plan. Jeff had never been consciously dishonest with anyone, but now he delighted in the opportunity to play the James Bond type. Thoughts of simply telling Jennifer the truth ran through his mind, but they were quickly dismissed when he remembered the harm that guilt by association could render. And God forbid her wrath if she refused to believe the truth! Jennifer couldn't see evil in anyone she loved, and it was apparent to Jeff that she loved Peter.

"Hi, Jeff," Jennifer said when she opened the door. "C'mon in."

"You ready for lunch?" he asked, following her to the kitchen.

"Yeah." She threw a light jacket over both shoulders, leaving it unbuttoned. "So have you found anything out about a halfway house for my men?" she asked as they walked to Jeff's car.

"Wait, we better take your car. Mine's about out of gas," he said, leading the way to the Subaru. "Instead of a halfway house, you'd be better off establishing a foundation. You'd be making a venture into a corporation. There's some financial risk, but I think you can do it."

Jeff opened the driver's door to watch her slide behind the steering wheel.

"What's the difference?" she asked, turning the key and giving the car a little gas as Jeff piled into the passenger's side.

"Well, for one thing, our state doesn't provide funding for half-way houses, and it doesn't sound like it's going to start," Jeff said, after listening to several failed attempts to turn the engine.

"One of these days, I'm going to get rid of this beast of burden!" Jennifer declared. "There's nothing worse than a car that won't start."

"Unfortunately, I'm no mechanic. But it's okay. We'll just put gas in mine and be on our way. It'll make it to the gas station around the corner. I'll call for a mechanic to fix yours while we're eating lunch," Jeff said.

They drove to Annabelle's, which served quick hot lunches but was still far removed from being fast-food quality. Privately, Jeff praised himself for using so little effort to accomplish his first step of deception, but deep down, the anticipation was growing—so was the guilt.

"I guess I could just call Peter," Jennifer said, taking a seat in a window booth.

"Peter's an awfully busy man, Jen. Let me call someone who relies on this kind of stuff to make a living." He pulled his cell phone from his pocket, and said, "Jen, I'll have to step outside to get good reception. I'll be right back."

"You want me to order for you?" she called out.

"Yes, please do."

He stepped outside where he knew he'd get some privacy before he called Jubal Tanner and said, "You did a great job. By the way, what did you do?"

"We just loosened the battery cable," Jubal said.

"Just make sure it's fixed by the time we get back," Jeff said before hanging up and going back to his table.

"So let's say I open a foundation for the newly released inmates. So what are the advantages and what would I have to do?" Jennifer asked after Jeff sat down.

"Well, for one thing, you'll be able to set your own standards, rules, and regulations. I think the prison here would use your facility exclusively because placement service is getting harder and harder to find, and the ones that do exist have never proven to lower the recidivism rate," he said. "By the way, what'd you order for me?"

"Let it be a surprise," she said, smiling with charm. "Don't worry, it's not health food, well, not per se." She watched him swallow hard. "So what do I do next? I mean, I can't afford a foundation on my salary."

"There were organizations in town that supported the Homeward Bound Program, and they would probably help get you started. The Lions Club, the Sertonas, Masons, Kiwanis. If it's a success, the general public may want to pitch in a little too. Maybe their need to feel safe will override the need for punishment."

"There's several large vacant houses on Old Main Street. I could probably get a good rent structure on any one of them because they're in desperate need of repairs. The men could help fix it up as part of their rent obligation to the foundation," she said, her eyes lighting his face.

The love and enthusiasm she brought to her work always warmed his heart. It was this side of Jennifer he fell in love with first. "And I bet we could get Robert to donate some legal services," Jeff said as the waitress set two tuna salad sandwiches and iced teas on the table.

"What *is* this?" Jeff asked with humorous suspicion, furrowing his brows. "Is this chick food?"

"Just eat. It's good for you," she said, biting into the sandwich.

*****

After lunch, while driving back to Jennifer's house, Jeff felt lost. *How do I approach the new car idea without nurturing suspicion?*

"Maybe I ought to get a new car," she said as they pulled into the driveway, noticing the Subaru had been moved.

"Well, they must've fixed it," he said.

"But for how long? Besides, I'm starting to feel that my car is a jinx. You know, Jeff, I've only had but one accident—until I bought this car," she said as Jeff turned off the engine.

"Well, if you think it's the best thing to do, we could check out Mac's Auto. It's just down the street," he said, restarting the car. He wondered if he wasn't being a little presumptuous. "Grab your title, just in case."

"Good idea. I'll only be a minute." She opened the car door as they both heard the phone ring. "I won't be long, I promise."

Anxiety plagued him now. This had all gone down too easily, and the long anticipating wait brought him to the conclusion that the phone call might have broken the good luck spell, especially if it was the obscene caller. He briefly had the urge to go in and grab her before she could change her mind, but Jennifer appeared at his car door just as jubilant as before the call. Ah! Jeff thought. Everything's going to be okay.

"I guess we better take both cars so they'll know what you have in the way of a trade-in," Jeff said. "And afterward, you won't need to take me home."

Cal, the salesman at Mac's Auto, reminded Jeff of an overzealous game show host who was next expected to ask Jennifer to choose "door number one, door number two, or door number three." It was decided that Cal's few premature gray hairs at the crown of his head were probably well-earned, and the longer-than-fashionable hairstyle was there to hide his extraordinarily long ears. Obviously, his bright, colorful shirt and clashing tie were designed to ensure that no one would mistake him for anything but a car salesman. Only the tight-fitting Levi's contradicted that image.

"Look, all I'm looking for is a car that never breaks down and can make mountain drives with no effort," Jennifer said, wishing to avoid as much of the sales pitch as possible.

"There's just one answer for that, little lady," Cal said with exuberance, flashing a big toothy smile and pointing both arms high. He looked like a referee at a football game who just called a touchdown. "It's our brand-new Ford Taurus! I'll just run in and get the keys and we'll take this little baby for a spin."

This pleased Jeff. The perfect car.

As they waited for Cal's return, Jennifer asked with a snicker, "Why is it that car salesmen always act as though they just dropped a hit of speed?"

"It's a prerequisite for the profession, just like not using a last name," Jeff said, sharing her humorous observation. "But don't let him push anything off on you. Make sure you really like it before you buy it."

Jennifer fell in love with all the enticing aspects of the new-car feel, including the new-car smell, the spotless blue-gray tweed interior, and a windshield that wasn't old enough to have any pit marks and scratches. It was Jennifer's car after the first mile, and Jeff and Cal both knew it.

While Jennifer spent time in the on-lot finance office, Jeff strolled around the showroom floor, hoping to find Cal.

"I could put you in this red convertible Mustang today," Cal said with a robust voice, slapping the hood. "Let's take this little baby for a spin."

"Cal, today is your lucky day," Jeff smiled, assured in the knowledge that if people ever stopped buying cars, Cal could always prosper by running for public office. "I want to buy Jennifer's Subaru—as is. What kind of deal can you make me?"

"As is?" Cal asked, squinting. "Why didn't you just buy it from her?"

"She needed it for trade-in value, I just want it for sentimental reasons. She doesn't need to know that, does she, Cal?" Jeff asked, winking.

"It's no one's business but yours, sir," Cal said. He smiled but still looked confused.

"Good. Get the blue book price on it and add a little for your trouble, and I'll be back in a half hour. And Cal, there's a $500 bonus in it for you," Jeff said, feeling amused at any ability to leave a car salesman speechless.

Jennifer walked out with a bounce in her step, wearing an ecstatic smile. She waved the keys to her new car. "C'mon, Jeff, follow me home."

"Okay, but just for a minute," he said. "I have some errands to run this afternoon." He got into his car and nodded at Cal, then followed Jennifer home.

As they walked into her kitchen, Jeff said, "It looks like you have a message on your phone."

"Oh, that's probably just Peter calling again," she said with gaiety before pushing the play button.

Again? Jeff's mind said, giving the word *strict* attention. But instead of hearing the expected voice of Peter Winslow, a raspy-sounding threat intruded into their otherwise capricious day: *You haven't lost me yet. You still have to pay for ruining my life.*

Jennifer felt a hideous black cloud land on her high spirits, trapping her in a cold, vacuous gloom. Fear replaced feelings of exhilaration, and she subconsciously edged closer to Jeff. The carefree day she'd so much enjoyed and felt deserving of now had turned into a torturous moment—one she wished would vanish as quickly as it had appeared.

"I shouldn't have let my guard down," she said, feeling guilty for allowing herself the high price of vulnerability.

"This isn't your fault," Jeff said, putting his arms around her. "Don't let that monster ruin this moment for you. You can't be expected to be on guard every minute. How would you function?" Jeff said, holding her for comfort. He felt helpless to protect her, just as he felt powerless to control his rapid pulse and heartbeat fluttering.

He no longer was able to separate his feelings of wanting to comfort from those of lustful desire; they seemed to be intertwined. The fine, granite-etched boundary line between being protective and just being there for Jennifer was growing more ambiguous even though he had begun to think that he could feel her hidden desire. Nonetheless, it didn't alter the hunger.

"Will you be okay if I leave?" asked Jeff, feeling her tense muscles begin to relax.

"Yeah. Besides, Peter's coming for dinner," she said as she walked Jeff to the door.

He raced with the beat of his heart back to Mac's Auto. He didn't see the Subaru when he parked, so he figured Cal was so happy to have the immediate cash that he stored the car for safety.

"You won't believe what happened!" Cal said as Jeff jumped out of his car and walked up to him.

"A guy came in here and offered me blue book price *plus* $3,000 more! Is that unreal or what!" Cal said with excitement as well as bewilderment.

"No! What's *unreal* is that you promised it to me," Jeff said, feeling the anger rise up in his throat and lash out. "How much would you sell your mother for?"

"It wasn't like that! Really! The guy said he was an insurance adjuster and he needed it for evidence," Cal said.

"Did this guy have a name?" Jeff asked, seething through his teeth.

"We can't give out that information," Cal said, indignant of the question.

"Did he pay you for that too?" Jeff felt his irritation rising to dangerous levels. He didn't wait for an answer before jumping into his car. He slammed the door and sped away.

Cognition indicated that driving in his present state of mind was nothing short of an unintentional hysterical suicide attempt. So when he spotted the coffee shop on the corner, it was like finding an oasis where his sanity could be replenished, and another offensive play could be born. After parking, he reached for the cell phone.

"Hi, it's me, Jennifer," he said, sounding calm after hearing her voice. "How did Peter like your new car? Was he surprised?"

"I don't know if he likes it or not because he hasn't seen it yet. But he won't be surprised because he knew you and I were going to the car lot. He was the one calling when I ran in to get the title," she said, wondering what Jeff's real reason was for calling. A pause followed while she listened to him breathe. "Are you okay?" Jennifer already knew he wasn't.

"Yeah, I'm okay, I guess. I'm just learning some things about myself that aren't exactly flattering. After a short pause, the next set of words flowed out, allowing Jeff to release whatever had a hold on him. "I just want you to know that I love you."

"I think I knew that," Jennifer said in a voice so soft that Jeff felt titillated. "But I'm—"

"I know, engaged to someone else," Jeff said, not really caring what her marital status was. He only needed to get the words out. "Talk to you later."

His next call was to Robert Henderson, inviting him to meet for coffee. He knew if he ever needed a friend, this moment would qualify. He waited for Robert inside the coffee shop in a corner booth, realizing he hadn't given much in the way of information on the phone. That's what friends are for.

"As usual, I can tell by the look on your face that this isn't going to be good news," Robert said as he joined him in the booth.

Jeff rambled, repeating himself as he unfolded the day's events in the order that impacted him the most, but not necessarily chronologically. Robert had never seen Jeff like this and was having trouble deciphering what had happened and when. But somehow he knew that together, they'd be able to put things in proper perspective, and Jeff would be able to catch his breath.

"Tell me about Jennifer's new car," Robert said, trying to find a beginning.

"It's a Ford Taurus, front-wheel drive, sits low to the ground, and has a low bumper. It virtually has no room for a black box. But the best thing is that it'll be under warranty for the first few years, which means the dealership takes care of all the upkeep, including oil changes, rotation of tires, and things like that."

"For free?" Robert asked.

"Well, no, not for free, but the customers that buy their cars here get preferential treatment, which Jennifer really liked. So Peter won't have any reason to have the new car in his possession," Jeff said. Robert watched his friend become calm enough for rational thought.

"So first you went to Mac's Auto with Jennifer, and then you went to Jennifer's house, right?" Robert waited for Jeff to nod before continuing. "But when you returned to the dealership to buy back Jennifer's car, the salesman had sold it to someone else because they offered more money." Again, Robert waited for a nod. "And you're surprised?"

"And then I called Jennifer," Jeff said calmly.

"Why? I mean, why did you want to talk to Jennifer at a time like that?" Robert asked.

"I had an overwhelming desire to tell her I loved her," Jeff said.

"You said *what*?" Robert asked in horror, eyes bulging.

"*You* told me to tell her," Jeff said.

"Yeah, I know, but I was hoping for better timing," Robert said, now snickering.

"I'm glad I told her. Maybe she'll hesitate on marrying Peter," he said, feeling good about what he had done.

"Well! You've had yourself quite a day." Robert chuckled softly with compassion.

"But what are we going to do? We now have no physical evidence," Jeff said.

"I don't know," Robert responded. "Maybe we can find out who bought Jennifer's old car. Cal's a car salesman. Money talks."

"I already know who bought it." Jeff watched Robert's facial expression go from studious to quizzical in a nanosecond.

"How do you know that?" Robert asked.

"Because Cal said he sold it to a guy who is an insurance broker."

"No wonder you became unraveled this afternoon," Robert said. "Who told Peter that it was for sale?"

"Ironically enough, Jennifer. We both heard the phone ring as she was going into her house to look for the title. She turned to me and said she'd only be a minute. It didn't occur to me to ask her who was on the phone. Since I waited in the car, I overheard nothing. I was just happy that it wasn't the obscene caller."

"You know, this puts a brand-new spin on things. We have to handle this with kid gloves," Robert said as Jeff nodded in agreement.

*****

Meanwhile, Jennifer was planning dinner for Peter, allowing one agonizing distraction after another to interfere with the preparation. Was she having unsettling differences about Peter? Or was she simply allowing Jeff's words—*I love you*—to interfere with how she felt? *Jeff would never do anything that would stand in the way of my happiness. What could I possibly be thinking? Jeff's my best friend, my closest ally, under any circumstances. Maybe he's just a little confused right now.*

But under it all, she knew Jeff wasn't confused. She *did* feel something when Jeff told her that he loved her. A few years back, she would've responded differently. She'd heard that once you have loved someone, you'll always love them at some level—even if you have gone through the divorce from hell. But she and Jeff had never had a crossword between them; they hardly ever had a difference of opinion. She tried so hard not to fall in love with him after they had met, but she was unsuccessful. He was married and his wife was dying, but she didn't see that as a welcome mat; besides, she had fallen in love with Jeff before his wife had cancer. Jennifer remembered all too well how difficult it was to get past those feelings, and she didn't ever want to go through anything like that again. To ensure that from happening, she wouldn't let the words he had said to her go to her heart.

But that aside, she knew that Peter had started to change and that lately he looked gaunt and seemed more distracted when they were together. Instead of working out at the gym three or four days a week, he now only went once or twice. Maybe his loss of appetite and mood swings were because of business problems, or there was some other logical explanation. And maybe his absolute attentiveness was reserved only for the first few months of courtship. She'd identified the male's fear of commitment many times while in private practice, but the contrary thought was that Peter wasn't showing *any* signs of being afraid of commitment. In fact, the obsessive way he hounded for a wedding date was troublesome. *I'm not pregnant. What's the hurry?* She snorted chuckle.

*****

"Hi, Peter," she said, greeting him at the door with a kiss. "C'mon in and watch me play Julia Child in the kitchen."

"I know it'll be delicious, it always is," he said, watching her cut the celery and radishes for the tossed salad.

"You nervous about something, Peter?" she asked, watching him pace.

"Uh . . . no, why do you ask?" Peter sat down at the table and fidgeted with the silverware.

"Listen, why don't we have a talk? Dinner won't be ready for a while yet," she said, taking a seat next to him. "How's work going?"

"Why'd you ask *that*?" he asked, snapping at what he viewed as an interrogation.

"What's the matter with you tonight? I've never seen you so jumpy," Jennifer asked.

"I'm sorry," Peter said. "It would be a good idea for me to go home early tonight and get some much-needed sleep."

"Okay, but is there something worrying you? Can I help?" Jennifer asked in a compassionate and nurturing tone. But when she didn't even hear a one-liner comeback that almost always followed an uncomfortable question, she asked, "Is this one of those bruised male ego things? You know, the kind I wouldn't understand even if you told me?"

"No, not exactly, but close," Peter said. "I mean, it's been so long since we've discussed setting a wedding date, other than a tentative one that you probably don't even remember." He pouted like a kid.

"When do you want to get married?" Jennifer asked.

"Six months ago," he said. "How 'bout you?"

"Well, I was thinking more along the lines of six months from today," she said. She felt proud that she was able to be honest instead of using the patronizing tone that was becoming an uncomfortable, familiar role when dealing with Peter.

"So what do we do? Compromise and get married tomorrow?" he asked facetiously.

"Gosh, I don't think I can. I have a dental appointment tomorrow," she smiled.

"Well, at least you haven't lost your sense of humor."

"Look, Peter, let's wait at least until my program ends, okay?" she pleadingly. "That's got to come first right now."

Jennifer was aware throughout dinner that Peter was upset. He'd made no effort to hide his feelings, wearing a facial expression similar to a distressed Third World poster child. She chatted casually as they nibbled appetizers and enjoyed the fruits of her labor, hoping that somewhere between the mashed potatoes and roast beef he would show signs of life, like the old Peter. But he seemed determined to portray himself as a victim. He picked at the food on his plate and acted like a high school sweetheart who'd been turned down in marriage. After she devoured a slice of strawberry cheesecake, which he declined, Jennifer thought that his idea of going home early was a very good one.

After Peter had left, she began to wonder if this new behavior was just a small compromise for the sake of the relationship, like accepting constant tardiness. Or was it an ongoing codependent association that she had unintentionally helped to nurture? The fine line between the two concepts blurred and spun brain wave activity until weariness gave way to sleep. A new day would begin, and Peter's behavior would somehow seem justifiable, or at least tolerable.

*****

Monday was a welcome sight for Jennifer, a way to leave the weekend behind and dive into her work aggressively. Counseling others not only produced a sense of worth for Jennifer, but watching the self-esteem rise for her clients was also a tremendous reward in itself. As a psychologist, she had been enlightened by people from every walk of life, and that had allowed her an infinite number of angles from which to view the complicated mind. It was like a continuous jigsaw puzzle that grew bigger and clearer as each piece intertwined with another.

The only dark cloud hanging over the day was the note Perkins gave her upon arriving at the prison, which requested her presence at an unexpected mandatory meeting with the review board. Warden Ellsworth wouldn't be attending.

The long oval table was surrounded by review board members sitting, chatting, and drinking coffee, all except for Tuttle, whose chair was conspicuously vacant when Jennifer entered and took a seat. The atmosphere had changed. People smiled, nodded, and asked if she'd like some coffee. The only strange face at the table was an arbitrator from Special Operations, Myrtle Hammond, who the review board elected to chair in the warden's absence.

"The board expects this meeting to be short, Ms. Collins, and only a few pertinent questions need to be answered," Ms. Hammond said as the group settled into silence. She tugged her fitted black skirt over both knees. "I'll read each question aloud. After your answer, the rest of the review board may continue with the same line of questioning or add comments. Do you have any questions before we begin?" She swung her long blond hair over both of her shoulders.

"No, Ms. Hammond," Jennifer said.

"Now that you're nearing the end of the Homeward Bound Program, can you give us a percentage rate of estimated failures? This means, how many of your men will return to prison within a year?" she asked, speaking slowly and distinctly as she prepared to take notes.

"I don't think any of them will return," Jennifer said. "It could happen, but only because of the way our criminal justice system works."

"Can you explain that?" Ms. Hammond responded, sounding interested.

"Because the paroled inmate doesn't have a clean slate when he leaves here, the laws are different for him than for you and me. Let's say one of them gets busted for smoking marijuana or drinking alcohol. I'm well aware that this kind of behavior is a parole violation. I'm certainly not condoning it. But on the other hand, I don't think the violation should be treated as though they robbed the First National Bank with an Uzi either. The parole board needs to keep things in perspective. I don't want the parolees to be sent back here to finish out their sentences on minor infractions of the rules. It wastes time and taxpayers' money, not to mention the ineffectiveness of locking them up again and again and again. A structured two-year rehab stay would get them the medical attention they need. As far as I'm concerned, judges should give that to the offenders who have more than once been in trouble with the law where drugs and alcohol were involved. Then maybe the offender could skip prison altogether. Ms. Hammond, do you know what I'm saying?"

"Yes, Ms. Collins, I do." Ms. Hammond looked around at the faces at the table and asked, "Does anyone have any questions for Ms. Collins?"

"Isn't it true that some of your men are in here for violent crimes?" Ms. Hammond asked earnestly.

"Yes, but that doesn't mean if any of them are sent back here, it'll be for a violent offense. In fact, the United States Bureau of Justice reports very low statistics on any reference to that type of recidivism. While the recidivism rate in our state prisons is 75 percent, only 17 percent return for violent crimes," Jennifer said.

Again, a hand went up and Hammond nodded permission to speak. "Can you guarantee us that none of your men will ever kill again?" the same review board member asked.

"Of course not, no more than you can guarantee that *you'll* never kill—or have to kill or be killed. But there's less than a 5 percent chance that anyone who has murdered will murder again, excluding mass murderers and serial killers, or terrorists, which none of my men were," Jennifer said.

"In your opinion, are we about to free anyone in the HBP that is capable of committing another violent crime?" Hammond asked.

"Everyone's capable—you, me, and even Mr. Tuttle—under the right circumstances. But no, I don't believe any of my men will commit another violent crime," Jennifer said.

"What is your prognosis for the men in the HBP who have a long history of street crimes, such as burglary?" Hammond continued.

"According to our justice department, street crimes cost us about $19 to $20 billion annually, but white-collar crime is costing us somewhere between $130 and $472 billion annually. Now in no way does this mean I condone street crime. I'm merely suggesting that, with proper job training, street crime could be lessened by as much as 80 percent. My men have planned their own careers," Jennifer said, noticing the dubious looks around the conference table. *Why is it such a leap of faith to believe these men could have careers?*

"I know your study isn't complete yet, but could you recite some possible reasons for our high recidivism rate?" Hammond asked.

"My study will never be complete because of its complexity. But so far, I've found recidivism is the result of many factors, all equally hazardous to the inmates' freedom," Jennifer said. "The inmate is virtually set up to recidivate while still in prison because the infrastructure suggests that punishment and revenge are 'just desserts' for anyone breaking society's laws. The infrastructure of the prison isn't set up for dispensing tools that promote healing, which is the missing paradigm for lowering the recidivism rate. Therefore, it becomes almost impossible for the inmate to function lawfully on the outside after years of confinement, considering all they ever witness is punishment and revenge. You see, Ms. Hammond, society insists that the inmates are punished the *entire* time they're here, but then it expects them to show no hostility or resentment when they get out. It just doesn't work like that in the real world. We are what our environment is, and until we have enough guts to stand up and say, 'That's enough!' then nothing's going to change.

"Another growing reason for the high recidivism rate is insanity, which has gone undiagnosed and untreated in over half of those who are suffering from mental and emotional illnesses. Prison isn't going to help these people.

"After that, there's a long list of entrapments for the newly released: committing small infractions of the law; lack of education and job training; lack of mandatory and continuing drug and alcohol counseling; lack of maturity, self- esteem, and self-confidence; returning to the same criminal environment that brought them here; lack of a decent place to live and of family and societal support."

"Which of these problems could place your men in jeopardy of recidivism?" asked Hammond.

"I don't feel any of them will," Jennifer said confidently.

"Ms. Collins, we'll be speaking privately with each of these men before their release. Do you have a problem with that?" Hammond inquired.

"Absolutely not."

"Thank you, Ms. Collins. Our meeting is over, and we'll let you know the day and time in which we plan to meet with your men," Myrtle Hammond ended, folding her notebook and bringing closure to the meeting.

Jennifer walked the long corridor bewildered. *What was that all about? And what happened to the almighty Ol' Man?* She was actually glad that this meeting had been called and felt deprived that all of the other update meetings were not ran the same way.

Chapter XII

Jennifer was still confused by why the arbitrator from the Special Operations Division conducted a review meeting and about the attending board members' congeniality. But she was determined to focus on her last session of the day with Ronald Bookman.

"I didn't know a lot about him. Only what Mom told me," Ron said, referring to the relationship with his estranged father. "He lived through the depression years as a migrant worker, so he really wanted something better for me. He married Mom after World War II and got a job in a tire factory. For thirty-five years, he worked in a place that made him miserable. I don't really think he hated himself. Maybe he just thought he was worthless and that if he didn't stay right on me all the time, then I'd end up worthless too." Ron started to laugh. "And look where I ended up!"

"Do you think you're worthless?" Jennifer asked.

"Not as much as I used to. I mean, like I know I'm not the smartest person in here, and I do have problems with reading and writing, but I never intentionally hurt anyone," he said, watching Jennifer's eyes widen. "I'm not claiming to be innocent of robbing convenience stores. I'm just saying that I didn't think stealing could hurt anyone."

"What about the woman who died in the process of you and your buddy robbing?" she asked.

"Why can't you believe me when I tell you that I wasn't the one who pulled the trigger?" he asked with pleading eyes. "I've never even held a gun in my whole life."

"Maybe you didn't pull the trigger, maybe you didn't even realize what your partner was going to do, but the clerk is just as dead, isn't she?" Jennifer said. "It's hard to forgive yourself for your part in that if you can't admit you *had* a part."

Ron cupped his hands around his face while Jennifer listened to soft sobs. "I know that now. I've written the family an apology letter," he said, pulling a piece of neatly folded notebook paper from his pocket.

"This is really good," she said as she read the letter. It was written in simple English with no misspelled words. She realized that he had put a great deal of time and thought into this. "I'm very proud of you."

"Can I send it?" he asked, wiping his wet face with one sleeve.

"No, I'm afraid not. It might not be taken the way you mean it because of your parole hearing that's coming up. But writing this letter isn't for them nearly as much as it is for you. Keep it, always," she said.

"Ms. Lily," Ron said, "I sent my drawings to a publisher. There's a group of people who write children's books and they're interested in me doing drawings and sketches. I guess you didn't think that would ever happen, did you?"

Jennifer's face beamed. "That's great, Ron! And yes, I always knew you could do it!" His smile broadened, and she could see the self-esteem rise from his body and soul just as though he'd sprung wings and was now ready to fly far above any place he'd been before. The Ron Bookman Jennifer met months ago had somehow disappeared and a new one took his place. He may have mental disabilities, but with the right environment, he would surely blossom.

*****

Jennifer had scarcely taken the time to notice spring had sprung, seemingly without the usual preliminaries. The warm weather had gone unnoticed and unappreciated until today. For many, springtime in the Rockies was an extraordinary time. Mother Nature was ready to show off her colorful scenery in daffodils and tulips, along with hundreds of wild flowers. Jennifer felt a sense of cleanliness and renewal as she saw spring imitating life by renewing itself. Every spring she would wonder why April doesn't have the honor of bringing in each new year.

Jennifer's rows of flowers surrounding the east side of her house felt the twinges of neglect. Fall's dead aspen leaves were still embedded around them. Small violet clumps of pansies were sprouting up along one side of the driveway—not perennials, but simply volunteers that survived a warmer-than-usual winter. Signs of new foliage of her favorite flower, the columbine, were peeping through the ground under the dead debris that winter's chill had turned brown. The glass hummingbird feeders, chaise lounge chairs, and the white plastic table that supported a multifloral- patterned umbrella remained unassembled on a garage shelf beside the sprinklers and wound-up garden hoses.

"Well, Jennifer, I don't usually see you out here anymore." Angela Colder's surprise voice was startling.

"I know. I was just thinking the same thing," she said, feeling urges of agitation crawl over her. "I'll have to call the young man I had last year. He was wonderful."

"Is that Patricia's friend?" Angela asked.

"Patricia is friends with his parents, I think," Jennifer said wondering why this would matter to Angela.

Jennifer felt the warmth of the sun penetrate through her clothes while browsing around each flower bed. She hoped it was becoming apparent to Angela that she had no interest in visiting with her, but no such luck.

"My flower beds are all cleaned out already." Angela marched up close to Jennifer to make sure the announcement couldn't be ignored.

"I'm happy for you, but if you'll please excuse me, I need to be taking some notes on what needs to be done for spring restoration," Jennifer said, pushing past her.

There just wasn't going to be enough time to devote to her flower beds and rose bushes as in years past. No one will be stopping by to tell her how great the yard looks, not this year.

She heard the phone ring and knew that it must be divine intervention as she waved bye to Angela and sent a quick thank-you to the one above.

*****

"Hello," she said, a little winded.

"Hey, how 'bout lunch with two good-looking men?" Jeff asked.

"Will you be there too?" she inquired, holding back a snicker.

"Very funny," he chuckled. "I thought we'd spring Robert out for an early lunch and talk about the foundation."

"How 'bout Nino's at noon?" she asked. "You call Robert?"

"It's a deal. See you there."

Walking to her new Ford Taurus, Jennifer spotted the mailman in his truck and realized the mail hadn't been picked up for a couple of days. Waving, she heard him yell some obscenities that ended with "That's a lousy thing to do!" He laid rubber pulling away and shaking a fist.

"What the . . . ?" she said, opening the mailbox. A shriek that could be heard for blocks generated from her lungs and alerted Jubal and Ethan, who jumped out of their van and came running. Jubal looked inside the mailbox. Picking up a nearby stick, he poked something.

"It's okay, Ms. Collins. It's dead," he said, pulling a ten-foot rattler from the mailbox.

"My god! Who'd do such a thing?" She cupped her mouth and nose with both hands, her body trembling.

"That's what we're supposed to figure out," Ethan said, shaking his head. He stared at the ground as though the gesture would somehow suffice as an apology.

"What do you *do* all day? HALLUCINATE?" she screamed. Fear and anger turned both of her cheeks red. "How in the hell could something like this have happened—RIGHT IN FRONT OF YOU?"

"That's another thing we need to figure out," Jubal said. He was embarrassed and knew there wasn't an acceptable excuse.

Jennifer marched to her car, turning her head around briefly to put the final verbal touches on the show of outrage. "And Jeff actually *pays* you for this?"

Jubal and Ethan remained silent knowing the show of hostility was deserved and remembering Jeff's plea, "Please, don't pi—— her off for your own good!"

*****

She found the two good-looking men sipping iced tea in the corner booth of Nino's and wondered if this was a good time to bring up the snake in the mailbox. Maybe not. The lunchtime crowd would soon be arriving, and the snake story was too new to go public. She slid in the booth beside Jeff, forcing a cheerfulness to surface in the form of a smile. In the time it took to place their order with the waiter, she was sure the smile looked genuine.

"What's the matter, Jen?" Jeff asked.

"Nothing I can discuss right now," she said, wondering why she thought her feelings could be hidden from him.

"Yes, you can," Robert said kindly. "Is it about the sicko who's after you? Don't be mad at Jeff for telling me. I only want to help."

Obliging them with the snake story only seemed to renew her fury. Robert and Jeff hadn't deciphered if her anger was aimed at the maniac or the surveillance team, but it was probably both.

"I know I've asked before, but why don't you move in with me for a while?" Jeff asked.

"No, I'll be all right," she said, rubbing her forehead vigorously, ironing out the scrunched wrinkles.

"Should we postpone our discussion on the foundation?" Robert asked.

"No! I don't have time to waste. Who am I kidding? I don't have time to change the burned-out light bulb on my front porch. But most important, the men don't have time for any delays," she said. "I found a big house on Old Main Street and located the owners through the assessor's office. They're anxious to sell and would look at a contract for rent with the option to buy."

"You've done your homework," Robert said. "Do they have a real estate broker?"

"No, their listing agreement ran out six months ago, so they're happy not to have to pay any commission," Jennifer said.

"How can I help?" Robert asked.

"I need someone to negotiate a small rent structure for the first six months so my men can get started on the renovations, showing the owners my earnest intentions to buy the place within a year. Later, I'm hoping for other contributions from some clubs and organizations around town until the men are gainfully employed and can afford to pay full rent."

"First, let me check on all local ordinances and zoning laws, then we can take a look at this place, get a rough estimate on how much renovations will cost," Robert said.

"Is next week too soon?" she asked.

"No, next week is fine," he grinned. Infectious enthusiasm had replaced Jennifer's previous mood, and all was right with the world once more.

Robert spotted the confused, amorous smile on Jeff's face, the one that never seemed to vanish in Jennifer's presence. A sparkle, a glimmer, something in Jeff's facial expression looked very familiar. It was the same look that he wore himself whenever he was in Elizabeth Ellsworth's presence. Robert was convinced the entire room full of people could hear the sound of energy flowing between the two people sitting across from him. He silently confessed that he didn't have an understanding or an accurate definition of love—at least not in the contemporary, romantic sense. It wasn't tangible enough for definition. At least, not for him.

He saw an aura around Jennifer. This is what had touched Jeff's heart and captured it forever. It implied the woman was warm and joyfully embraced life with her heart. She didn't count the losses, only the efforts. Feeling this magic could be mystifying—or risky—as it had been for Jeff. But Robert had already discovered that all relationships held some degree of risk. If they didn't, what'd be the point in pursuing them?

Jennifer stood to leave. "Thanks, Robert, for everything," she said, leaning over to give him a quick kiss on the cheek in appreciation for helping her. "I need to get going."

"Wait a minute, we'll walk with you," Jeff said. Both men stood to pay the bill.

A few minutes later, as they were walking to the parking lot, Jeff asked, "So, Robert, how are things between you and Elizabeth? Should I be buying rice? Or bird seed would be the environmentally correct purchase."

"Probably, but don't go shopping just yet," Robert said, beaming.

"How's Charlie Bremmer's case going?" Jennifer asked, feeling uncomfortable with Jeff when the subject of marriage came up.

"Well, if we could find Eddie Wallace, the jury would almost have to set Charlie free, or at least free him of death row," Robert said. "We've hired a private detective to locate him. The problem is he has more aliases than politicians have excuses."

"Oh! There's Mr. Perkins walking toward us," Jennifer said, surprised.

"Well, hello, Ms. Collins. How ya doin'?" Perkins asked, stopping to chat.

"I'm fine. You remember Dr. Hanes and Robert Henderson, right?" she asked as the men shook hands. "Are you off today?"

"No, I'm just taking personal time to take care of some business with the insurance company because of a minor fender bender," he said.

"Was anyone hurt?" she asked.

"No, and luckily my agent at Winslow Insurance said it wasn't my fault and my premiums won't go up. Peter Winslow called me personally to assure me he'd expedite the repairs, and he did. I'm going to pick my car up now. He even lent me his car while mine was being repaired. That's not something any other insurance company would do," he said, not noticing the looks passing between Robert and Jeff.

"Peter's a good friend of mine," Jennifer said.

"No kiddin'? He's a good friend to have," Perkins said as he turned to leave. "See you this afternoon, Ms. Collins."

After Jennifer jumped in her Ford Taurus and headed for the prison, Jeff and Robert stood in the parking lot, talking.

"Let's just cut to the chase, okay?" Jeff said, knowing they had both put the puzzle together. "Peter replaced Jennifer with Perkins."

"He certainly can't expect to have the same control over Perkins's car that he enjoyed with Jennifer's," Robert said. "You know, this might be a blessing in disguise."

"I don't see how setting up Perkins for a potential drug bust could be a blessing."

"We can tell him what we know. He'd be protected and be the key witness in putting Peter away," Robert said, watching Jeff eventually nod.

"Good idea," Jeff said. "Let's go back to my office and you can make some calls."

*****

Jennifer's drive to the prison became distracted by thoughts of how she would approach her counseling session with Derek Coleman. Telling him he was a victim of child abuse could allow Derek justification for self-pity, or worse, it could intensify his denial of being abused by his father. It had to come from him, or the progress she'd been hoping for would not materialize.

"Hi, Ms. Lily," Derek smiled as he took a seat in the counseling room next to her. "What's the big grin for?"

"All of you guys seem to be in pretty high spirits lately," she said.

"Yes, we're getting out of here pretty soon," he said, then paused. "Well, probably." He flipped his hair from his eyes.

"We're going to spend some time talking about that in our next group session this afternoon. For now, let's just talk about you," she said. "How's your twelve-step program going?"

"Funny you should mention that," Derek said as though something had been on his mind. "There's a guy in my NA meetings that started talking about the forgiveness he's found for his mother. I guess she used to whip him with a belt for dumb stuff, like not cleaning his room and getting bad grades. It all sounded a little hokey to me."

Finally, she thought, *saying a quiet prayer for thanks!* "Hmm, to me, it sounds like he's done a lot of growing if he's able to forgive abuse," she said.

"You honestly think anyone could forgive something like that?"

"Sure. *I* did. Besides, he already took the first step by admitting it happened," she said.

"*You*, Ms. Lily? *You* were abused?" Derek asked, looking stunned. "You never told us that before."

"I didn't need to until now."

"You'd go that far just to get me to admit that my father abused me?" He was overwhelmed by her compassion.

"Hey! Whatever it takes," she said with a grin. "I needed to hear that as much as you needed to say it."

"How long did it take you to forgive?"

"Too long. I tried to drink it away, just like you tried to drug it away. But I finally got there. You will too. Just keep going to your meetings," she said. "How long have you known?"

"In reality, I think I've always known—or at least by the time I was eleven or twelve," he admitted. "I knew my friends' dads didn't hit them like that. Most of them didn't hit—period."

"Did you tell them that yours *did*?"

"What do you think?" He smiled shyly while flipping the hair out of his eyes.

"The other guys are coming for group," she said, hearing the thunder of feet and the distinct chatter of schoolboys on the last day of school.

The effects can be far reaching with child abuse, and Derek and Jennifer would have to spend much more time dealing with all the properties surrounding it, starting with low self-esteem and self-respect. What always bothered Jennifer the most about these men was that had there been an intervention, there probably wouldn't have been prison time for any of them. Could've, would've, and should've are just ways of beating yourself up because those feelings always happen after the fact. Derek would be able to pick himself up, brush himself off, and go on. Although she noticed that at times when they would discuss the abuse in detail that tears would well up in his eyes and he let his head hang down. Jennifer would remind him that the shame wasn't his to bear; that belonged to his father and, to some extent, his mother. His responsibility was forgiveness, healing, and living his life with utmost spiritual joy he could find, then passing it along.

*****

"Who can we call?" Jeff asked Robert as they settled into the privacy of Jeff's office.

"I still have some contacts at the district attorney's office. A little chat with them will keep Perkins free of any—" Robert began to say as the phone rang.

"It's for you," Jeff said after answering it. "It's Elizabeth."

Robert perked up like he'd won the lottery. He took the phone from Jeff's hand and covered the mouthpiece before whispering, "She can't live without me."

But soon the excitement faded; the bright face that had lit up like a neon light drained to an ashen color. Robert's head fell forward as he placed his open hand across both eyes. Jeff could only hear Robert's voice ask "How?" and "Was he hurt?" Slowly dropping the phone into the cradle, Robert looked at his friend. "Perkins has been arrested on possession with the intent to sell cocaine, meth, and pot."

"No way! How could something like that have happened?" Jeff asked.

"His tire blew out on the way back to the prison on Old Mountain Highway and the car landed on its side. He had left his cell at work, so he had to walk almost a mile on a broken ankle to get to a phone. When the police arrived, well, you know what they found," Robert said, falling into a chair.

"The black box," Jeff said, rubbing his eyes with the palms of his hands. "Damn! Did he have any other injuries?"

"I'm not sure. Elizabeth said they hadn't finished examining him yet at the hospital, but they plan on keeping him overnight for observation with a policeman on duty outside the door. He asked the police to call Elizabeth, and of course, she posted bail," Robert said.

"Why am I feeling so responsible for this?" Jeff asked.

"You're not alone," Robert said, shaking his head. "I hadn't told Elizabeth about Peter's drug involvement because of Jennifer's tenuous situation at the prison, but I don't think she believes Perkins is in any way involved with drugs."

"Who would!" Jeff exclaimed.

"That's what I'm going downtown to find out right now," Robert said, standing to leave. "I've got to convince them to pick up Peter for questioning. And I hate to say this, but it's showtime for you too. You need to have a talk with Jennifer. Today."

Jeff nodded with reluctance and muttered, "Yeah, I know."

*****

Peter Winslow was summoned to an emergency meeting in the same abandoned shack on the dark side of town. Hank Poovey sat at the table, grateful not to be the one in the hot seat.

"Did you see the paper today?" Lark asked.

"Uh, no. Why?" Peter asked.

Lark slammed the *Clear water Springs Daily* newspaper on the uneven table and pointed to the article that read, "House Bill 134 and 135 Passed at the House."

"That doesn't mean anything," Peter tried to explain. "Both bills still have to be passed at the Senate and even then it's not a done deal until the governor signs it, which may never happen. Look, Jennifer has already told me that she's getting out of prison work as soon as the Homeward Bound Program ends."

"Oh, she is, huh? So the two of you can ride off into the sunset together, right?" Lark questioned, giving Peter a chance to come clean about his relationship.

"Okay! So we want to get married! What difference does it make? She won't be working in the prison system anymore."

"The point is that, first of all, you weren't supposed to fall in love with Jennifer Collins. And second, you weren't supposed to get strung out on the stuff. I tried to tell you how addictive the junk is," Lark said. "Look at you. You look like hell."

"Who cares? Once the HBP ends, we're gone," Peter said overconfidently.

"You're dreaming," Lark stated, shaking his head in disbelief. "Breezy has it from a reliable source that Collins carries more weight on the hill than what we first thought. Her with her big college degrees and promoting prison programs doesn't keep Breezy's pockets lined. He would become very unhappy if the cons quit buying drugs. I've watched a few people make him unhappy. They ain't walking around today."

Peter never met Breezy, never even knew his last name. He heard of the man who dispensed brutality as casually as most people order ham and eggs. Drugs may have made Peter a little delusional, invincible even, but he still knew that if Breezy ever came after him that there would be nowhere to run, nowhere to hide. He'd be better off being killed by a hit man than to face the torture of Breezy.

"All I have to do is talk with her and she'll realize that they don't need her on the hill," Peter stated as a matter-of-factly.

"They do need her, and they'll do anything to keep her," Lark stormed.

"Well, I need her too!" Peter claimed. And I'll do anything to keep her."

The meeting broke up, and Peter drove away, trying to imagine how he was going to keep Jennifer from contributing on the hill since she doesn't even know that he's aware of what she's been doing there. He surmised that Jeff probably knew, but that would be the only person she would trust, which bothered him to some degree. He knew she and Jeff had a lot in common, but their chosen careers are what had always glued them together. Peter had never been jealous of Jeff—not outwardly anyway. He wondered what other secrets they shared that were not work related. Maybe he should ask. After all, wasn't it an unwritten rule that married people aren't supposed to keep secrets from each other? Wouldn't that also apply to engaged people?

As the rest of the men gathered around the table, Jennifer scanned her notebook. She listened to their sounds of pleasant chit-chat, which demonstrated the camaraderie among them that couldn't have been heard a few short months ago. It was encouraging to see them bonding. In their solidarity, the men talked about new careers, which of the guards were on their case this week, and how happy they'd be to never have to eat at the Poke in the Choke again, a prison moniker used for the food served in the lunchroom.

Even Michael Bishop's reserved demeanor was put aside now when the six of them got together. Much to Ronald Bookman's delight, they'd ceased any harsh ridicule over his adolescent questions, which continued to pop out without genuine thought. Tomas Gonzales's happy disposition was starting to rub off on Grumpy, a name used to describe Travis Talltree. Kent Beasley's serious side appeared more often in group now, and hiding feelings through sitcom dialogue had almost vanished. Through laughter and a little healthy teasing, the others let Derek Coleman know when his ego got the best of him in the form of gross boasting, overexaggeration, and the need to monopolize every conversation. He was beginning to learn how to laugh at himself through their eyes.

"Okay, guys, let's settle down and get some work done today," Jennifer said, setting her notebook down. "I have something I want to talk about before we begin group discussions."

"Is it about us gettin' outta here?" Ron Bookman asked, giggling and rubbing his hands together between his knees.

The others only shook their heads and chuckled at Ron's enthusiasm at the thought of being released.

"As a matter of fact, it is," she said. "I'm opening a foundation for newly released inmates and you're all invited to live there, provided you'll sign a two-year contract."

"What are our other options?" Travis Talltree asked.

"Out-of-state halfway house."

"You mean, there's not one halfway house that will take us in Clear Water Springs?" Michael asked.

"They're willing to bend the rules a little for a thirty-day stay if you sign with the new foundation," Jennifer said. "But the parole board is going to ask for at least six months of in-house monitoring before they let you go."

"I ain't got nowhere else to go," Kent Beasley said.

"Me either, but what are the rules at the foundation?" Tomas Gonzales asked.

"In the beginning, pretty much what they are here, except you won't be behind bars and you'll have more responsibility," she said.

"You're not exactly painting a picture of paradise," Derek Coleman said.

"No, I'm not. It's going to be a lot of hard work, so if you're looking for an easier, softer way, don't choose the foundation," Jennifer said. "I found a place big enough for all of us. But to say it needs work is an understatement. We'll all be working together—probably for months. Yes! It needs that much work, but it's structurally sound and has been approved by the county. They'll be checking in on every step: plumbing, electricity, roofing. Everything will have to be signed off on before we continue the next step."

"Can we talk this over just among ourselves?" Michael asked.

"Absolutely. I recommend it," she said. "We can save this particular subject for next week and begin our group session now."

*****

Driving home, Jennifer felt the weight of the week balancing on both shoulders with a heaviness brought about by tension coupled with deprivation of sleep. Peter would be coming over tonight, and she could only hope he'd settle for something less than a night out on the town, hobnobbing with the elite. Unfortunately, leisure time alone would only create the perfect opportunity for another debate about the timetable of their marriage. Neither option sounded conducive for getting rid of the headache that seemed determined to bloom into a full-fledged migraine.

"Damn! I've got to get that porch light replaced," she said as she pulled into the driveway. But she immediately realized that she was driving a new car now, and the headlights automatically stay on long enough to light the path to the front door before shutting themselves off. Jennifer grabbed her purse and briefcase and headed for the door with only one thought in her mind: soaking in a hot tub. She unlocked the door and walked in and flipped on a light.

Immediately, that familiar eerie feeling swept up her spine and tingled at the back of her neck.

The sense of imminent danger flooded through her veins and spiraled into a rapid heartbeat just nanoseconds before a familiar-smelling hand clamped across her mouth. Terror was paramount to the intense pressure she felt as he twisted her left arm back. Adrenaline sped through her body, providing strength that grew to a powerful force for kicking, gouging, and scratching the intruder. Her eyes flashed on the blood trickling from his face as she continued to twist and turn, using survival instincts. Managing only to dance them closer to her philodendron family, the struggle ended in a grand finale when all the greenery came crashing to the floor in one fell swoop. Handmade pottery bounced on the carpet as fresh dirt flew everywhere in blizzard-like style.

Gaining physical control of Jennifer from behind, the familiar, raspy male voice said, "I'll let you go, but if you make one sound, I'll just kill you now."

Leaving no doubt what the intentions were, she feigned calmness, encouraging the gradual release of his right hand first, which covered her mouth and tasted of gritty car oil. Then came the gradual release of her left arm, which had been painfully twisted back.

Jennifer began scanning the house for an escape route before bolting for the front door. She immediately felt a determined hand grab the hair on the back of her head, jolting her body to a stop. Directly following was a violent blow to her right cheek, which made her feel as though her eye had popped out. Her body crumbled to the piled carpet.

Dazed with blurred vision, Jennifer heard boisterous words. "You're a stubborn bitch, aren't you?" He grabbed her from the floor and threw her on the couch, and she could finally see the angry face of a dark-bearded, long-haired man. He was wearing a pair of faded blue jeans and a dirty, torn T-shirt advertising a mini-brew beer. Spying his arms with grotesque tattoos of frightful-looking snakes sent shivers down her back. He was now brandishing a 9 mm semi-automatic with one hand while wiping the blood from his face with the other.

Slamming his chubby body down next to her, he said, "Lori and me, we was doing just fine until you interfered." She now knew the intruder was Sol, Lori Watkins's former abusive boyfriend. As he grabbed her chin, pulling the big brown eyes closer, the strong odor of stale beer on his breath turned her stomach into nauseating disgust. "I know who your boyfriend is, and I know he's coming here tonight," he whispered with sadistic pleasure, pulling her even closer to his foul-smelling mouth. "When I kill him, then *you'll* know what it's like to watch someone you love disappear forever." He pointed the weapon at the front door before swinging it back to her face. "But I gotta admit, lady, you do have nice neighbors. One let me in to your house a way back. And again tonight. What'd you do, screw with her 'ol man or something?"

Now, Jennifer could put it together. Angela found a way to let this monster into my house! Why? Because she can.

What the hell are Jubal and Ethan waiting for? An autopsy report from the coroner?

Finally releasing her chin from his jaw-breaking grip, Sol laid the gun on Jennifer's lap, his hand holding it in a shooting position. He toyed with the trigger, saying, "I'll tell you what I'll do. You give me Lori's new address or phone number, and I'm outta here."

"I thought you got that information when you broke in before." Jennifer needed that confirmation.

"Oh, so you knew that was me, huh? Were you scared?" He needed to hear her admit she was. "Your neighbor was quite accommodating. What's her name? Angie something. She knew you had a window in the back that didn't always lock like it should. She didn't even ask me who I was, but I told her I was a repairman."

Knowing Peter would soon be at the door, a distraction was necessary. "I'll get you Lori's number. It's in my office. I'll go get it," she said, starting to stand.

He got up and pulled her down the hall toward her office. Jennifer could feel the barrel of the semiautomatic pressed firmly against her back. Sol rambled on, very much like a madman. "I'm going to get Lori back, and you're going to mind your own business.

You shrinks are all alike. She'd never have left me if it hadn't been for you."

Jennifer rummaged through the files, hiding her panic the best she could. He had to know that there was just as much chance of her giving him Lori's address as there was of stumbling across the Hope Diamond. Terror ripped through her when she heard Peter knock on the front door.

"Get up! Now!" Sol yelled, yanking the hair on the back of her head.

"You don't need anyone else. I'll find the address for you!" she pleaded as he dragged her to the front door.

"Open it and invite him in so we all can have a little chat," Sol whispered, standing behind the door. He pointed the revolver at her head. "And maybe I won't have to kill you too."

Jennifer laid a trembling hand on the doorknob and gradually unlocked the dead bolt. She barely opened the door.

"Hey! What happened to you?" Peter asked, standing in the dark. He didn't know whether to laugh or be concerned.

"Go, Peter! Run!" she screamed, slamming the door shut with the full weight of her body.

"You bitch!" Sol shouted. The pistol whipped her face twice before Peter burst through the door, landing on Sol. Just a few feet away lay Jennifer's motionless body, curled into a fetal position.

Peter's two quick punches to Sol's face took him by surprise and immobilized him. Peter was able to wrestle the gun from Sol's hand and stood up. "Stay right there," Peter said, pointing the weapon three feet away from Sol's face. Both hands shook as he fumbled for his cell phone.

"Hell, you ain't got the nerve to shoot," Sol said as he lunged at Peter like a cannonball blasting out of its chamber. The pistol and cell phone went flying in different directions.

The two formed a rolling mass of punches, kicks, and twists until Sol landed on top of Peter. He clutched Peter's neck with both hands, choking him till Peter shot a fist thrust to Sol's throat, finally breaking the deadly grip. Air filled Peter's lungs as adrenaline surged through his veins. He jerked his knees forward and sent Sol flying, then scrambled for possession of the revolver, Sol at his heels. They both grabbed the gun, and the sound of an explosion brought Jennifer back to consciousness. Both men continued to hold on to the revolver, pushing and shoving as pictures and table lamps fell to the floor.

Finally, Peter jabbed his left elbow into Sol's flabby belly, sending the pistol flying once more; this time it landed at Jennifer's feet. Grabbing the weapon with bloodstained hands, she pulled the trigger, firing into the ceiling before leveling the semiautomatic at Sol. "Stop or I'll shoot you like a rabid animal!"

Jubal Tanner and Ethan Waters appeared at the open door, guns drawn. Jennifer dropped the pistol and made her way to Peter's side, blood oozing from his face and upper arm.

She glared at Jubal and Ethan. "What the hell were you two waiting for, a hand-carved invitation?" She didn't want to hear their answer. "Make yourselves useful and call an ambulance!"

*C*hapter XIII

The two mumbled something about calling 911 when they heard the first shot, requesting an ambulance and police car. "We also called Dr. Hanes."

Peter had already left by ambulance and Sol was in handcuffs when Detective Malloy arrived. "Well, it looks like the war is over," he said, observing the piles watched his joke fall flat. "By the way, I got a couple of patrol officers to bring me here in their squad car as soon as I knew it involved you, Ms. Collins."

"Where you taking him?" Jeff asked Detective Malloy as they watched two officers lead Sol to the police cruiser.

"After I ask Ms. Collins a few more questions, I'll deliver him personally to the Clear Water Springs Jail." Wearing tan Dockers topped with a chocolate cardigan sweater, Malloy looked more like a college junior than a well-seasoned detective.

Eyeing Jennifer's lacerations and growing bruises was almost more than Jeff could handle. Vicariously feeling the pain of her ripped and bruised face, he knew for the first time what it felt like to be capable of murder. It was exhilarating! As he felt the adrenaline rage, he knew that killing Sol would somehow be justifiable because of the trauma visible in Jennifer's big brown eyes. *Who could blame me for killing a person like him?*

But rationality began to win over the novelty of this kind of feeling and he realized that killing the monster who may have permanently scarred the woman he loved would put him on the same level as a diseased dog—and *that*, he couldn't live with. Emotions gave way to civility, vacating any barbaric intentions. But for those few seconds, he knew he felt what other murderers have experienced, and he never wanted to undergo anything like that again.

"Do you know the intruder?" Detective Malloy asked.

"No, but he mentioned Lori's name, and he also used the exact same threats that I've been receiving by phone, so I'm assuming it must be Sol," Jennifer said.

"Sol's the guy that was abusing one of Jennifer's clients, Lori Watkins, until she reached out to Jennifer for help," Jeff interjected. "And we were trying to find him before he could find Jennifer. But as you can see—"

"Sol who?" Malloy asked.

"I don't know. We weren't formally introduced," Jennifer said with reasonable cynicism. "Doesn't he have identification on him?" She held a bag of ice to her bruised and bloodied face.

"Yeah, he does, except the name on his driver's license isn't Sol," the detective said.

"But it's probably the same man Lori knew as Sol," Jennifer offered.

"Does he have any priors under the name on his license?" Jeff asked.

"No, no priors," Malloy said, closing his small notebook. "That's about all the information I need for now, but, Ms. Collins, you need to be checked out by a doctor."

"Don't worry, she's going to the hospital right after I walk you out to the car," Jeff said.

"Good enough. See you later, Ms. Collins," Detective Malloy said as he turned to leave.

"What name is Sol using now?" Jeff asked as they reached the police cruiser.

"Let me see," the detective said, flipping through his notebook. "Um, Edward Wallace." He sat down in the passenger's front seat of the patrol car, not yet shutting the door.

"Eddie Wallace!" Jeff screamed. "He's the guy, never mind. How long before he makes bail?" He scrutinized the bloody face in the back seat. The man's hands were handcuffed behind his broad body as an officer sat next to him.

"It'll be up to the judge tomorrow morning at Wallace's arraignment, but I'm booking him tonight on everything from attempted rape to attempted murder. And just for good measure, I'll probably throw in breaking and entering, phone menacing, using a public utility to threaten bodily harm. By the time he's fingerprinted, he'll also be looking at assault and battery charges and assault with a deadly weapon," Malloy said in Clint Eastwood style.

"And don't forget murder," Jeff said.

"Who did he murder?" asked Malloy.

"I think you'll find out that he killed a man named Stix. It's a ten-year-old murder—"

"Oh God! Wallace killed the man that Charlie Bremmer is sitting on death row for murdering!"

"I knew you'd remember," Jeff said.

"Wallace won't ever be hurting anyone again," Malloy said. "They'll be piping sunlight to him for the rest of his life, if he doesn't get the death penalty. His parole officer won't be born for another ten years, just in case you're worried he may get paroled someday." Malloy shut the car door, and his patrol officer drove off.

Jeff stood in the driveway, watching the patrol car drive out of sight. His legs felt numb while his percolating mind remained bewildered and shocked, but he was mostly filled with disgust. Images of Charlie Bremmer sitting on death row for ten years and a jury who didn't want to believe a man named Eddie Wallace existed burned Jeff. He condemned the judicial system for all its flaws, prejudices, and inconsistencies; for having the audacity to make human errors; and for all the lives destroyed and lost through a less-than-perfect system. Finally, feeling his legs beginning to come back to life, he made tracks for the house.

"What's the matter? You look like you've just seen a ghost," Jennifer said. She grabbed more ice and another clean cloth to soothe her quickly swelling face.

"Let's get you to the hospital, and then I need to call Robert. I'll tell you all about it on the way," Jeff said, looking pale.

Driving to the hospital, Jeff told her about Eddie Wallace.

"The criminal justice system isn't perfect," Jennifer said. "We're simply told that it's the best there is, but how can you rate the efficiency of a judicial system using *that* kind of scale?"

Jeff fell silent, holding back the tears that begged to flow. But right now, he just wanted to be strong for Jennifer.

"Let's talk about something else, okay?" Jennifer asked, almost pleading.

"I suppose by now you've already heard about Perkins," Jeff said, wiping an eye with his sleeve.

"No, what about him?" Jennifer asked.

"He had an accident this afternoon on his way to work. I thought you knew," Jeff said.

"No, no one told me."

"Well, probably under the circumstances—"

"What circumstances?" Jennifer asked, giving him a hard look.

"I-I just meant that maybe Elizabeth didn't tell you because—"

"Elizabeth knows?" she interrupted in disgust, feeling the pain of the warden's unjustifiable mistrust. "I guess I shouldn't be surprised. It's not as if she's ever confided in me anyway. So how is Mr. Perkins?"

"I don't know really. I heard they were keeping him overnight for observation," he said, knowing now the subject shouldn't have been mentioned.

*****

While Doc Beadle tended to Jennifer's wounds, Jeff called Robert, giving him a fast rundown of the evening's events leading to Eddie Wallace's capture.

"I just thought you'd want to know, so you can get over there and do whatever it is you have to do to hold him," Jeff said. "I hope this does it for ol' Charlie."

"I'll call Elizabeth right away," Robert said.

"Better yet, take her with you," Jeff said.

"Before I go, I want you to know that I've notified the authorities and told them everything we know so Peter will be questioned, whether he's in the hospital or not," Robert said. "Have you told Jennifer about him?"

"No, I think she's been traumatized enough for one night, don't you?" Jeff asked.

"Okay, tomorrow then," Robert said.

"Tomorrow."

*****

Lying flat on a hospital gurney in emergency room 3, Jennifer endured a few head stitches between her eyebrows and on her scalp. Several butterfly Band-Aids placed carefully over microstitches on her face. Then she was able to sit up to enjoy the bundle of sympathy mixed with puns and physician's jokes as Dr. Beadle finished tending to her cuts and contusions on both arms and legs.

"You kids sure play rough, considering your ages." Doc gave a quick smile and wink to Jennifer. "There's a chance you may have a concussion. How 'bout you spend the night?"

"No way," Jennifer said.

"Not with me. I mean in the hospital," he said, allowing the infectious laughter to spread throughout the other emergency rooms.

Jennifer couldn't help but chuckle, shaking her head. She said slowly, "I didn't see that one coming."

"You never do. I get you every time," Doc said with enjoyment.

"Maybe you could answer something for me."

"I'll certainly try," Jennifer said, bracing herself for the question.

"I don't understand what it is about my patients. They just do not want to spend time in our hospital. They have a clean bed, total control over the TV remote, nurses at their beck and call, their own landline, no dishes to wash, no cleaning to be done, and food brought to their bedside upon request. Doesn't that sound like a vacation?" He put the last bandage in place and patted her knee while chuckling. He pulled a drug from the shelf and said, "Now I want you to take these as directed and stop by and see me in a day or so, okay? Call me if the pain intensifies. And take a week off from everything."

"I'll do that," Jennifer said, watching Doc's unconvinced eyes. "Okay, I'll *try* to do that."

"Do I need to talk with Jeff?" he said with a smile.

"No, but you could tell me how Peter is doing," she asked.

"He'll be home in two or three days. He's got three broken ribs, contusions over 50 percent of his body, and a bullet hole through his left arm. It missed hitting any bones or tendons, which was a stroke of luck. You kids need to find some safer games to play," Dr. Beadle said, laughing out loud.

"When can I see him?" she asked.

"Don't you think you've enjoyed enough excitement for one night?" Doc asked, watching Jennifer's impish grin appear. "How about tomorrow? He'll still be here."

"Okay, but how's Mr. Perkins doing?" she asked as they headed for the outside door where Jeff was waiting.

"Sammy? Oh, he's all right. A minor fracture to the ankle and some bruises, but he's fine. I set the broken bone and decided to send him home. He didn't want to spend the night any more than you do," Doc said, rubbing his chin. "I guess I just don't understand you young folks today."

"Is there a cop stationed at his home?" Jennifer asked softly.

"No, your Ms. Ellsworth is taking full responsibility for ol' Sammy," he said, walking down a long corridor that lead to the outside door.

"Hey, Doc, let me ask you something," Jennifer said with a quizzical look. "Did Angela Colder used to work here in the hospital?"

"As a matter of fact, she did. Do you know her?" he wondered.

"Can you tell me if she was let go?"

"Yes, she was," Doc said.

"Can you tell me why?" she asked.

"Well, just between you and me, she rejected authority, making everyone's life miserable."

"Hi, Jeff," Doc said, shaking his hand. "Are you going to be taking care of this little lady tonight?"

"I'm going to try," he said.

"Sam, huh? I never knew Perkins's first name," Jennifer said.

"You probably didn't need to," Doc said.

*****

Opening the front door and seeing all the damage, Jennifer realized what she'd been through seemed like a nightmare complete with monsters trying to kill her. The physical evidence brought her back to reality, denying her the luxury of illusion. Gaping silently at the destruction, her memory began to play back the night's events, and the harsh certainty of the evening became all too real.

"Don't worry about the mess," Jeff said, putting his arm around her shoulders. "If you're up to it tomorrow, I'll help you clean. For now, let's just go to bed."

Jennifer jerked her head up to witness the seriousness of the suggestion.

"I didn't mean *together*. Well, unless you . . . I'm just kidding!" Jeff said, chuckling. "But I think it's best if I stay tonight in the spare bedroom. Do you need to take something for sleep?"

"Yeah, Doc Beadle gave me something," she said. "It's pretty mild because there's a chance I might have a concussion."

"Good, now get some sleep," Jeff said, kissing her forehead. "I'll check in on you from time to time. I'll ask you some questions and then let you go back to sleep."

Jennifer hated to admit it, but she did feel safer with Jeff there.

*****

The next day started for Jeff before the rising sun officially debuted. He'd brewed fresh coffee and devoured a slightly stale jelly-filled pastry before searching for the right words to tell Jennifer about Peter. His mind spun through a dozen imaginary dialogues, trying to find one that would hurt the least, but none seemed to fill the requirement and postponement was no longer an option.

"Good morning," Jennifer said. She poured herself a cup of coffee before joining Jeff at the kitchen table. "You sure look deep in thought."

213

"Yeah, I guess I am," he said, noticing the bright daylight intruding through the white lattice kitchen curtains. "Can I fix you breakfast?"

"Maybe in a little bit. You know, you look like I feel . . . and I feel like I've been hit by a semi." She stretched both arms out further than they were willing to go, hoping to find relief for sore muscles. "I look worse today than I did last night," she said.

"You look fine to me," he said in a barely audible voice.

"Are you okay?" she asked.

"I'm fine, don't worry." He got up to rummage through the fridge, hoping food would lessen his anxiety.

*****

After breakfast, they began removing fragments of lamps, hand-painted pottery, and crushed light bulbs from the bloodstained carpet that used to be immaculate beige. The much-cherished claw-legged tables with glass tops that had paid homage to the paisley camelback sofa were now nothing more than kindling. Jeff filled several garbage bags with unidentifiable trashed valuables, including a lampshade that had more twists and turns than a roller coaster.

Jennifer slipped into the kitchen, placing every last possession in perfect order before sweeping and mopping the floor. The dreaded chore of cleaning the office made her feel the most violated. Once a meticulously organized room, it had once had the ability to lessen the pressures of a chaotic world; now it seemed to only add to the confusion and discontent. How long would her nose insist that the dreadful stench of car oil and alcohol were embedded into the walls and carpet? She coughed sporadically while reorganizing until each labeled file was in its proper place.

Jeff sat on the sofa, taking a coffee break, his face resuming the anguished expression worn during breakfast.

"Well, I think we've got everything done except for the carpet and bullets in the ceiling," Jennifer said, trying to laugh. "I'm calling professionals in for that. Not that long ago I was wondering where I'd find someone to help me with the flower gardens outside."

"Did you try to hire that same kid from last year?"

Tilting her head down, she said, "Yes, but his parents heard from Patricia—in church no less—that I wasn't the kind of person he should be working for. So much for Christianity. Thank you once again, Angela Colder."

"I'm so sorry, Jen, that these women here treat you like this. It's so unfair. I've heard of jealousy from other women, but this is ridiculous," he said patting her hand. "You really don't live in a Christian neighborhood, do you? Well, except for the McCaron's and Allison's."

"It's okay. What could happen that God and I couldn't take care of?" she said.

He watched her sadness and wondered how in the world he was going to tell her what had to be said.

"Hey, you okay?" she asked again, nudging him gently. She wondered what thoughts were clouding his ocean-blue eyes.

"Yeah, I'm okay. It's just that there's something I need to tell you," Jeff said, watching the steam rise from the black coffee mug.

"So tell me," Jennifer said.

Jeff only sighed long and hard, avoiding eye contact.

"Tell me!" she said, forcing his chin up from the coffee mug.

"Okay. Peter deals drugs out at the prison and he's been using you for the transportation," Jeff said, blurting out the words without any cushy preludes. He knew it was the only way he'd be able to say it.

"Have you lost your mind?" Jennifer said as she stood up straight.

"I'm sorry, Jen, but it's the truth," Jeff said, trying to calm her with his sedate voice.

"Have you forgotten that if it wasn't for Peter, I'd probably be dead now!" She wanted to scream loudly, but knew it would hurt too much. "Where was your damn surveillance team? Counting the few brain cells they have left?"

"Calm down, Jennifer," Jeff said. "Let's talk—"

"No! *You* calm down! I can't believe you'd stoop this low! Look, Jeff, you may not like Peter, but I do. I'm going to marry him!" she shouted hysterically.

"Jen, *please*," he begged her calmly.

"Get out of here! I mean it. I just want you to leave. I don't want to listen to your lies!" she said as she ran into the bedroom and slammed the door shut. She fell on the bed, crying uncontrollably into her pillow. Jennifer felt the tears burning her stitches as they soaked the pillow.

She wasn't just crying because of what Jeff said about Peter, but for everything that had been happening: Coralee dying in a car she'd been driving, the stubborn Ol' Man, the warden not wanting to be friendly, Mr. Perkins's car accident, the maniac that left threatening messages and almost making them come true, Peter being shot to save her life, having to tolerate her neighbors hatefulness. She cried until sleep won over her weary body, mind, and soul. She slept all day and through the night.

Jeff slumped back on the sofa, tear drops rolling down his face. He couldn't remember ever feeling this sad, except for when his wife died. His body and mind seemed as though they were on separate highways: his mind wanted to go in one direction, but his body wanted to go in another. There'd be no sense in trying to talk this out—not now anyway. He slowly got up, gathered his things, and went to his car. He convinced himself over and over that there was no other way. She had to be told about Peter transferring drugs out to the prison. If he could've found a way to be kinder, gentler . . .

*****

Jennifer didn't go to see Peter at the hospital the following day or the days to come, nor did she talk with anyone, except Dr. Beatle, whom she promised she'd stop back to see about her injuries.

After a little over a week had passed, Jennifer was able to apply small dabs of liquid makeup to the week-old cuts and bruises after the doctor had removed the stitches. She lightly brushed on a little face powder on both cheeks, blending the facial colors to perfection—almost. Taking one step back and then one step forward, she inspected her image in the mirror to observe her artistic ability. Staring with approval at the final product, she knew no makeup artist in the world would be able to portray her face the way it used to look—at least, not yet.

Walking to the car, she automatically looked at the empty parking space across the street where Jubal Tanner and Ethan Waters once parked. How much longer would her head snap in that direction? Was the annoying involuntary reflex now an obsession? Maybe it would become like the sound of her phone ringing and simply lose its authority to produce apprehension. She clung to the philosophy that time would heal all wounds, and as far as Sol went, time wounds all heels.

*****

Driving up to the prison, reoccurring projections of the men's reactions ran through her anxious mind. How well they could handle her assault would depend on how far they'd come in the program. As repetitive playbacks scanned over and over, she hoped their emotional growth was genuine and could survive the truth. Reaching Rec Room One, Jennifer made the conscious effort to hold her head up, but the startled looks from the men almost destroyed the positive attitude.

"Ms. Lily, what happened?" Ron Bookman blurted out before she could take a seat at the table.

"We're going to talk about that, Ron," she said, watching the remainder of the group gape in silence, their eyes glued to the not-yet-healed face. "Once upon a time, there was a man who couldn't control his anger." She took a seat. Telling the story, feeling the men's discomfort, an array of roller-coaster emotions surfaced. At first, there was just bewilderment and wiggling bodies. Then Travis Talltree and Derek Coleman's expressions began to verge on anger, then suddenly settled on sympathy as though remembering their past history with abuse and how they handle it now. Ron Bookman's face glazed over, spelling disbelief and sorrow. Kent Beasley and Tomas Gonzales demonstrated looks of guilt and embarrassment as their heads tilted down, then a tint of anger wrinkled their foreheads before their eyes focused on her bruised face again. Michael Bishop bit his bottom lip, hoping to prevent the tear-filled eyes from spilling, saving himself the embarrassment his feelings could cause. Even now, he couldn't allow certain emotions to show in front of the guys.

"I feel like my past just jumped up and bit me where the sun don't shine," Tomas said. "I remember the times I hit my mother, 'cept I'm not that person anymore."

"I know what you mean," Kent said. "I used to hit my wife, but somehow I was blind or just too insensitive to look at her pained face."

"Yeah, the one I used to wear," Travis said.

"I'd like to punch the guy that did this to you, Ms. Lily," Derek said, "but would I be punching him for what he did to you, or for what my dad did to me? All I'd really be doing is perpetuating the violent cycle that we talk about in here."

"It's like when you're living on the streets, seeing violence every day, you are, like, numb to it," Ron said. "But things are different now. And you've helped change that for us, Ms. Lily. I'm not—we're not—numb anymore."

"Ms. Lily? What stopped you from pulling the trigger?" Travis asked.

"Well, like I said, help arrived, so there was no need," she said.

"I think most of us, out of sheer rage and revenge, would have pulled the trigger anyway," Travis said, watching the aghast looks around the table. "Well, I do. I don't think any of us are all that well yet, except for maybe Michael and Ron."

"Maybe he's right. You always say, Ms. Lily, that we are what our environment is, and right now our environment is tense," Tomas said. "We've learned about restraint, like not to strike physically or emotionally, but what do we know about self-defense? About using only enough physical force to stop someone from hurting us? None of us has been put in Ms. Lily's situation."

"If you can handle the environment here without violence, then you have a very good chance on the outside," Jennifer said. "I never want to believe that any of you are going to be a danger to society when you're released, whether a situation like mine arises in your life or not."

"How many of us honestly know for a fact that his anger will not go into a violence mode if provoked enough?" Travis asked, watching Tomas stumble on an answer.

"Last week, I would've said it wouldn't. Last week, Ms. Lily hadn't been beaten."

"Remember, it's my responsibility to do the forgiving, and I have," Jennifer said. "It over. It's a done deal."

"Oh, c'mon, Ms. Lily," Kent said. "Even *you* have to feel some resentment. How do you feel when you walk to the parking lot, or when you go home alone and turn out the lights at night? You wouldn't be human if you weren't scared now. And as you have told us, fear grows into resentment, right?"

"It can, if you let it. I admit most definitely that I have some insecurities," she said, and then added quickly, "but I don't have to react to the anger negatively because I know how to pray for forgiveness."

"I don't think any of us are that healthy yet," Travis said.

"It takes time and practice," she said.

"Remember when we were all talking about what emotion comes first in any confrontational situation? Is it hurt or anger?" Kent said. "Before we could get honest with ourselves, we believed that anger was the first emotion because we learned how to be comfortable with that emotion. It was what we knew, it was what was familiar. But as time went on, we realized that there was one other emotion we felt first. We couldn't recognize it right away, but we do now. We learned that first you pause. Once you do that, the realization of hurt comes first. Then comes anger, and that can turn to resentment."

"Try to remember that pain is inevitable, resentment is optional," Jennifer looked around at the eyes in the room. "The only way I was able to guide you to the point of nonviolent behavior was because I worked the steps. There are steps for grieving, steps for quitting drinking, and steps to control anger. I'm sure in your twelve-step meetings, you were given the same tools to recognize the pattern of violence as you were the steps to prevent it. Of all the forgiving you've learned to do through a power greater than yourselves, leaving this place—free of resentment—will be your biggest challenge, *not* forgiving the maniac who did this to me. Yes, I've worked through the anger. I can't say I'm not afraid sometimes, so I'll just say that I'm more cautious. That's good enough for now," Jennifer said, wondering about Michael's silence.

"What would you do to this maniac if you could?" Ron asked.

"I did it. I prayed for him," Jennifer said.

"But you still have the pieces to pick up," Kent said.

"Yes, and I've taken the first few steps," she said. "I'm surely not going to try to convince you that physical violence, as well as any other violence, just goes away because you worked some steps for a day a two. It doesn't work like that! Especially if you're a novice. It takes hard, consistent work. It comes down to this for you guys: you either want to get out of prison, or you want to stay out of prison. The ball's in your court."

"You know, Ms. Lily, in our last session, you asked us to talk over moving into the foundation," Kent said. "We'd already pretty much agreed it would be best, but now I think it's a must. None of us are really ready to make it on our own or move into an out-of-state halfway house, which would be the same as making it on our own. I think we can all admit we need one another—and you."

"None of us wants to finish out our time without you," admitted Ron.

"I'm really glad we're going to be together a while longer," Jennifer said with a smile, thinking that time would no longer have the power of an enemy. "Our last day together will be on Friday, and your parole hearings are all scheduled for next week, but the prison board members will interview you first individually."

"Will you be there?" Ron asked.

"For the parole hearing, absolutely. But the board wants to interview you alone," she said.

"Why?" Derek asked with suspicion.

"Why not?" she asked. "All you have to do is be honest."

"I wish you could be there," Ron said in a hushed, fearful voice.

"You'll do just fine, all of you," she said.

"Even me?" Tomas asked.

"You are all going to be just fine, I promise. Truth always wins out."

"Ms. Lily, may I be excused please?" Tomas asked. "I have to finish some work I didn't get done this morning."

"Okay then, let's call it a day. Michael, I'd like you to stay for a minute," Jennifer said.

A discussion of the foundation and plans for living on the outside of the concertina wires loomed in the halls while an atmosphere of hope reigned in each man's voice: the chance for freedom once again grew near. But this time, a slight opportunity for success would accompany it. It was all up to them. They'd heard those words many times but were unable to put any specific meaning to them—until now.

"I think I'll move over here next to you, Michael," Jennifer said, after the others had gone. "So what's going on? You're awfully quiet."

"I just didn't know what to say. When I saw you like that, I just wanted to cry," Michael said, perching both elbows upright on the table, cupping his face with both hands.

"It's okay, Michael, it's over now. I'm fine," she said, putting an arm around his shoulders, ignoring the stipulation of the HBP that forbids any physical contact.

"I've grown to love you, just like the ladies that helped raise me," Michael said, listening to the guard tap on the window.

"I'll take that as a compliment," Jennifer said with a smile, waving a hand in the air to let the guard know things were okay.

"I protected them if a John roughed them up, but I wasn't there to protect you," he said, watching the guard tap harder on the window until it rattled.

"It wasn't your job to protect me," Jennifer said, withdrawing the arm to pull his chin toward her face. "Do you understand?"

"I think so, but I don't want you to get into trouble," Michael said, watching the guard's furious face turning red.

"Don't worry about it. What are they going to do, cancel my program?" she snickered standing to leave.

"You are *bad*, Ms. Lily," Michael grinned as he walked with her to the door.

"Yeah, well, some rules are unrealistic," Jennifer said.

Remaining in the doorway, she watched Michael walk back to his cell.

"You are such a sap when it comes to these bums," said Hank Poovey, the guard who Jennifer tried to make believe didn't exist.

"You have a nice day too, sir," she said, walking back to the guards' station to connect with Richard, a new guard she'd seen only once.

Richard Vaughn was young, bright, and eager to be helpful—characteristics that alienated him from his peer group in the prison. To most, Richard probably seemed like a lanky kid who always had more questions than what there could ever be answers for. It wasn't just his incessant curiosity that bothered them but also his chipper attitude that they didn't feel fit the profile of a prison guard. His choice of hope over despair also annoyed them. For Jennifer, Richard was a breath of fresh air that was long overdue in the prison's dysfunctional atmosphere.

Richard's biggest crime was being "green" to the prison system—a temporary condition the guards used to humor themselves. Granted, he was a little naive about life, but he possessed qualities that couldn't be taught, only instilled at an early age. Jennifer hated the thought of the end product if Richard chose to remain in the current prison system. He'd still be Richard, but with Hank's attitude.

"Which way you headed today, Ms. Collins?" Richard asked.

"To the administration building. I've got to get all my files and go home to write recommendations for next week's parole hearings," she said.

"Am I foolish to want to do the kind of work you're doing, Ms. Collins?" he asked, bouncing out the door to hold it open for her. "The other guards say I am."

"I don't think so. How much formal education have you had?" she asked, thinking a place at the foundation would suit his personality and benevolent character better.

"I have a bachelor's in sociology from Metro State University. Would that qualify me for a place at your new foundation?" he asked.

"Do you read minds?" she asked in jest.

"Do I need to?"

"No, but it helps," she said, snickering as they walked. "How did you know about the foundation?"

"There aren't any secrets in prison," he said.

"Yeah, I've heard that. Why don't you stop by the foundation in about three weeks, and we'll work something out, okay?"

"Thanks, Ms. Collins." He wore a winning jackpot smile.

"You're welcome, Mr. Vaughn," Jennifer said sweetly.

"Richard," he said. "You can call me Richard."

"And you can call me Jennifer," she said, shaking his hand.

Reaching the doors of the administration building, Richard asked, "Jennifer, why do the guards see the inmates as hopeless?"

"I don't know, exactly. I guess because it's easier to be sarcastic or cynical about social problems and injustices than it is to try and change them. Everyone's looking for an easy way out these days—and not just the inmates," she said, bidding him goodbye.

As she walked down the hall, she dreaded knowing that seeing Elizabeth right now would be difficult, at best. The pain of betrayal by keeping Perkins's accident confidential burned enough resentment that even basic civility felt like an impossibility. The warden's absence of support for the HBP, which had been made embarrassingly apparent from the get-go, should be all there was to endure. What was she trying to prove anyway, that the temporary psychologist wasn't a trusted confidante? She had already made that perfectly clear.

"Hi, Ms. Ellsworth," Jennifer said, entering the warden's office. She walked briskly to the locker. "I won't be long. I just need to grab these files."

"Hi, Jennifer," Warden Ellsworth responded, looking up from the desk. "You did hear about Mr. Perkins, right?"

"Yeah! Eventually!" Jennifer said, not turning to address the question.

"You know, I think it's time you and I went out for a long dinner. Is tonight a possibility?" Elizabeth asked, leaning back in her chair. She twirling her yellow pencil with both hands.

What could this woman be thinking? "Ms. Ellsworth, you don't owe me anything. It's just that I thought in this situation, concerning

Mr. Perkins, that some common courtesy would've prevailed over any sense of privacy you think you deserve."

"We'll talk about that and a few other things over dinner. Tonight?" she asked.

"Fine," Jennifer said, gathering her files and leaving.

"I'll call you," Elizabeth said before Jennifer was out of hearing range.

You do that, Jennifer shook her head at the idea of them having dinner together. *I guess she forgot that most people having dinner together usually talk.*

Chapter XIV

A sense of weariness sunk into her aching muscles as Jennifer zapped a cup of coffee in the microwave. She slumped into a chair at the kitchen table. Her mind became a spiral of interrupted thoughts, like an afternoon soap opera with too many story lines for successful continuity. Ignoring the blinking light on the answering machine, she sat in what would have appeared to be a meditation mode, only in meditation, you don't let your mind focus on anything but a mantra, let alone allowing it to skip from one problem to another. She hated the feeling of being out of control even though she knew somewhere deep inside that people aren't the ones who are in control. People make plans; God laughs. She'd been grateful for all the years that her God had a sense of humor.

Without permission, her mind broadcast brief scenes of her six men and all the problems that were ahead for them. Would they make it? Did they depend too much on her and lack the faith in their Higher Power that they had all learned about in their twelve-step meetings. Then her brain jumped to an imaginary apology from Jeff.

The harder she tried to let go and let God, the more she was distracted with trivial matters, such as why in the world would Elizabeth invite her to dinner? The warden hadn't shown any interest in her before. Not real interest! So why now? Jennifer was starting to think that it was a little too late for the warden to do the right thing now. But because of her strong resolution that "it's never too late to make something right," she would go to dinner with Elizabeth. The only thing she feared now was what she might say that would jeopardize the HBP.

"Jennifer," she said to herself, "don't say the things you've been dying to say to her. If you do, you'll unravel everything you've worked so hard to make happen. Just let Elizabeth take you to some prissy restaurant, and occasionally nod politely, as though you agree, and then you can go home.

She looked at the blinking light on the phone and then pushed Play.

Elizabeth had already called to say she'd be by at seven; Jeff Hanes hadn't called, which was still appreciated. Robert Henderson called, not leaving a detailed message, but Jennifer felt sure that the message had something to do with the new foundation and returned Robert's call.

"Hi," Jennifer said. "Got your message. What's up?"

"I have great news. Can you meet me tomorrow in front of your new foundation?" Robert asked.

"It's mine?" she squealed with delight, forgetting all of the worries and woes that seemed to be so important five minutes ago.

"Pretty much. We've got a couple of details to take care of, but yeah, it's yours," he said, hearing a "Yes!" on the other end of the phone.

"How 'bout nine tomorrow morning?" Jennifer asked.

"I'll be there," he said, before hanging up the phone.

*****

Much to Jennifer's astonishment, Elizabeth drove them to the Eight Ball, a restaurant known for its younger crowd, late hours, and frequent cameo appearances of men dressed in blue who wore badges and toted guns.

"What made you choose this place? Have you ever been here?" Jennifer asked with a laugh before getting out of the car.

"No, but we *need* this tonight," Ms. Ellsworth retorted with confidence as they entered the clamor of new-wave music, along with its hairdos and local slang.

Although it was hard to hold out much hope of salvaging what appeared to be a nonexistent friendship, Jennifer thought the night was bound to stimulate interest. Besides, the least she could do is extend the courtesy to go along with whatever the warden had in mind.

The three-level establishment with its barnlike decor bore a striking resemblance to a 1950s twelve-family garage sale, except the garage sale would've looked more organized. Once the decision was made to sit at a table closest to the ceiling, the treacherous trek to get there was made by climbing up two sets of rickety wooden stairs with raw timber railings waiting to carve splinters into both hands. Once there, they settled in for a clearer view of the havoc that portrayed itself as a restaurant.

The nostalgic furnishings consisted of every trinket known to mankind in farming communities as far back as the Dust Bowl. Beaten-up washtubs, ancient tricycles, and milk buckets, along with antique horse harnesses and oxen yokes, covered the A-frame rustic ceiling. There were other objects that reeked of obsolescence, but Jennifer couldn't identify them with any certainty. Elizabeth's eyes widened with exhilaration, examining relics left over from an era Jennifer wasn't privy to, except from a high chair, eating meat from a spoon.

"This is just like the early fifties, isn't it?" Elizabeth asked, eyes full of sentiment engulfing every detail of the motif.

"Where? In Hanoi?" Jennifer said, a smile creeping over a gaped mouth.

"Oh, c'mon, Jennifer! There's more to life than dining at Nino's Café."

A waiter—or what they thought was a waiter—appeared at the table. He wore faded blue jeans that hung off visible bare hips; the pants would only stay in place if the need for sneezing didn't arise. The knees of the jeans were missing, probably with the help of a blowtorch. The acronym on the off-white T-shirt read CU something. The remainder of the message was covered by a red-and-blue plaid flannel shirt that looked as though it hadn't been washed since Bush Sr. was president.

"What'll it be, girls?" he asked, pad in hand. He pulled a pencil out from behind his pierced ear—that is, the left pierced ear.

"I'd like a . . . You don't drink, do you, Jennifer?" Elizabeth asked.

"No," Jennifer said. "But you go ahead."

"Thanks, I'll have her share too," Elizabeth said. "Bring me your jumbo margarita with an extra shot of silver Patron, some chips and salsa too."

"I'll have club soda with a lime," Jennifer said, watching the waiter's hips sway to the next table before she began to wonder how many different sides there were to the warden.

"Okay, Jennifer, now I'm ready," Elizabeth said. "I'll answer every single question you've had in the last six months and even some you didn't know you had. But first let me say the reason I didn't tell you, or anyone but Robert, about Perkins's accident was because the police found large quantities of cocaine in his car. The other reason was because your ordeal happened just a few hours later, so I didn't get the chance."

Jennifer's mouth fell open. "I don't believe it. *Not* Mr. Perkin! This has to be some kind of a mistake," she said, noting the reasons why she hadn't been informed of his accident.

"I agree and that's why I called Robert. He said the charges will be dropped. Just how, I have no idea," Elizabeth said. "But in the meantime, Perkins is only on leave for medical purposes."

"I miss him at work," Jennifer said. "I have had some very interesting talks with him. He's quite an observer. Not much gets passed him."

"He's my right arm," Elizabeth said as the drinks arrived. They were placed on cocktail napkins that looked and felt like burlap. Jennifer uttered a short snicker before lifting the square-sized material to her nostrils, then quickly set it aside.

"What a turn of events, just to find Eddie Wallace," Elizabeth said.

"Ms. Ellsworth . . . "

"Please, call me Elizabeth," the warden interrupted, sipping the margarita and reaching for the chips and salsa.

"Elizabeth then," Jennifer softened. "Does Charlie Bremmer know?"

"We told him right away, and Burt Walker too."

"Will Charlie be free now?"

"I don't know about free, but Burt's hoping to get Charlie's sentence commuted to life in the absence of Eddie's full confession," Elizabeth said.

"What about you and Robert?" Jennifer asked. As she reached for the chips and salsa, she imagined Elizabeth's eyes squinting at that question.

"O-o-oh! Me and Robert," Elizabeth said, smiling with romantic fascination. "He's my best."

"Your best what?" Jennifer asked.

"Where do you live? Do you need illustrated graphics? You know, draw you a picture?" Elizabeth asked, giggling with the thrill of titillation.

"No!" Jennifer said. "I got it!"

"My best *friend*," Elizabeth held her chin high and laughed.

"So you and Robert," Jennifer inquired. "You said I could ask anything."

"We're getting married right after my long overdue retirement," Elizabeth said, watching Jennifer's eyes bulge.

"Wow! Wait! *What* retirement? When? Why?" Jennifer asked the questions in rapid succession.

"You should've been a reporter, Jennifer." Elizabeth laughed. "Friday, and you should know the *why* by now!" She sipped the margarita from the side of the glass that still had salt. "But what you don't know is that I was within one day of handing in my resignation when you brought the proposal for the Homeward Bound Program proposal to the prison."

"You're right. I didn't know that," Jennifer said, confused. "I didn't think you saw any value in my program. Where was your support?"

"Jennifer, if I would've openly supported your program, it wouldn't have passed. Had I verbally agreed with you at the review board meetings, they would've brushed us both off as 'a good ol' girls' network," Elizabeth said.

"Well, ain't that the pot calling the kettle black?" Jennifer said, recognizing the irony. "It's no different from what the men do in the business world."

"Oh yeah, I know," Elizabeth said. "But whether you know it or not, these ears were listening to everything you had to say."

"I thought *we* were past gender bias," Jennifer said as she shook her head.

"No, not really, but that's what *they* would have you believe," Elizabeth said with a confident smile. "The glass ceiling is still there—and thriving."

"That's crazy! I mean, you're the *warden*," Jennifer said. "They have to listen to you."

"I'm a *woman* warden," Elizabeth said. "I'm the system's token that shows the State of Colorado that the criminal justice system isn't biased or prejudiced. They patronized me. Surely you've noticed there are few women in Special Operations who are invited to attend the review meetings?"

"I met *one*," Jennifer said.

"Myrtle Hammond? Nice lady. We had a little chat about what's been going on in those review meetings," Elizabeth said.

"Oh! So *that's* what happened!" Jennifer said. "But anyway, you mean you liked my proposal from the beginning?" Jennifer asked, watching Elizabeth nod. "Well, knowing *that* is better than eating dessert here." She pretended not to notice Elizabeth's expression and instead allowed both her feet to shuffle through the peanut shells that carpeted the barnwood floors.

"Of course I liked your HBP. It made *sense*," Elizabeth said. "If nothing else, it left us with an alternative instead of just simply warehousing. Besides, I knew you had the spunk to turn heads, upset the proverbial prison protocol, and hopefully create enough havoc to force them to reevaluate their barbaric belief system that they seem determined to hang onto. Let me tell you, you were a *hoot!*" Elizabeth laughed, throwing her head back before finishing the last drop of her margarita. "Now let's have dinner."

Jennifer had dreamed of this time when the two of them could just talk about anything. And they would laugh and exchange ideas and learn from each other. During dinner, Elizabeth asked Jennifer about what should be done with serial killers and mass murderers. She was surprised with Jennifer's answer but agreed. Jennifer explained that there are human beings that either weren't born with a conscience or no one was there to help them develop it or lost what they had of humanity due to excessive abuse.

"It's unfortunate that serial killers and mass murderers, along with terrorists, are irretrievably damaged," Elizabeth stated. "I believe these kinds of people should be put to death for their safety and ours. But expiration of a life shouldn't be a sideshow. Only a handful of witnesses are needed when the needle is stuck in the arm."

"I know what you mean," Jennifer agreed. "If you think for a moment that their victims' families and friends receive gratification from watching their death, you'd be wrong. Just hours b*efore* the execution, the victims' friends and relatives talk on and on about retribution, an eye for an eye, and they want him/her to hurt the same way their loved one hurt. It's only fair, they'll say. But have you ever seen these same people who are interviewed on their way to the parking lot after the execution is over?"

"Absolutely!" Elizabeth said with certain sadness. "Relatives and friends of those who were murdered can barely speak even when reporters put words in their mouth, 'So do you have closure now?' They don't look like they have closure. They look like someone who had just witnessed a human being put to death. And somewhere inside of them there is a small voice that says they would have been better off spending the last few years healing from the death of their loved one, instead of carrying around the hatred they had for the killer."

When every last morsel of the beef and chicken fajitas had been devoured and dessert was passed over, Elizabeth and Jennifer sat back and enjoyed hot coffee.

"You look tired, Jennifer," Elizabeth said. "You want to leave?"

"Not before you tell me why you want to retire now, just when there's hope," Jennifer said. "Look, I've seen positive changes in the men due to the HBP. Maybe after they prove they can stay clean, sober, and free, the prison will hire *two* psychologists to run the program, instead of just one. That would help twelve men instead of only six, and maybe a domino effort could continue to occur."

"Like Jeff always says, you *are* the eternal optimist," Elizabeth smiled. "But, Jennifer, it'd take *time* to change, what do you call it, the mind-set of a hundred generations. The problem is that most of the men on the board have been there for twenty years and any replacements would have to follow their ideals. In other words, they'd have to keep quiet and kiss Tuttle's you-know-what. If your program is a groundbreaker, it's got to break ground without me. By the way, speaking of Jeff, what's going on between the two of you?"

"Hasn't Robert told you?" Jennifer asked.

"No, but I know he knows," Elizabeth said.

"Oh, great," Jennifer said, sighing with exhaustion. "Robert and I are getting together tomorrow to work out some details on the foundation. I'm in no mood to talk about Jeff—with anyone."

"Don't worry, he won't give you a hard time," Elizabeth said. "But Jeff's cared about you for a long time, so go easy on him."

She looked at Elizabeth as if to say, "Are you deaf!"

"I know, I know. We don't have to discuss it." Elizabeth nodded with an understanding smile. "But tell me about the neighbor that helped this guy break into your house."

"She's one of those people that won't have to answer to anything. She'll just say she thought she was helping me. And trust me, *my* neighbors will believe *her* and so will everyone else in town!"

*****

That night, alone in bed, thoughts of Jeff's healing kindness and magical feel-good potions, which he could produce with mere words, dominated Jennifer's whole being. Hoping sleep would triumph over an exhausted body, images of his understanding smile appeared before her and refused to leave. Sleep was becoming more remote with each half hour that past. But she just kept thinking, *How could he say the things he said?* Jennifer knew him as a man with integrity, not maliciousness. She just knew that there had to be some kind of misunderstanding! *I can't lose any more sleep over this.*

She hugged a nearby pillow, forcing images of Peter to surface, remembering how he'd saved her life. But how sure was she about marrying him? Did their relationship fit her unspoken definition of what real love was—or what she believed it to be? Did she and Peter think as one, have the same desires for the future, believe and live by the same standards and values? Had they even discussed anything resembling that kind of intimacy? Her restless mind replayed a line from a movie, *It Takes Two* (1994) starring the Olsen twins, where a symptom of being in love is a feeling described as "can't eat, can't sleep, over-the-fences, World Series type." She wished love was just that easy; in high school it was.

Jeff had been her friend for a long time; Jennifer couldn't picture her life without him in it, and that thought alone made a good night's sleep difficult, if not impossible. She knew that being with Peter wasn't like being with Jeff, and there was no way to explain the difference, no way that she was willing to admit just yet. But she knew intellectually that being in love in the adult sense was so much more than just a one-liner from a kid's movie.

When morning arrived, bright sunshine glared through the windows, announcing a new day. Jennifer showered and gulped some coffee before driving to Peter's house to see if he needed anything, remembering she had a meeting with Robert Henderson at 9:00 a.m.

She knocked on the locked door leading to the kitchen, hoping to be heard over the loud heavy metal music pulsing through the walls. With no answer, her hands plunged into her purse, digging deep to find the key he had given her months ago.

"Hello!" Jennifer yelled out after entering. "Anyone home?" *The music is so loud, no wonder he can't hear me.* Gradually making a path down the hall leading to the bedrooms, she called out once more. The din grew louder as she entered Peter's bedroom. The earsplitting volume of the music came from his bath off the master's bedroom, and the door was opened only slightly. Jennifer laughed at herself, amused that she had tiptoed to the bedroom.

Cautiously, because she didn't want to scare him into another injury, a chuckle erupted as she heard Peter stretch his vocal cords into high pitches in his effort to imitate the voice booming from the box on the edge of the tub. Peeking through the steam from the hot tub, she saw his reflection in the wall-size mirror. But what she saw next would remain cemented in her memory for eternity.

There on the edge of the tub was a vial filled with a white substance. Peter tapped the contents out on a small, flat piece of glass to form a straight line before inhaling it up one nostril and then the other.

Jennifer's body felt numb; both feet took steps backward without the mind consciously knowing. Shocked and revolted from what must be a nightmare, she prayed someone would be kind enough to wake her. Jennifer could no longer hear the music; the only sound she heard now was that of her racing heartbeat as she stumbled out of Peter's bedroom and down the hall to the kitchen. Reality began to register, and feelings of immobility were fading. Reaching for the wall phone, she dialed 911 before leaving.

After reaching her car, tears burned down both red cheeks as if they were acid. The key seemed to go into the ignition automatically, and the engine started. This climatic finalization of their relationship made her feel as though she just buried a loved one, and in a way, she had.

Wiping the last tear away, Jennifer pulled into her driveway feeling a strong urge to call Jeff. The need to talk to him outweighed the excitement of her upcoming meeting with Robert Henderson. *But how can I do that? He tried to warn me.* She heard her phone ring while opening the front door.

"Hi, Jennifer," Robert said. "Did I catch you at bad time?"

"No, it's okay. What's up?" she asked.

"Can we meet a little later today? Something's come up that I've got to take care of," Robert said in a cryptic tone.

"Are you okay?" she asked, remembering that the best way to survive a tragedy is to help others.

"I'm fine, it's just that I have things to tend to that can't wait," he said.

"What about four this afternoon?" Jennifer asked.

"Are *you* okay?" Robert asked.

"Yeah, I guess I'm just a little tired."

"Okay then. I'll see you at four."

Jennifer fell down gently on the camelback couch, closed her eyes, and waited for a surrender that would take her into a dream of utopia. Sleep followed, and she woke refreshed a few hours later. Now she could tackle the evaluations with enthusiasm for the men in the HBP, and by four, she was waiting for Robert parked in front of what was to be the new foundation.

"Am I late?" Robert asked, opening her car door.

"No, I'm early," she said. "Can we go in?"

"Sure, but afterward, can we talk about a problem I'm having?" he asked.

"Yeah, of course." She was a little surprised—and honored—since Robert usually turned to Jeff for guidance.

They toured the house, taking notes on needed repairs. They knew the place would have to meet certain building codes before a certificate of occupancy would be given. It was an older three-story wood frame with a porch extending the full width of the house. Robert reviewed his notes, counting all the hours needed for extensive repairs and speculating on the financial burden the house could become.

Jennifer's review consisted of making *ah* and *oh* sounds. She saw every problem—doors with missing hinges, boards that protruded up from the floor and cracked tiles in the bathrooms—as already remodeled, an insight that she thought everyone had.

Stepping outside for one last look at the exterior, Jennifer said, "This is so perfect, don't you think?"

"Well," Robert said, pausing, "I'm sure it *could* be, eventually."

"You'll help me with the legalities, right?" she said, marveling at the house while Robert wondered why it hadn't been condemned.

"Of course, but you know this isn't the best neighborhood, right?"

"Yeah, I know, but it's all I could handle for now," Jennifer said. "But you have to look at the assets the house has. It's on Old Main Street, so there will be little traffic because the city cut off half of the original Main Street to take traffic in a different direction. The house will give the inmates ample opportunity to work for their share of the rent, food, and utilities. They'll love it! I know it. And once all of the repairs are made, it really will be home to them."

"Yeah, we'll put it together somehow," Robert rubbed his chin wistfully.

"Good. Now let's have that talk over coffee. I'll meet you at Nino's."

Robert and Jennifer headed for the café; Jennifer grabbed the one parking space left in front. She wondered if it was simply a choice made of convenience or a rebellious act aimed at Peter to reclaim her liberation. Taking a table inside, Robert soon joined her.

"What kind of a problem could you possibly have that I'd be of any help?" she asked, wondering if he wanted to talk about Elizabeth.

"Jennifer, you know about Peter, don't you?" he asked, watching the brightness in the big brown eyes fade.

"Well . . . I-I mean . . . Jeff said . . .," Jennifer said.

"No, I mean, you *know*, don't you?" he asked. "The police got a tip from a 911 call earlier this morning. It came from Peter's house, and I think we both know *he* didn't make the call. We were going after him today. He'd been questioned while in the hospital. The call only confirmed what we already knew."

"How'd *you* know?" she asked in an unintentional whisper before clearing her throat.

"The surveillance team initially," he said.

"Well, I guess they were good for something after all," she said sarcastically and apologized immediately, but only because it was Robert.

"That's okay, Jen," Robert assured her. "Jeff has pretty much told me how you felt about them, but you got to admit they sure came in handy finding out Peter's involvement with the drugs out at the prison."

"That's true enough."

"I need to apologize for pressuring Jeff into telling you before you were ready to hear about Peter's drug problem. Neither one of us wanted to hurt you. We were trying to protect you," Robert said.

"Protect me from *what*?" she asked.

"From Peter, naturally. You and I both know what you saw this morning, and we both know who made that call," he said. "Will you please tell me what happened?"

Jennifer took Robert through, step by step, of what still felt like a nightmare, pausing intermittently to wipe a tear away. "Now quid pro quo. Tell me everything you know," Jennifer said.

Robert started at the beginning, with the suspicion that Peter kept current on the progress of the HBP through the local newspaper, then arranged the fender bender with her Subaru. He told her what Jubal Tanner and Ethan Waters found underneath her car. As he continued to rattle off the sequence of events, Jennifer felt numb again. She pieced together some of the things that had happened when she and Peter were together: the sudden—as well as frequent—nosebleeds, including the first one she saw when they went skiing, his loss of appetite, and nervousness, an extremely high energy level, then there was him not wanting her to park on the street but only in a back parking lot. Why he was always ten minutes late for every occasion. But the worst thought was him asking her to marry him so she wouldn't have to testify against him in case he was discovered. The signs of drug abuse were right there, under her nose. She felt more foolish than she could ever remember.

"Jennifer, the only reason Jeff got you to trade your car in was to protect you from any evidence in the event that Peter was busted. By the way, Jeff had arranged with the salesman to buy your Subaru, and we were going to keep it for evidence. But Peter beat him to it. When we knew we had enough evidence was that day the three of us had lunch together, and afterward we ran into Mr. Perkins. Do you remember that?" Robert asked, watching Jennifer's slow nod. "From there, it wasn't hard to see the writing on the wall. Then we knew that Peter was using Perkins's car to get drugs to the prison."

"How could I be so stupid?" Jennifer was dumbfounded. Shocked. "He never really loved me at all. I was just a . . . a . . . " She paused for fear of crying.

"I think he probably *is* in love with you as much as anyone like that *can* be in love with someone," Robert said. "And as far as you being stupid, well, let me give you some of your own advice: don't be so hard on yourself. And don't overcompensate with the next poor schnook that falls in love with you." Robert smiled.

"The next?" she questioned in a tone of intense doubt.

"Or should I say, the *other*," he said with a grin.

"You mean, Jeff?" she asked.

"Ye-ah!"

"I guess I owe him some amends, don't I?"

"You two will find a way to work it out," he smiled. "Remember, love *is* blind, but that's not always a bad thing."

*****

By Friday, Jennifer was driving up to the prison for the last group session. It would also be the last time she'd see the men in a prison surrounding, except for supporting them during parole hearings.

The legal aspects were taken care of concerning the new foundation, and her dream would soon become a reality. The only concern now was filling positions for the board. An offer would be made to Robert and Elizabeth, but there were still two more to be filled. Somehow the dream didn't seem complete without Jeff's involvement.

As she pulled into the designated parking spot, Hank Poovey was taking the sign down that read PSYCHOLOGIST. Just a few quick turns of a wrench exposed the original sign, STAFF MEMBER. Edward Tuttle's idea, no doubt.

The thought of Perkins not being there to escort her on the last day set in uncomfortably. She'd sent a get-well card to him and wanted to go visit, but she felt guilty because of Peter. And now it seemed inappropriate for Hank to be the one walking her to Building A.

"Ms. Ellsworth wants to see you," Hank said.

"Okay," Jennifer replied, scampering up the steps to the administration building.

An odd feeling swept through her as she walked down the long dilapidated corridor that lead to the warden's office. It was the first time neither a rehearsed dialogue nor a line of defense was going to be needed.

"Hi, Robert," Jennifer said, walking into the office and looking around. "What have you done with our warden?"

"She'll be right back. I'm glad you stopped by. I've got a couple of things to tell you. First, I'm inviting you to Elizabeth's surprise retirement party tomorrow."

"Surprise Elizabeth? Isn't that an oxymoron? You know, like jumbo shrimp, amicable divorce. She probably already knows about it." Jennifer grinned.

"Probably," he smiled before a serious look appeared. "Jennifer, Peter will only give a full confession, complete with names, dates, and places, if you'll be there."

"Is he crazy?" Jennifer's eyes bulged.

"That's pretty much been established," Robert said, throwing a quick grin. "But we *need* this." He got serious again. "Will you do it?"

"Will it help Mr. Perkins?" she asked.

"Very much."

"Then I'll do it. But I want Angela Colder there too, and I don't care what you got to do to make it happen."

"Good. I'll meet you at your place after group session today," Robert finished as Elizabeth walked into the room.

"Where are you two going?" Elizabeth asked with a smile. "Jennifer, are you moving in on my territory?"

"No, Ms.—I mean, Elizabeth," Jennifer said, laughing at the thought of the warden having a compatible sense of humor. "Did you want to see me?"

"Elizabeth, I've got to get going," Robert said, heading toward the door with a wave of one hand. "Jennifer, I'll see you in a couple."

"Right," she replied.

"Let's sit down a minute," the warden spoke in a tone that pushed Jennifer back into the defensive mode. "I don't know how to tell you this, so I'm just going to come right out with it: Mr. Tuttle is stepping in as the temporary warden until one is appointed."

"No way! How could something like that happen?" Jennifer said, feeling like she'd been sucker punched in the stomach.

"It's called male bonding and male networking. It's not a perfect world, Jennifer," Elizabeth said. "And we both know it won't really be temporary. The position will provide him with what he's always wanted: more control over the inmates' daily lives."

"At least my men won't be here," Jennifer said.

"No, but you need to know that Tuttle will be at the parole hearings next week," the warden said.

"No! Why?" Jennifer said.

"He wants to make sure *everything* is reviewed on your men's pasts, not just the last six months," Elizabeth said. "I've made arrangements to be there. At least I'm not sending you into the lion's den alone anymore."

"Well, this oughta be interesting," Jennifer said with a quick snort. "Does he know you'll be attending?"

"No," the warden said with a coy smile.

*****

As Hank Poovey escorted Jennifer to Rec Room One, she wondered why the usual noises of chatter and laughter couldn't be heard. None of the lights had been turned on. *Are my men in lockdown?* She stepped into the room and felt around for the light switch. She was getting very curious about her situation. All at once, the room lit up, her eyes felt like someone had just snapped a picture using a large flashbulb.

The men were all standing in a straight row in front of the big round table, looking neat, clean, and freshly shaven. They waited with silent anticipation for the inspection. Cautiously stepping closer, Jennifer put her hands on her hips and bent a little closer. First she spotted Derek Coleman's short haircut and asked, "Who's the new guy?"

"It's Derek, Ms. Lily. It's Derek with a haircut," Ron said, giggling.

"Very good, Derek. No more whiplash, huh?" she grinned. And looking at Tomas, she said, "I can see your face."

"I shaved," he said coyly.

"Looks good," she remarked. "Now does anyone want to tell me what's going on?"

"It's a party! For you, Ms. Lily," Ron said like an anxious child barely able to control his excitement.

She gazed at the decorated cake on the table and sighed deeply, preventing the tears from spilling. Michael handed her a large poster board featuring all six men's faces, which Ron had drawn with colored pens. Each of the men printed a message of thanks below their portrait.

"It's not much, Ms. Lily, just a token of the thanks we owe you," Michael said.

"It's beautiful!" Jennifer wiped a tear that slipped by.

"Cut the cake, Ms. Lily," Kent Beasley said excitedly.

"So does anyone have a knife?" she asked, watching them break into laughter.

"Sure, in my back pocket," Travis said, snickering.

Hank Poovey offered a butter knife, then left the room to stand guard outside.

Jennifer cut the cake, and the men poured coffee before gathering around the table one last time. She was astonished by how quickly they were devouring the cake.

"Don't they feed you in here or what?" she asked, taking a small bite.

"You'll feel better if we don't tell you what the food's like in here, trust me," Derek said as they all shook their heads in agreement, stuffing their faces.

"I trust you." She smiled. "How did you arrange this little party anyway?"

"The warden helped us," Michael said.

Jennifer smiled again before saying, "Let me fill you in on everything that's going to happen in the next two weeks."

"What's the foundation called?" Travis Talltree asked.

"I don't know. I haven't thought about that yet," she said, seeing growing smiles aimed at Michael. "Okay, Michael, what'd you name it?" She grinned.

"The Tiger Lily Foundation," he said, scooping up the last piece of cake.

"I know better than to ask, but tell me why," she said, snickering.

"When you first came here, we all thought of you as Lily White, but we soon learned our lesson. You came in strong and determined to change things. You showed us how to change ourselves. And it's all the little things we talk about now, things you taught us. 'The word is *yes*, never *yeah*,' you'd say. You insisted that we respect one another even when we didn't agree. We now know that stuffing feelings doesn't really work, not in the long run. It actually creates new problems, but six months ago we wouldn't have ever believed that or even understood it. We do now. Now we all think of you as Tiger Lily," he said as the other men all stood and clapped until their hands were tired.

When the room settled down again, Tomas asked, "Ms. Lily, what'll happen to the HBP now? Will it continue?"

"I don't know. I guess it'll all depend on the results from this experiment."

"She means if we all stay out of prison, it might continue," Derek said. "We won't let you down."

"I know you won't," she said.

"Did you find what you were looking for?" Kent asked, watching Jennifer's perplexed expression. "You know, the causes for the high recidivism rate?"

"I didn't know you knew about that."

"Oh, c'mon, Ms. Lily, there are no secrets in prison."

"Right, I found many of them," she said. "I learned a lot. I hope you did too."

"You ought to write a book about us—all of us," Ron said.

"Maybe I'll do just that," Jennifer responded, smiling.

*****

She felt no desire to make small talk with Hank Poovey as they walked to the car. They had never seen eye to eye on the politics of the prison system. As they passed an elderly inmate who'd been working on the grounds all morning, Hank spoke up.

"Hey! Where do you think you're going?" he shouted onto the inmate's face.

"It's lunchtime. I'll be back out to finish," the inmate said.

"No! You finish now!" Hank sounded like the Ol' Man.

"But the cafeteria closes at—"

"I know when it closes. If you would've worked a little harder, you would've had this done by now!" Hank bellowed.

As the inmate returned to raking, the two continued down the sidewalk. "That's what's wrong around here," Hank said. "There's no discipline. They all want to be treated like prima donnas. And I bet *you* feel sorry for them."

"No, it's *you* I feel sorry for," Jennifer retorted. She hurried to her car and drove away.

Chapter XV

As Jennifer and Robert walked into the small interrogation room, she saw Peter and his defense attorney sitting at an oblong wooden table. Detective Malloy entered, and much to Jennifer's surprise, he was wearing a white shirt with a wide blue-and-red-striped tie, which accented his black dress slacks. He and another detective were at the far side of the room speaking softly.

The walls, like Jennifer's face, were ashen-colored even after seeing Peter's seductive smile. Her mixture of sorrow and pain outweighed any temptation to try to understand or dissect his personality. To hell with him! All she really wanted to do was walk to his table and reach over to slap the shit out of him. Ironically, a line flowed through her mind from the play *The Mourning Bride* written by William Congreve (1697): "Hell hath no fury like a woman scorned."

"Before we begin, Detective Malloy," Robert started, "Ms. Collins and I will be meeting with Angela Colder in another room after we're done here, right?"

"Yes, sir, Mr. Henderson," answered Malloy. "I will be there too. That meeting will be well supervised and recorded. Ms. Collins will have the opportunity to press charges if she wants."

"Thank you."

"Shall we begin?" Detective Malloy asked, turning on the tape recorder. "Remember, the recorder can't hear you nod or shake your head. Mr. Winslow, you may begin, starting with last July."

Jennifer sat stiff in a chair next to Robert and sometimes felt agitated, hearing Peter talk about his involvement with drug pushers who were hired to rear-end her Subaru. As he talked about the way he found to meet Jennifer, she felt embarrassed and humiliated; she couldn't wait to get out of the room.

"I didn't count on falling in love with her, but I did. And I still love her," Peter said, trying to make eye contact with the woman who felt only contempt for him.

"Define *love*!" Jennifer snapped at him.

"Shhhh," Robert whispered, placing an arm around her.

"Okay, you got the chance to say what you want to say, Mr. Winslow, so go on," Detective Malloy said.

Jennifer felt astonished, hearing Peter's monotone voice explaining in detail how and why he attached and maintained the black box. The tone of exuberance had vanished, just like his drugs.

"Who received the drugs for distribution at the prison?" Malloy asked.

After clearing the lump in his throat, Peter said, "Hank Poovey."

Jennifer's face looked anemic as she tossed a startled look Robert's way. He held her shoulders a little snugger.

"Jennifer's parking spot was permanent, and it made Hank's job easy," Peter said. Jennifer's mind flashed back to the day she saw Hank Poovey by her car. How foolish she felt now. Why was she willing to act as though she believed his story about picking something up that he had dropped? She knew he was lying, but she had no idea that it had to do with her car being the transport for drugs.

"From whom were you and Poovey getting the drugs?" Malloy questioned.

"I never heard their full names, probably not even their real first names," Peter said.

"What names did they use and what did they look like?" Malloy grilled.

"They called themselves Lark and Breezy, but I never met Breezy. Lark was about five feet, ten inches, brown hair, slender build," Peter said.

"What nationality?"

"My guess is that he's from the Middle East." Peter struggled to keep eye contact with Malloy. He noticed Jennifer's scowl and knew that she only felt contempt for him and that he had to learn to live without her. That was a lot to take all at once.

"What about Mr. Perkins's accident?" Robert asked, knowing Jennifer wanted out of there as soon as Perkins was cleared.

"The first one I arranged because Jennifer had turned in her Subaru for a new car. I bought it, destroyed the evidence, and sold it out of state. The second one really was just an accident. You have to believe me. I didn't want the stuff to be found, so of course I didn't arrange the accident," Peter said as he watched Jennifer stand up to leave. "Please don't go. Can't we talk? I love you!"

"Sure! I'll come every visiting day at the prison so you can humiliate further," she said, clenching her hands and teeth before feeling Robert grab her around her wrist to lead her to the door.

"We've heard everything we need to hear," Malloy said to Robert as the detective pointed to the door. Then Robert walked out swiftly with Jennifer beside him and headed for the next meeting with Angela Colder.

"Lock him up. I can't stand looking at him!" Malloy said to the uniformed officers.

Jennifer was apprehensive as she and Robert walk to the next room where Angela and her "yes" people were already seated—ready and waiting. She wished to the point of praying that just this one time that they all could skip the drama that seemed to be as much a part of Angela as her DNA. Jennifer could feel that Robert was about ready to give consolation as his arm went around her shoulder.

"It's okay, Robert," she assured him. "I know what to expect. I've been living around the town crier long enough to know what she's going to say before she says it."

"As long as you remember that the truth is all that matters, you'll do fine," Robert stated. "That and don't lose your temper."

"Oh, I won't. I still got it," Jennifer said, looking up at him with a grin.

Robert smiled at her as he opened the door to see an oval table full of people. They were bewildered by the stacks of files that Detective Malloy was carrying as he came in through another door.

"Let's take a seat, shall we?" Malloy said, setting the files on the table.

Angela had been trying to make small talk with the right people, but she soon found that she was no longer dealing with sheep who only followed, but professionals who led. All that coy grinning was for nothing.

"Ms. Collins, Ms. Colder is being represented by her attorney, Mr. Black," Malloy announced. Jennifer simply nodded, but Black stood to greet her and Robert with a handshake although Robert had met him several times back in the days when he was the prosecuting attorney.

"Do you know why you are here today, Ms. Colder?" Malloy asked.

"Because Jennifer thinks I helped Sol break into her house," Angela answered.

"Did you?" Malloy asked.

"Don't answer that," Black instructed. "Detective Malloy doesn't have sufficient proof that Ms. Colder did any such thing. All he has is hearsay from someone who was being assaulted and held against her will by an unstable person."

"So my testimony doesn't count!" Jennifer spoke out.

"You were understandably under duress, Ms. Collins," Black pointed out. "And since you were the only witness—"

"Not quite, Mr. Black," Malloy stated, laying his hand on the stack on files. "The man that calls himself Sol, a.k.a. Eddie Wallace, has confessed to everything in detail, including the fact that Ms. Colder helped him get into Ms. Collins's house."

"Because he said he was her cousin he hadn't seen in years," Angela defended. "I didn't see any harm letting him in through an unlocked window."

"Did you ask to see any ID? What about the second time, Ms. Colder? Didn't it occur to you that, by then, he should have had his own key if he was a welcomed guest?" Malloy wanted to know.

Stone-cold silence filled the room as Angela bowed her head to weep.

"This is Ms. Colder's first and only offense, so I'm asking for—"

"There'll be no need to ask for leniency, Mr. Black," Jennifer said. "I'm not pressing charges. I'm not even going to ask her to live up to her part in slandering me all around town for the last seven years. But I am going to warn her that what goes around comes around, and she won't always be able to keep her hatred for me a secret, not even in our naive neighborhood. Jealously doesn't look good on anyone, Angela. You'd be better off ridding yourself of self-pity by using all your excess time you seem to have on your hands to help the poor and needy. That would be something you and your guppies could really be proud of."

"Ms. Collins, do you want me to file restraining orders on Ms. Colder?"

"No, that won't be necessary, will it, Angela?" Jennifer said.

*****

Robert Henderson had said that Elizabeth's surprise retirement party was informal. *But how informal?* Jennifer wondered, pulling tight-fitting blue jeans over slim hips and shoving both feet into new Reeboks, tying them snugly. Pulling a pink beaded sweater from the drawer, she held it in front of her for viewing in the mirror. Not satisfied with the look, a blue blouse was held up for inspection. In all, eight tops failed to achieve a rave review. Then it was finally decided that the pink beaded sweater was best. Large heart-shaped blue-and-pink earrings that held a touch of glitter were placed with care in each ear lobe. Then she brushed her brown curls up on the sides of her head and secured them with a blue-jean-colored clip, leaving some curly tresses to hang loose around her face. *Well, this looks casual, doesn't it?* She took a long look in the mirror at her choice of clothing. *I got to get out more!* she thought humorously as she shook her head. *I have no sense of fashion.*

Jennifer glanced down at the three-carat diamond engagement ring lying on her dresser. She didn't know what to do with it; she didn't know anything about protocol with diamond rings. Should she give it back? Dear Abby says that once you give something to someone, then it is theirs to do with as they wish. But on the other hand,

Dear Abby has also said that the woman has to give the engagement ring back if she breaks the engagement and doesn't plan to marry the man. So Jennifer decided the only decision she was qualified to make was to grab her small denim handbag with a few essentials every woman needs and head for the party.

The decision on the three-caret diamond ring would wait, but not for long. If the truth was ever known, the ring went a long, long way in helping to restore the Tiger Lily Foundation and filling two refrigerators and three freezers with healthy food. There would be no more Poke in the Choke food ever served to the men again.

The loud knock at the front door was unsettling, and the familiar eerie feeling flowed through her body. *Oh no. This can't be good.*

"Good evening, Ms. Collins," Detective Malloy said. "I'm sorry to bother you. I know you're on your way to Ms. Ellsworth's retirement party."

"Please step in," Jennifer said. "What can I do for you?"

"Ms. Collins, you were bound to hear this sooner or later and I didn't want you to hear it in a roomful of people. I'm sorry to tell you that Peter Winslow is dead. He was murdered in his cell this afternoon," Malloy said with compassion. "We suspect that it had something to do with his confession and giving names, dates, and places. He didn't have to give us those names, you know. He did it for you."

Malloy watched her rub the back of her neck. "I feel numb," she admitted. "Peter wasn't a bad person. He just let himself get caught up in something that he eventually had no control over. I was no help. Me, the trained professional." Jennifer's eyes filled with tears.

"You can't be responsible for the whole world, Ms. Collins," he said. "Think about your successes—the six men who will now have real freedom."

"Thank you, Detective, for bringing this to me personally. I appreciate that," Jennifer said solemnly, closing the door behind him.

Her only worry now was how Jeff would react to her at a social gathering, a gathering that would force both of their hands, leaving Jennifer in unfamiliar territory.

Robert had chosen the community center a couple of miles out of town, and every parking spot was already taken. Actually, Jennifer felt relieved at not having to jump up and yell, "Surprise!" She found a parking spot on the side of the road. Stepping in the door and gazing at the number of admirers, she waved after spotting Robert chatting among the guests.

"Glad you could make it!" Robert said as he gave Jennifer a hug.

"Well, was she surprised?" Jennifer asked.

"Why don't you ask *her*?"

"I would if I knew where she was."

"You're kidding, right? Who do you think this beauty is holding my hand?" he asked, chuckling.

Glancing at a light-brown-haired woman who was wearing a large grin and patting the fresh new-colored, cut, and curled coiffeur, Jennifer squealed, "My God! It's *you*, Elizabeth! You look beautiful! Wherever did you find that darling outfit?"

"Thanks, Jennifer," Elizabeth said, whirling to show all sides of her makeover and new sense of clothing style.

"So did you already know about the party?" Jennifer asked.

"Well, sort of," Elizabeth said with a guilty grin, walking Jennifer away from Robert's earshot. "I've got something to tell you," she said in a schoolgirl whisper.

"You've set the date?" Jennifer asked.

"July first, but that's not the big news," Elizabeth said. "Eddie Wallace has confessed to killing Stix. Charlie's free!"

"How'd that happen?" Jennifer asked.

"Well, Robert says Eddie was under the impression the police already knew that it was him, but personally, I suspect it was Robert who gave him that impression," Elizabeth said mischievously.

"Yes, but Robert really did have proof because of the pictures that couple took that were timed and dated," Jennifer reminded.

"I think that's the evidence Robert showed Eddie Wallace while he was still in jail." Elizabeth nodded. "Therefore, Robert could convince Eddie that he didn't stand a chance. But Robert knew that a very sharp attorney could turn that evidence into some kind of smoking mirrors."

"I'm so glad it turned out the way it did," Jennifer said. "Oh, you just look so good, beautiful really." Jennifer couldn't help but staring at her; there was such a discrepancy between Elizabeth now and the one Jennifer knew for the past six months.

But Elizabeth's eyes roamed somewhere else. Noticing Jeff across the room, she said, "Hey! I know someone who'd like to see you." She motioned with a snap of her head toward Jeff. After studying Jennifer's face for a few seconds, Elizabeth said, "At least go say hi to him."

"Yeah, I was just thinking about that," Jennifer said as she slowly started across the room.

Big brown eyes captured the ocean-blue ones staring back. A mutual, knowing smile electrified the air between them, and they slowly sauntered toward each other. The music started and the dance floor became jammed in seconds, pushing Jeff and Jennifer to opposite sides of the floor. There were people everywhere. How was she going to get to him now?

Spotting Perkins sitting alone at a small table where he was eating, she sat down next to him. "It's nice to see you looking so good. I wanted to come and see you," she said, ruefully.

"So why didn't you?" Perkins asked.

"Oh, I don't know. I-I . . . " she said, letting her words drift away.

"You know, you weren't responsible for what happened to me," Perkins said.

"I can't tell you how sorry I am that you were ever involved in such a mess," Jennifer said, almost in tears.

"But it's over now. Ms. Ellsworth and Robert Henderson told me everything." Perkins reached for Jennifer's hand. "Listen to me. You had no way of knowing about Winslow. None of us did."

"You're very kind, but It's my Job to know people, *really* know them. Normally, I have good insight," Jennifer said, "and excellent intuition, if I say so myself."

"Yes, you do, Ms. Collins," Perkins started to explain. "But remember, you're not in love with your clients. Being in love is a lot like being, well, it's a lot like being insane."

"You mean love *really is* blind?" she asked, snickering just a little.

"I don't believe real love is blind, but infatuation can certainly be very misleading," he said. "Either way, Ms. Collins, love seems to be electrifying.

"Thank you, Mr. Perkins," Jennifer said, smiling at his wisdom.

"You can call me Sam if you like," he said.

"I'd like that a lot, Sam," she said. "And you can call me Jennifer, okay?"

"You got it," Perkins said as he watched Jeff head their way.

"Anyone for pizza?" said a voice coming from behind Jennifer. "It has double cheese."

"Aaaah! Double cheese," Jennifer said, turning to see Jeff's hopeful face.

"Someone told me you liked double cheese," he said as he set the pizza down on the table.

"Who's spreading such vicious lies?" she coyly smiled.

"I've been told he's an angel who recently fell from grace, even lost his wings," Jeff smiled. "I was also told he's trying as hard as he can to win them back."

As they sat there, staring into each other's eyes, Sam pulled the pizza his way, saying, "I'll take care of the double cheese. You two can dance."

Elizabeth nudged Robert and pointed at Jeff and Jennifer dancing cheek to cheek while everyone else bounced heartily to keep time to a Beach Boys song.

"I think I'll go cut in," Robert said, teasing.

"You'll do *no* such thing," said Elizabeth, holding his arm. "You're bad."

"I'm sorry I didn't believe you about Peter," Jennifer whispered into Jeff's ear as he held her closer.

"I'm sorry I had such bad timing. But Robert—"

"Yeah, I know, he told me," she said. "He admitted he'd pushed you too hard, too fast to tell me what I needed to know without looking at what it might do to us. I wish I could've believed you, but when I accidentally overheard you talking to Robert in your office one day about how you really felt about me, I—"

"I should've told you when I first suspected that I was in love with you," Jeff said.

"We've never danced like this before," Jennifer cooed as she listened to the vibrations coming from both of their hearts.

"There's many things we've never done before." Jeff wished that he'd quit trembling.

"Do I really have to play the damsel in distress to get your attention?" she asked.

"No, not ever."

"Jeff, I've loved you for a long time, and I tried so hard to get over you," Jennifer said quietly.

"How'd you make out?"

"Not worth a damn. I was afraid that if I told you how I felt I'd lose your friendship and I'd die," she said. "By the time I overheard you confess to Robert your feelings for me, I became confused."

"It seems as though we've been feeling the same way for a long time," he said as he looked into her eyes.

"I think we should set some time aside in a quiet place and practice some rigorous honesty." Jennifer waited for a response, but it was as though Jeff didn't hear what she said and continued to hold her close and dance.

"You know what I think?" Jeff finally responded. "I think we need to get out of here before someone yells, 'Get a room!'"

*****

Driving out to the prison for the parole hearings, Jennifer still felt uncomfortable about Tuttle's plan to be present. Was he going to attempt to provoke or anger the men? The thought of them being set up to fail went through her mind while running up the steps of the administration building. There she met Sam, who was using a cane to walk.

"You're back to work already?" Jennifer asked.

"Just for today," he said, knowing an explanation wasn't needed.

"Where are the hearings being held?"

"Right down this hall," he said, pointing. "I'll take you."

"What would you say if I asked you to spend your last few years before retirement working at the Tiger Lily Foundation?" she asked.

"I'd be honored," he said with a big smile. "I understand Ms. Ellsworth and Robert Henderson will be on the board of directors."

"And Jeff Hanes," Jennifer added.

"Good group of people," Sam said, nodding. In a moment, they arrived in the foyer filled with men, waiting.

The uneven triangular-shaped foyer was vacant of furnishings, except for one long wooden bench stretching the length of the shortest wall. The same unkempt chipped tile seen in the corridor leading to the warden's office dominated the scene, along with the unpleasant order. One oak-framed picture of Theodore Roosevelt hung cockeyed, and the words "Speak softly and carry a big stick" rang with irony in Jennifer's mind as she greeted Elizabeth and the men. She scanned the area for Tuttle's mustache.

"Well, are you ready?" Jennifer asked.

"More ready than I've ever been," Tomas Gonzales said.

"You all will do fine," Elizabeth said, noticing Tuttle march into the foyer. He looked at Elizabeth as though she didn't belong there.

"And in what capacity are *you* here?" he asked her in a brisk air of confrontation.

Jennifer shuffled the men to the farthest corner, allowing Elizabeth the space and time to say what should've been said a long time ago.

"I'm here in support all the men," Elizabeth said.

"You know, I *am* the acting warden now," Tuttle said, twisting one end of his mustache as he stood erect, chest puffed out.

"Then act like one," she said. "Don't make the same mistakes I did."

"I'm only here to find out what profound things these cons did to deserve freedom," he said.

"They *tried*," Elizabeth responded. "They worked very hard for the past six months. They deserve a chance to live a full life, which includes making their own living and paying taxes, which, by the way, pays your salary."

"I have no idea what you're talking about, but you certainly don't buy into all the expensive expenditures brought about by that dumb, bleeding-heart liberal over there, do you?" Tuttle asked, pointing at Jennifer. "Do you know what our prison budget looks like?"

"Well, first let me say that, other than paying a qualified psychologist to help these men be all they can be, there *was* no other expense. And you're asking me if I know what the prison budget looks like? I'd have to be deaf if I didn't! That's all anyone ever cared to talk about in the last thirteen years. That and the fact that we're always overpopulated. No one wanted to see the correlation between the two problems. Until the initiation of the HBP, no one was willing to think in terms of healing inmates so that they would have a chance of unequivocal freedom. Instead, we enthusiastically prepared for their return by building more warehouses," Elizabeth paused and then added, "Speaking of *dumb*!"

"Now because of overpopulation, our prisons are letting inmates out even earlier and aren't bothering to check if they've had any violent convictions anywhere, and if so, how many?" Elizabeth was aware that Tuttle couldn't get a word in edgewise and he knew better this time to think she would just walk away. He'd never seen her like this. "People have been raped, causing pregnancies, stabbed, and killed because of poorly run prisons, especially privatized prisons, because they keep their eyes on the bottom line even more than you do. You'll get a paycheck every week whether the prison expenses go up or not, thanks to the good ol' State of Colorado."

Elizabeth was on a roll after thirteen years of keeping it all inside. "It wasn't all that long ago when an inmate was let out early in a Colorado prison, and he ended up killing a policeman in Texas after just three days of freedom. So sending the inmates out early, based on the prison budget, is nothing but irresponsible. And the irony is that the reason these men are here is because of their own irresponsibility. What message does this send? It sends a message that it's okay for the state to act irresponsibly, but the inmates certainly won't be allowed to."

"My expertise lies in accounting and—"

"It ought to lie in accountability," Elizabeth said, using her infamous piercing eyes to drill a hole through his deceitful words. "Don't you think I *know* why my office was refurbished yearly? Why the guards' lunchrooms were remodeled at the first sign of discontent? Why guards are given free rein over disciplining inmates? Why the inmates are crammed into smaller and smaller quarters? Why mental health and social programs are cut to the bone? Why our salaries go up 15 percent a year while food nutrition for the inmates suffers at the same declining rate?" Elizabeth stepped closer to Tuttle as she continued, "*Every* entrepreneur wants privatization of prisons. There's money to be made and you know how they intend to do it, don't you? They'll run the prison the same way *you* do!"

"I beg your pardon!" Tuttle said indignantly, rubbing and twisting the mustache.

"And you should!" Elizabeth articulated. "You know, Edward, no matter how many times you were beaten up by bullies as a kid, it won't be erased by the brutality of your guards with the inmates. And one more thing. We both know it's not too late for me to rescind my resignation. You stay out of the parole hearings, and I'll remain retired. Get it!"

Jennifer and the men looked at Tuttle's red face and watched his neck veins pop out in rage. Then he walked past them in a huff, mumbling something about "a prison should be a prison and . . . "

As Ron Bookman watched Tuttle stomp away, he asked, with the innocence of a child, "I wonder what it is that I don't like about that man?"

"Roots!" Jennifer laughed, and the other men chuckled.

"Huh?" Ron asked.

"Never mind. It's time, and you're first," she said, walking with him into the room where the decision of freedom would be made.

*****

The parole hearing usually consisted of one person whose intake of information from each eligible inmate was shared with five other members of the parole board at a later date. Only then was a consideration for parole made. But today, all six parole board members were eager to be present at Elizabeth's request.

"Because it's unusual for a warden to request a presence at these hearings, we'd like to know what you have to say before we begin our line of questions," the senior parole officer said.

"I'm not only here to support these men but also to give full support to the Homeward Bound Program," Elizabeth began. "I've had five in-house psychologists on staff over the past thirteen years before budget cuts. In that time, their only job was intervention of suicide. In my opinion, the HBP is a success, whether 20 percent of the six men remain free or not. They've built tools together that'll stay with them forever. Simply warehousing these individuals is not the answer to lowering the recidivism rate, if indeed that's your real goal. Sapping the life and dignity from them is not conducive to releasing well-adjusted men who are ready to be a productive part of society," she finished.

"Our understanding from your letter of request to attend the hearings today is that you intend to be a part of their ongoing life at the Tiger Lily Foundation," the officer said.

"Yes, both Robert Henderson and I will be active board members, arranging twelve-step meetings and counseling sessions and promoting education," Elizabeth finished.

The strict two-year-supervision contingency weighed heavily in the decision to parole all six men. They were shipped off first to halfway houses, then finally to the doorstep of the Tiger Lily Foundation.

*****

Jennifer and Elizabeth waited anxiously outside for all six men to arrive for the Grand Opening of the Tiger Lily Foundation, along with Robert, Jeff, Sam, Richard, and many of the townspeople who had contributed time and money. The foundation needed lots more work, but they managed to get their certificate of occupancy with a few contingencies.

Richard Vaughn had already moved in and proven he was valuable by setting up tables and chairs and arranging for food and beverages. Sam Perkins helped decorate with streamers and a painted sign that read, WELCOME HOME.

Finally, they arrived. As the men stepped out of the van, the crowd grew large and noisy and Jennifer lost sight of them. She stood back, hoping to see their faces, and then she caught the familiar eyes of Michael Bishop coming her way. She hugged him before seeing the doubtful look that said another rule was being broken. "You're not in prison anymore, Michael. A real home deserves realistic rules." She saw the other men making their way through the crowd, and they formed a circle for a group hug—their first but not their last.

About the Author

Betsy Tutchton and her husband of twenty-five years enjoy residing in Colorado. Their daily lives include the viewing of the San Juan Mountain range, which provides them with much inspiration and spirituality. Besides the love she shares with Joe, Betsy's other adorations are reading and writing; she thoroughly enjoyed researching and writing *Ms. Lily White*. She also enjoys photography and has framed and hung much of her lifelike work all throughout her home. Loving to work with wood, she refurbished all of the couple's kitchen cabinets and much more. The spring earth begs her back to the wholesomeness that the earth offers: digging, weeding, planting. The Columbine, the state flower, is her favorite, and her well-groomed rose bushes portray their meaning: love.

Betsy wanted to be a writer since seventh grade, but there were just too many forks in the road, too many unguided decisions. Many opportunities for detours. She's happy to proclaim her happiness for her past. It's what gave her the courage and then the stepping stones that first lead her to a college door, the door she felt had already been closed. Then it led her to become a writer. There never has been, and there will never be, a greater teacher than *life*: pain and all.

Betsy's best advice to anyone wanting to be a writer is to never give up because you don't know what's around the next corner.

CPSIA information can be obtained
at www.ICGtesting.com
Printed in the USA
LVHW04*2144220518
578159LV00002B/38/P